IN THINGS UNSEEN

GAR ANTHONY HAYWOOD

In Things Unseen

A Novel

SLANT

IN THINGS UNSEEN
A Novel

Slant
An Imprint of Wipf and Stock Publishers
199 W. 8th Ave., Suite 3
Eugene, OR 97401

www.wipfandstock.com

HARDCOVER ISBN: 978-1-7252-7999-5
PAPERBACK ISBN: 978-1-7252-8000-7
EBOOK ISBN: 978-1-7252-8001-4

Cataloguing-in-Publication data:

Names: Haywood, Gar Anthony.

Title: In things unseen : a novel / Gar Anthony Haywood.

Description: Eugene, OR: Slant, 2020.

Identifiers: ISBN 978-1-7252-7999-5 (hardcover) | ISBN 978-1-7252-8000-7 (paperback) | ISBN 978-1-7252-8001-4 (ebook)

Subjects: LCSH: Religion--Fiction. | Miracles--Fiction. | Children--Death--Fiction. | Fiction--Thriller--Supernatural. | Fiction--Suspense. | Thriller--Suspense--Fiction.

Classification: PS3558.A885 T48 2020 (print) | PS3558.A885 (ebook)

Manufactured in the U.S.A.   AUGUST 17, 2020

For Donna

Your faith is my salvation

HE WAS A BEAUTIFUL LITTLE BOY, but the young woman with him was not his mother. She was just an adult he trusted, perhaps as much as he trusted his own parents. He thought of her as a friend, and believed she felt the same way about him.

She had stolen him away from school today, in broad daylight. It was a kidnapping; that's what all the police and media people looking for them were calling it, though he thought they were just on an adventure. No one had told him she was deranged, and had anyone suggested she was dangerous—that she was angry and confused enough to do him harm—he would have laughed.

But the woman herself was not so sure. She was angry, so much so that outrage blurred her vision, and what had brought her to this place, to this crime, could not be excused as mere confusion. She was tired of being made a fool, and she didn't want to be tired a moment longer.

The boy could end her misery. He was the only one left who could. But kindness had gotten her nowhere with him, and time was running out for them both. If she had to become the monster they believed her to be to save herself, she would. She'd find the strength somewhere. As for the how of it, that remained a mystery.

Until she remembered the gun in the glove box of her car.

SUNDAY

IN HER DREAMS, the boy never returned at night.

It was always in the morning, as she was making breakfast, alone in the kitchen of the tiny house his absence had rendered so vacant. She would be at the coffee machine or the stove, idly stirring sugar into a cup or turning bacon in a pan, trying to lose herself in what for anyone else would be a menial, automatic task. The quiet, as usual, would be suffocating. And then she would hear his footsteps as he entered the room, and turn to see him climb onto his favorite chair at the table, wearing the pale blue pajamas she had packed away long ago with the rest of his things. His little face would betray nothing, answer not one of the questions she had been struggling to answer for herself for nearly a year.

And that would be fine. Because the questions would no longer matter. Their place in her life, like the pain they engendered, would immediately cease to exist.

When the miracle she'd been praying for was finally granted, it came against all her expectations, not in the light of day but by the cover of night. As she always did, she went to check the boy's room before turning in, and there he was, fast asleep in his bed, exactly as she remembered him. Not a hair on his head had changed since the last time she'd seen him, silent and lifeless and dressed for his own funeral.

Tears came first, then relief, followed by an overwhelming wave of gratitude that brought her to her knees and kept her there.

She wanted desperately to touch him but didn't dare. Acts of God were fragile things. Taking the child in her arms, cradling his face in her hands, could be perceived as a need for proof that what she beheld was real, and she knew this was hardly the time to demonstrate such lack of trust. Her faith had brought her this far; it would take her to the coming dawn at least.

Tonight she would sleep, in her own room, in her own bed. Life was worth living again. Her son was home.

TUESDAY

ONE

BEFORE HIS DEATH, Adrian Edwards had been Laura's favorite student. She had been teaching for only two years, but Laura had the feeling her fondness for the boy would withstand the test of time. She couldn't say why. What had made Adrian special should not have struck her as particularly endearing. He was droll rather than precocious, serene as opposed to happy, and his sarcasm had a bite no seven-year-old had any right to possess. Adrian was silent in the face of chaos and resolutely neutral in all playground disputes. If he hadn't been the heart and soul of Laura's second-grade classroom at Henry Yesler Elementary, he had at least been its spiritual compass, the true north she had always been able to count on.

Eight months had passed since the accident that took his life. His classmates had long since moved on, the ensuing weeks of tears and questions and memorials thankfully forgotten. But Laura was still recovering her balance. Lost innocence had come for her far too soon. At twenty-six, she was still unfettered by the doubt and pessimism that eventually afflicted so many in her profession, and she had planned to remain that way for many years to come. But the tragedy of a dead child proved to be a great equalizer. It ended any illusions of control she may have had, any hope that the children in her charge were hers to shape and mold. She could see now they weren't hers at all, any more than they were their parents'. They belonged to fate. As it had with Adrian Edwards, fate could take a hand at any moment, turn Laura's designs for this child or that one to dust.

Once, she would have laid the blame for such random cruelty at the feet of God. She'd been raised a Presbyterian, taught to believe He (it was always a *he*) was behind everything that happened in the world, both good and bad, big and small. But Laura had lost the capacity to embrace such fantastic notions many years ago, while she was a senior in high school.

The more educated she became, the more aware of the world around her, the less she could reconcile a belief in an all-powerful, all-knowing God with an abiding faith in the provable universe. She found increasing comfort in only those things the science of man had established as incontrovertibly true. It made the injustices of pain and suffering, illness and death easier to accept because they required no explanation; they were simply inexplicable parts of an inexplicable whole.

So Laura hadn't searched for reasons when sixty-eight-year-old retiree Milton Weinman—or was it Weisler?—hit the accelerator pedal rather than the brake one Saturday last March and plowed his car into the playground at Lakeridge Park, killing Adrian Edwards instantly. She knew there were no reasons to be had. Adrian's death was not a mystery to be solved but a blow to be absorbed, a natural disaster that could be survived but never fully understood. She braced herself for the pain of his loss and let it come, comforted by the knowledge her grief would someday pass.

Of course, the same could not be said for Adrian's parents. Their grief, Laura knew, would be everlasting, a cloud over their lives that would diminish over time but never completely subside. It had already taken a heavy toll on the boy's mother in particular. Prior to her son's death, Diane Edwards had been that rarest of rarities, a stay-at-home mom who seemed at peace in her own skin, a woman with bright blue eyes and an infectious laugh who was neither bored by nor resentful of her station in life. Though she'd carried more weight than Laura could have tolerated and, from all appearances, spent her days running the same household errands over and over again, only a Buddhist monk could have projected more spiritual contentment than Diane Edwards.

But now that woman was gone. What Laura had seen in her place, on those rare occasions they had run into each other after the funeral, was a specter: a wispy outline in human shape that moved like rolling fog and spoke in halting whispers. Adrian had been Diane Edwards's only child and sole purpose in life, and when he died, he took all but a hollow shell of his mother with him.

If Adrian's father had been similarly devastated, Laura was unaware of it. It was rumored Michael and Diane Edwards were separated now, and sightings of Michael were rare. A recording engineer by trade, he had always been painfully taciturn in Laura's presence, a big man with slits for eyes and a granite chin who seemed perpetually on the verge of being rude. The last time she had seen him, in her classroom at the first of two memorial events she'd organized for her kids in Adrian's honor, Michael Edwards had appeared only slightly more surly than usual. His words to the children had been kind and sincere enough, but he'd had little to say to Laura and the other adults, save for a few standard expressions of gratitude for their sympathy and support.

In any case, however he and his wife were coping with the loss of their son eight months after the fact, Laura was confident she was farther along in returning to a life of normalcy than either of them. These days, she thought of Adrian only occasionally, and almost never for very long. In the beginning, his empty chair in her classroom would stop her cold, cause words to catch in her throat mid-sentence. Tears would come and her legs would threaten to give out. It could be hours before she was right again. But now that empty chair, still there by the window in the midst of the other children, held little sway over her. She thought of Adrian only when something or someone in her class evoked a fond memory of him, and the twinge of sorrow she felt was mercifully fleeting. It seemed her days of being haunted by Adrian Edwards would soon be over.

Or so she had thought.

This morning, ten minutes before the start of class, he walked through the door of her classroom and took his old seat, exactly the way he had a hundred times before that day last March, and Laura realized in an instant he had only begun to place his indelible mark upon her life.

TWO

"WHAT THE HELL do you make of it?"

"I don't know. I really don't."

Howard Alberts, Yesler Elementary's principal, and Betty Marx, his vice principal, were huddled on the walkway outside the main office. As word spread of Laura Carrillo's breakdown, one teacher after another was coming into the office to find out what had happened, and Alberts, having few answers for them, was now deflecting them back to their classrooms the minute they reached the door.

"Has she been under any kind of strain lately?" he asked Marx. "Either here or at home?" A tall, gangly man who resembled a stork, he had to fold at the waist to meet Marx's gaze.

"No. Not that I'm aware of."

"There must have been something. A person doesn't just suddenly lose their mind like that for no reason."

"You think she's lost her mind?" A short, cherubic woman with an ample bosom and red hair crowned with a bun, Marx seemed horrified at the thought.

"Well, you heard what she said. She thinks the boy's a ghost. That he was killed in a car accident last spring. She's *convinced* of it. If that's not insanity, what is it?"

Marx didn't know and she was loath to guess. It sounded like madness but she wasn't a doctor. Laura was in Alberts's office now with Sonia Fedin, the school nurse, and Sonia was better qualified than Marx or Alberts to make assumptions about the young teacher's state of mind.

That something had gone seriously wrong for her was obvious. Twenty minutes ago, Laura had rushed into the office in an apparent state of shock, having committed the cardinal sin of leaving her kids unattended. "I can't go back in there. I won't," she told Edie Brown, Yesler's desk clerk.

Edie immediately thought something had happened to one of Laura's children, but Carrillo shook her head. "He's in the room right now," she said, eyes as wide as two dinner plates. "Go see for yourself."

"Who?" Edie asked.

"Adrian. He just walked in. I know it sounds impossible, but. . . ." She pointed in the direction of her classroom. "Go look. He's just sitting there." She started to sob. "He's just sitting there."

Edie had called Alberts out of his office. Marx, who'd been on the phone, was right behind him.

"What's going on?" Alberts asked.

"Something must have happened to Adrian Edwards," Edie said. "Somebody needs to go check on Ms. Carrillo's kids right away."

Marx volunteered and took off.

* * *

Alberts, fearing the worst, searched Carrillo's face and body for blood and was momentarily relieved to find none. "Laura, what happened? What's wrong?"

She barely registered the question. Her gaze was vacant and unfocused, and she was listing like a drunk who could drop to the floor at any second.

"Laura—"

"He's dead," Carrillo said. "I don't understand. How can he be in my room if he's dead?"

"Oh, my God." Edie brought a hand to her mouth.

Alberts told her to call 911.

The clerk was talking to a dispatcher when Marx reentered the office, recognized what she was doing, and shook her off. "The children are okay," she said. "They're all okay."

"Are you sure?" Alberts asked. "She says Adrian's—"

"He's fine. Everybody's fine." As Edie hung up the phone, Marx glanced at Carrillo, who remained oblivious. "They're a little confused and frightened, but they're all okay. I put them in with Mr. Gianetti's class for the moment."

"Fine?" Carrillo flared. "He's *not* fine. He's dead! How can you say he's fine?"

"Laura, what are you talking about?" Alberts demanded. "Adrian isn't dead. Nobody's dead."

"You're wrong. I went to his funeral. You did, too." Glaring now, she turned to Marx. "And you." Then Edie. "We were all there."

She studied their faces, saw the same mix of pity and disbelief on each one. "Why are you all looking at me like that? You're acting like you don't *remember!*"

Their silence told her that was exactly the case.

"Oh, my God." She buried her face in her hands and began to weep.

Alberts and Marx sat her down in Alberts's office and tried to console her. On Alberts's orders, Edie summoned Sonia Fedin to join them. Eventually Carrillo grew lucid enough to answer their questions, and the story she told only made them fear for her well-being all the more. She said Adrian Edwards had died earlier that year at nearby Lakeridge Park, crushed under the wheels of a car driven by an old man who'd lost control. She continued to insist most of the school staff had attended the boy's funeral at St. Bernadette's Church six days later, including everyone presently in Alberts's office, with the exception of Fedin. She was able to describe the days and weeks that had supposedly followed in great detail, from the flowers she'd ordered for the service to the way some of his classmates had responded to his death. It all had the ring of truth, except every word was impossible.

At Fedin's request, Alberts and Marx left the nurse to talk to Carrillo alone, and now the two of them were here, standing outside the main office, struggling to make sense of Carrillo's behavior.

"Do you think Adrian might know what this is all about?" Marx asked. "Could he have said something, or done something to her—"

"To what? Put the idea in her head that he's dead? No. How could he?" Alberts had never been as taken by the boy as Carrillo was—he'd always found Adrian's unshakable calm to be unsettling in a child his age—but he couldn't imagine the boy disturbing the teacher to such a grave extent, deliberately or otherwise.

"I don't know. I just thought. . . ." Marx paused. "Why *him?* Why would Laura choose to believe such a terrible thing about Adrian?"

"You tell me. You just saw him. Did you ask him what happened?"

"Of course."

"And?"

"He said what all the other children said, that Miss Laura got scared and ran out of the room. He didn't know why."

"He didn't do anything to frighten her?"

"No. All he did was come in and take his seat. At least, that's what he and all the rest of the children say."

Alberts decided to go talk to the boy himself. As a precautionary measure, they were sending all of Carrillo's students home, but most of them, including Adrian, were still here, waiting for their parents to pick them up. Alberts found Adrian in Chris Gianetti's classroom, where Marx had left him, and brought him out to the vacant lunch area, where they could sit and chat alone.

As always, Adrian was clean and neatly dressed, today in khaki shorts and a crisp blue T-shirt. Dark-haired and hazel-eyed, of average height and weight, he would have blended right into any second-grade class photo. As they took their seats at a table, Alberts studied him, looking for some sign Carrillo's actions had upset the boy in some way, but Adrian appeared as eerily imperturbable as ever.

"Adrian, I just want to ask you a few questions about what happened with Miss Laura in class today."

"Okay."

"Can you tell me what happened? In your own words?"

The boy shrugged. "She just started yelling 'no.' And then she got up and went to the corner."

"No?"

"Yes. 'No, no, no,' like that."

"Do you know why she said that?"

Adrian shook his head.

"You told Ms. Marx she was afraid."

The boy nodded.

"What was she afraid of?"

"I don't know. But. . . ."

"Yes?"

"She was looking at *me*." He shrugged again.

"Why would she be afraid of you? Did you say or do something to frighten her?"

"No." His head swiveled emphatically from side to side, his Zen-like façade finally giving way to the hurt of a child falsely accused. "I didn't do anything to her."

"Are you sure?"

"Yes. I just sat down. That's all."

"And that's when she started saying no over and over and got up to . . . stand in a corner? Is that what you said?"

"Yes."

"And then she ran out of the room after that? Without saying anything else?"

"She said it couldn't be."

"It couldn't be? I don't understand."

"She said, 'It can't be.'"

Alberts's throat was suddenly dry. He took a moment to ward off a growing sense of unease. "And when she said that, she was still looking at you?"

"Yes. But I don't know why. I didn't do anything. I just sat down. Am I in trouble, Mr. Alberts?"

Adrian was almost in tears. Alberts was both ashamed and relieved to see the boy react, at last, with some genuine emotion. "No, no, of course not. You haven't done anything wrong, Adrian, I promise."

He got up and drew the boy to his feet, tossing an arm over his little shoulders. "Come on, we're done. Let's go back to class."

When they arrived at the classroom, Adrian's mother was there waiting for them. Alberts remembered her name was Diane, though they had met only once before, three months earlier at a Yesler fund-raising carnival. She looked concerned but not afraid, which struck Alberts as a little odd. Edie Brown had been instructed to offer people only the merest whiff of an explanation for sending their children home only hours into the school day, and the principal was expecting many parents to show up in a state of panic. Diane Edwards seemed significantly more relaxed than that.

"Are you okay?" she asked her son, hugging him close.

"Yes."

His mother turned to Alberts. "I understand Miss Laura had some kind of a breakdown. Is that right?"

"That's probably too strong a word for it, 'breakdown.' A slight panic attack would be more like it."

"Is she okay?"

"I'm sure she'll be fine. We're only sending the kids home because some were a little spooked by it all, as you might imagine. Adrian, included, I'm afraid."

"Adrian?" She looked down at the boy. "Is that right? Were you spooked?"

Before her son could answer, Alberts said, "He seems to think, because it happened just as he came into the room, that he had something to do with Laura's behavior. Of course, I've told him that's not possible. Is it?"

He had asked the question just to see her reaction.

"No. Of course not," she said. Choosing the exact words he would have chosen in her place—if he had been addressing Adrian. She should have been trying to reassure her son, but she'd been looking straight at Alberts when she spoke, as if hoping to allay *his* fears and not the boy's.

Alberts didn't know what it meant, or if it meant anything at all. And he chose not to care. He let Diane Edwards take her son home and turned his attention back to Laura Carrillo. Because whatever had caused the teacher's meltdown, it hadn't been a little boy risen from the dead.

Of that much, Alberts was certain.

THREE

THANK YOU.

Diane couldn't get the two words out of her head. All day Monday, she spoke them out loud and recited them in silence, with tears and without, a mantra of gratitude to the all-merciful God who had finally heard and answered her most improbable prayer.

Thank you.

Her son was back. In the flesh, whole and unblemished, the same little boy his parents had laid to rest last spring.

She spent the entire day in a state of dizzying euphoria, alternating between holding him in her arms and watching him at a remove, marveling at the miracle he represented. And surely that was the word for this: miracle.

She thought of all the times she almost gave up hope. Got up off her knees and made up her mind never to get down on them again. It had happened more than she cared to admit. The excruciating pain was unrelenting and her loneliness, especially after Michael left, pushed her ever closer to the breaking point. What use was faith if it couldn't provide the one thing, the only thing, you needed most in the world? But somehow she had always held on. Not simply to the hope but the *belief* God would do this incredible thing she was asking of Him. And now He had.

But how to tell Adrian's father?

From the moment she found their son in his own bed the night before, Diane had wanted to call her estranged husband to tell him what had happened. Keeping something so immense, so unimaginably wonderful, to herself seemed both selfish and impossible. But she never reached for the phone that night, and as of Monday evening, still hadn't. She waited for the dawn instead, fully awake in her own bed, trying to imagine what words she could use that would not make her sound like a madwoman.

Had she made a call to Michael, she realized now, it would have been a huge mistake. Because more than just the obvious had changed. Beyond the fact Adrian had returned to it, this was a different world than it had been before. With Monday's morning light, Diane had begun to see evidence of this everywhere she looked. Two days earlier, Adrian had been a child she only used to have, her home bearing few reminders of the place he once held in it. But on Monday, his closet was full of clean clothes and his hamper overflowed with dirty ones. His favorite foods were stocked in the kitchen again, and the shrine Diane had built for him atop her bedroom dresser had been reduced to a single photograph, the pamphlet from his funeral service conspicuously missing.

Time, it seemed, had been rewound to erase all signs of Adrian's death.

Even the boy himself had no memory of the event, as far as Diane could tell. He woke Monday as he always had on weekdays—on his own, prepared to go to school—and only agreed to stay home after Diane insisted it was a holiday of which he'd been unaware. As wary as ever of breaking the spell that had brought him back to her, she passed the hours on Monday studying her son with tender care, quizzing him only enough to ascertain he had no answers for any of the questions she longed to ask him. Wherever he had been over the last eight months, heaven or hell or somewhere in between, Adrian thought he had been right here, safe and sound in his family's home.

Like the timing of his return, this wasn't at all how Diane had envisioned it would happen. She had thought the world would remain as it was, and that the miracle of a dead child rising from the grave would simply turn it upside down. That she would have to draw on every ounce of her strength to protect her son from the towering wave of believers and nonbelievers that would come crashing down upon him, seeking answers he could not provide. The skepticism of the faithless would be relentless, and the curiosity of the faithful would be no less so.

But that was clearly not God's plan. The final proof was the call Diane placed to her sister Vicky early Monday night, after she'd put Adrian to bed. No one other than Michael had been more devastated by Adrian's death than Vicky, who lived seven miles away in Columbia City, and no one had ever taken greater pains afterward to avoid the very mention of his name. But on this night Adrian's aunt asked about him as if nothing more than mere hours had passed since she last placed a kiss on the boy's forehead. Hearing he was alive and well surprised Vicky not at all.

God hadn't simply reversed Adrian's death; He had undone it. But why? How could a miracle bring glory to God if God Himself had chosen to make a secret of it?

Diane ultimately decided she didn't need to understand and she didn't care to. She had spent every night of her life since that nightmarish day—every night for eight months—praying for one thing only: to have Adrian back. And now that God had seen fit to answer that prayer, she wasn't going to question the rhyme or reason of His methods. Instead, she would take comfort in the safe assumption her son was not meant to be shown off and displayed like a circus freak. He was proof of God's great love and mercy, His power to change the unchangeable, but he was not intended to lift the veil of unbelief from the eyes of the entire world. For the moment, at least, he was just a little boy who had once been lost and now was found, and all that was incumbent upon his mother was that she treat him accordingly.

So Tuesday morning, after sleeping beside him more soundly than she had slept in months, Diane resigned herself to follow the script Adrian seemed to be writing. Counter to her most fervent wish to hold him close, she sent the boy to school, exactly as she always had before the accident, and waited to see what would happen.

* * *

When the call from Yesler Elementary came, less than an hour after she'd dropped Adrian off, Diane had feared the worst. Had she misread the signs? Heard her sister say something she hadn't? Were the teachers and children at school thrown into a panic at the very sight of her son, their collective memory of his death fully intact?

No. From Edie Brown's voice over the phone, Diane had been able to tell that wasn't the case. Something unusual had happened, yes, but it had involved Adrian's teacher, Laura Carrillo, not Adrian himself, and nothing along the lines of a school-wide horror show had ensued.

The minute she arrived at Yesler to hear Edie's vague description of what had occurred, Diane realized Carrillo alone understood the import of Adrian's reappearance in her classroom. No one else had a clue. Diane could not imagine why the young teacher had been singled out to receive the gift of insight, but she suspected she would find out soon enough. In the meantime, Diane would pretend to be as shocked as everyone else by Carrillo's actions. When the right time came to speak the truth, Diane would do so gladly. But this was not the time.

Speaking the truth to Michael was another matter. Shortly after bringing Adrian home from school, it had dawned on Diane that her husband's memories of the last eight months, and the tragedy that preceded them, were likely to be as intact as those of Laura Carrillo. Because otherwise he'd be here with her, the disintegration of their marriage erased by God's hand like all the other consequences of Adrian's death. The boy had barely mentioned his father more than once since his return, apparently accustomed to his parents' separation and the reasons—another mystery in this new world—they may have had for brokering it. This seemed proof enough to Diane that Michael, too, must be living in a past no longer in effect.

He needed to be told.

Diane knew Michael would refuse to believe it. His love for Adrian had always been as boundless as her own, and he had mourned for the boy with a passion she would have thought was beyond him. His faith in God, unlike hers, had been an open secret at best, rarely mentioned and almost never demonstrated, but in the beginning his prayers—to wake up one morning and find the accident in Lakeridge Park was nothing more than a bad dream—made Diane's pale by comparison.

Eventually, however, as the reality of Adrian's death sank its teeth ever deeper into him, Michael lost his faith. His sorrow turned to anger, black and cold and insurmountable, and Diane found herself more alone than ever. Her prayers for Adrian went on, her own spiritual beliefs tested but never quite shaken, and her refusal to swallow the bitter pill of defeat finally drew Michael's ire and contempt. She couldn't hold him, and five months after laying their little boy to rest, she stopped wanting to.

Which was not to say she no longer loved Michael. She did. And she was certain he still loved her. But what Michael had needed from her—an admission they would never have Adrian back—was the one thing she could not give him.

And now she wouldn't have to. Any future they might yet have together suddenly depended not on her ability to accept a difficult truth, but on his. All he had to do was lay down the sword of bitterness that had closed her off to him and open his eyes. Trust what they would soon be telling him and believe in the impossible again.

Diane hoped there was enough light left in him to do so.

FOUR

ELLIOTT KNEW SOMETHING was terribly wrong when Laura called him home just after noon. Laura never called him at the office, and rarely went home early from school herself. He pleaded for some explanation but she wouldn't offer any over the phone. Her tone of voice, flat and lifeless, was one he had never heard before.

He arrived to find her in the bedroom, fully dressed and sitting atop the covers on their bed, a cup of tea growing cold in her hands. She was staring at the television but it wasn't on, and she only seemed to notice his entrance when he sat down beside her.

"Laura, what is it? What happened?"

Her eyes, rimmed in red and filmed with tears, slowly turned in his direction. "I don't know." She shook her head. "I don't know what happened."

Elliott guessed she was in shock. He'd imagined all kinds of horrible things on the drive home but this was more frightening than most. Laura didn't shake easily.

"Are you ill? Should I call a doctor?" He touched her forehead. Her temperature seemed normal. "Laura, talk to me."

"Adrian Edwards. He was run over by a car in the park and killed."

"Oh, Jesus—"

"Last March," she added. "We went to the funeral together. I said a few words for him at the service and slept for two days afterwards, right here in this bed." She searched his face. "Please tell me you remember that. *Please.*"

Elliott was confused. The name was familiar, of course. Adrian was one of Laura's favorite students and she talked about him incessantly. But this was the first Elliott had heard about any accident in the park, let alone the boy's death. And the only funeral Elliott had attended in the last four years was for his sister Jayne.

"I'm sorry, babe. I don't."

Her eyes flashed. "You're lying." She slapped him hard across the face, upending her tea into her lap. "You're lying! He's dead, you know he's dead. Why can't you just admit it?" Her voice cracked. "Why won't *anyone* admit it?"

She burst into tears as Elliott recoiled, cheek burning. "Laura, what the hell is going on? You're not making any sense!"

* * *

Slowly, word by painful word, it all tumbled out. She began with Adrian's appearance in her classroom that morning and ended with her dismissal from school, Howard Alberts sending her home for the day with the concern of a doting grandmother. In between, Laura recited all she could recall that was germane to the boy's death: the children's various emotional breakdowns in the classroom afterward, their questions about life and death that she could answer only in riddles, the time she saw a boy at the Willowbridge Mall who resembled Adrian so strongly that she nearly fainted. Elliott had been there with her that night, he *had* to remember it.

And yet he didn't. He didn't remember any of it.

It left Laura with only one conclusion, the same one she'd been terrified to face ever since she'd glanced up from her desk that morning to see a dead child walk into her classroom: she was going mad.

She cried for a long time in her fiancé's arms, not knowing what else to do. Elliott was as lost as she, but he didn't push. He was a man who always understood the value of silence, even in moments of crisis. He stroked her hair and face and held her close, offering an occasional word of comfort.

She sat upright again and met his gaze. "What's wrong with me, Elliott? Why is this happening?"

He showed her a brave smile. "I don't know."

"They think I'm crazy. Everyone at school, I mean. The district psychologist was called out to examine me. She questioned me for over two hours, treating me like a mental patient. She thinks I'm just overworked."

"Aren't you?"

"No. You know I'm not. And you know I'm not insane. Or am I?"

"No. Of course not."

"Then tell me what's going on. Adrian Edwards is dead. He died last March, exactly the way I've been saying he did. I'm not making it up and I'm not imagining it, Elliott. It happened."

Elliott shook his head. "That isn't possible, Laura."

She waited for him to go on, an unspoken dare.

"If the boy was at school today, and no one but you has any recollection of this accident in the park. . .it couldn't have happened. There's just no way."

"Then I *am* insane. Or I'm dreaming and this is a nightmare."

"You don't have to be insane or dreaming. You simply have to be subject to. . .to. . ."—he searched for the right phrasing—"some kind of delirium."

"Delirium?"

"You may not be overworked in the technical sense, but that doesn't mean you haven't been under a certain amount of stress lately. You take your work very seriously, babe, and you bring a lot of it home. Maybe you've just broken down a little. It happens. It happens to everyone."

"No." She shook her head defiantly.

"Wait. Bear with me for a moment." He paused for her to object. When she didn't, he pressed on. "You're fond of Adrian. You're always saying he's special in a way your other kids aren't. He fascinates you. So naturally, if your subconscious were to single out anyone to develop a fantasy around, however bizarre—"

"I'm not fantasizing about anyone. This isn't a goddamn fantasy!" The word turned her stomach. Even if this *was* her infatuation with Adrian gone wrong—she'd already considered that possibility without Elliott's help—that wouldn't fall under the description of *fantasy*. She started to tear up again.

Elliott said, "I don't know what you want me to say. I want to help but I'm not going to lie to you. What you're saying happened didn't happen. And this isn't a dream. That much I can tell you for certain." He gathered his courage and delivered the final blow. "I think you need to see a doctor. Whatever this is, it's more than we can handle alone."

If he were expecting another hand across the face, what she leveled against him—all the unfettered hatred she could bring to bear with her eyes—was meant to feel infinitely worse.

"Get out," Laura said. "Get out of here and leave me alone!"

"Laura—"

"I said, get out!"

He threw his hands up to fend off the teacup she hurled at his head. He looked for some sign of remorse and she showed him nothing.

"I'll be right outside if you need me," he said. "Try to get some sleep."

He left the room and closed the door.

* * *

Several hours later, a call came in on her cell, which was sitting alongside her purse on the dining room table where she usually left it. Elliott saw Howard Alberts's name on the phone's screen. Laura had fallen asleep and he was loath to wake her, but he was too desperate for answers to just let the phone ring.

"How is she?" Alberts asked after the two men had exchanged awkward greetings. They had met more than once but only briefly on each occasion.

"She's sleeping right now. I'm hoping she sleeps straight through to morning."

"She told you what happened at school today?"

"Of course."

"Any idea what could have caused it?"

"Not a clue. I don't even know what 'it' is. Maybe you can help me with that."

"Beyond an emotional breakdown of some kind? No. Is she still insisting—"

"That this boy Adrian Edwards is dead? Yes."

"Jesus."

"She said the district psychologist who examined her at the school believes she's just overworked."

"Yes. And I suppose that's as good an explanation as any. But. . . ." Alberts's sigh came in loud and clear over the phone. "It's more than that. I've seen teachers who are overworked. I've been trained to know the signs when I see them. And Laura's never given me any reason to believe she's been working too hard. Of course, you'd be in a better position to know than me."

"Well, she puts in a lot of hours and gets tired like everyone else. And sometimes she even complains about it. But if she's been overworked, I can't say it's been obvious to me. At least, not enough to explain something like this."

The two allowed a short silence to build.

"I assume you and this psychologist talked to the boy?" Elliott asked.

"Of course. Our first thought was that he'd done something to set Laura off. Played some kind of bizarre trick on her or something. But by all accounts, he never even spoke to her. She started screaming the minute he entered the classroom. Poor guy's just as baffled as the rest of us."

"Is he okay?"

"I think so. Some of the other children were a little freaked out, but Adrian seemed fine. Which is typical of him, as you may know."

"Yes. Laura says he's not your average seven-year-old."

"No. Far from it, in fact."

"The way Laura describes him, he sounds a little strange."

"Strange? No. Just. . .unusually reserved for someone his age."

"Reserved, strange. Either way, isn't that all the more reason to suspect him? I mean, don't the most innocuous kids turn out to be the most dangerous sometimes?"

"Sometimes, sure. But not in this case. I'm fairly certain of that." Before another stretch of silence could assert itself, Alberts said, "I know this is a terrible question to ask, Elliott. It *is* Elliott, isn't it?"

"Yes."

"I know this is a terrible question, but I have to ask—does Laura have any history of mental illness that you're aware of? Depression, schizophrenia. . . ."

"No." Elliott was unable to hide his offense.

"What about prescription drugs? Does she—"

"No. Laura abhors drugs." Which meant she was sometimes less inclined than Elliott to smoke the occasional joint while watching a movie at home.

"You understand—"

"Why you had to ask, yes. But the answer to both questions is still no."

"I'm sorry if I offended you, but here's the thing. I can't let Laura back in the classroom until we know exactly what happened today. And until I have a reasonable expectation that it won't happen again."

Now Elliott didn't care how pissed off he sounded. "Excuse me?"

"District regulations say once our psychologist has been called out, we have to get a clean bill of health from a certified physician before we can put a teacher back on the job. That's just the way it is."

"Are you serious? Laura's not a danger to anybody, least of all her students. She loves those kids!"

"I know she does. And I'm sure she would never willingly do anything to hurt them. But her behavior today strongly suggests she may not be in complete control of herself. She needs to see a doctor, Elliott. The sooner she does that, the sooner we can welcome her back to school."

Elliott felt he owed it to Laura to argue with the man, to defend her right to work against his thinly veiled charges of mental instability. But he knew Alberts was right—no one could say what Laura was capable of until they had some understanding of what had happened to her today. What was still happening to her.

"Have her call me when she's up to it," Alberts said. "Tonight or tomorrow, it doesn't matter. We only want what's best for her and the children. Please tell her I said that, will you?"

FIVE

MILTON WEISMAN WAS a changed man.

For most of his sixty-eight years, he had been a bad one. A terrible husband and a neglectful father. Work had been his only love, the single thing he considered worthy of his full attention, and he was happy to let everything else go to hell. In his youth, ambition was all the fuel he needed to keep going, but at some point alcohol superseded it, transforming him into an ogre of anger and resentment. His law practice suffered, his marriage crumbled, and his children began to hate him. He became someone his late mother, whom he had adored above all others, would have despised.

When his wife Shauna died four years earlier, after they'd been together almost three decades, his daughters had hoped the shock would move him to get clean. Janet, his oldest, had tried guilt to reach him, laying her mother's death directly at her father's feet. Her sister, Lisa, had taken a different tack, sending him self-help books and emails teeming with links to online articles about alcoholism. Neither approach worked. Milton was recalcitrant in his self-destruction. Shauna's death only served to isolate him further.

Then he killed that little boy.

Adrian Edwards, just seven years old. Last spring in the park. After reading the morning paper there like he always did, Milton had been exiting the parking lot when his foot slipped and tapped the Honda's accelerator instead of the brake. He recognized his mistake immediately but panicked, and in his attempt to stand on the brakes, he drove the accelerator pedal straight to the floor. By the time the car came to a stop, it had traveled thirty yards, churning up grass and sand and earth, clipping the ladder on a playground slide and rolling right over the child who'd been climbing it.

Most of what occurred immediately following the accident was lost to Milton, so great was his mind's need to protect him from the memory. What he could recall were only flashes of sight and sound and fragments of sensation: the screams of Adrian's mother and the only other woman in the park that morning; the pain in his right knee, shattered when the car finally slammed into a tree; and what seemed like thousands of questions. Witnesses, policemen, paramedics—everyone asking him what had happened, how it had happened, why it had happened. He had no answers for any of them.

Naturally, they tested him for alcohol before the ambulance could deliver him to the hospital. On any other day back then, the results would have cost him his life: his home, his retirement, and very likely, his freedom. But on this particular March morning, he had forgone the bottle and gone to the park sober. His impulsive choice that day to test liquor's hold on him could have been an omen, but Milton didn't believe in omens any more than he believed in God, so he had thought little of it.

It took him until the next day, lying in his hospital bed with machines tied to his every extremity, to fully grasp what he'd done and, comparatively speaking, how little he was likely to pay for it. He'd killed a little boy but had suffered only minor injuries. He was being reviled as a clumsy, senile old man but not as a homicidal drunk. He might be sued for damages but would almost certainly not be incarcerated. He even had the pity of some who would rather be thankful they weren't as old and pathetic as he than condemn him for being both.

In short, he was incredibly fortunate.

Or such was his initial view of things. He eventually came to see what had happened to him in a different light. Milton was a retired corporate lawyer, a man for whom gray areas did not exist, so the concept of luck, good or bad, was one he had always found laughable. People made their own luck, either by commission or omission, and ascribing the turns their lives took to anything other than their own actions was idiocy.

He thought much the same way about religion. His parents had been devout Jews, a stark contrast to those doggedly secular American Hebrews who treated Judaism like a mere tattoo, and Shauna had never missed a High Holy Day at shul in her life. Milton, on the other hand, had relieved himself from the shackles of faith many years ago, when it became obvious he could meet his professional goals just fine without wasting a minute's time on worship. As far as he could tell, the only difference between highly successful Jews who believed in Adonai and those who didn't was the freedom the latter had to sin at will. Milton was too busy to be bothered with such hypocrisy.

At first, nothing about the accident caused him to reconsider his atheism. If anything, the tragedy only served to further justify it. What god would allow such a thing to happen to a child and an innocent old man? But as the days and weeks wore on, something began to turn inside him. His guilt and anger, which had painted black his every waking hour since his first glimpse of Adrian Edwards's broken little body, gradually took on a new dimension, one that could only be described, insufficiently, as gratitude.

The closer he came to a complete recovery from his injuries, the more he believed he'd been spared the total devastation he could have suffered—*should* have suffered—for a reason. Instead of being dead or crippled or withering away in prison craving a drink he could never have, Milton had emerged from the accident with only a cane and a slight limp, and no amount of objective reasoning could convince him that fate alone was responsible.

Milton was as alive and free as he had ever felt, his alcoholism a shed skin he had somehow put behind him while still in the hospital, without deliberation or significant effort. He'd been well insured and Adrian's parents showed little interest in seeking greater compensation for his death than they'd already received. Having had his daughters gather around him after the accident, Milton was now closer to them, Lisa in particular, than he'd been since they were little girls.

It could have been argued Milton was better off today than he had been before killing Adrian Edwards.

How was this possible?

Milton didn't know. He only knew none of it was by chance. There was a plan at work here, one beyond his abilities to comprehend, and he was going to play his part in it to the fullest. He owed whoever or whatever had saved him that much, whether "God" was its proper name or not.

As he waited for the meaning of it all to shift into focus, he resolved to become a better person than he had ever been. A better father, a better citizen, a better man. Humility was the key. He'd never had much use for it—humility was a weakness to be exploited, not a strength to be admired—but he understood there would be no redemption for him without it. So he held the memory of what he'd done last March close to his breast. Not as a weight to be carried but as a reminder of his potential for ruin. He had developed a routine: two nights a week before bed, without fail, he turned on his computer and searched the web for stories about Adrian Edwards.

He always found something. The story was a local sensation for weeks. There were YouTube videos of television newscasts covering the tragedy, newspaper stories, feature columns, magazine articles, message board threads, and blog posts. In all but a few, Milton was portrayed as either a hapless old fool who had no business possessing a driver's license, or a cold-blooded child-killer who had gotten away with murder. Voices sympathetic to his position, to the guilt he was left to carry, were few and far between. When he'd been allowed to speak for himself, his words were turned against him, bent and twisted to fit the image of a delusional old drunk.

Subjecting himself to this public flaying every Tuesday and Thursday night helped him appreciate how far he'd come. To hedge against remission, a return to the selfish, unfeeling man he used to be, it was necessary to weigh his present against his past, to keep the flame of guilt that had fueled his spiritual transformation alive and well.

It was not always easy. Some nights, he just wasn't up to the task. Tonight was one of those. He'd had a difficult day, littered with melancholy and capped by a stupid and unnecessary argument with Janet about his diet, and by eight o'clock, he was dead on his feet. After bathing and dressing for bed, the last thing he wanted to do was sit down in front of his laptop and revisit the darkest hours of his life.

But he turned the goddamn computer on, anyway.

SIX

THE PAIN WAS CONSTANT. It changed shape and color daily, but never its depth. It always cut straight to the bone, blackening everything it touched.

Michael had never known anything like it. He'd lost his mother when he was fourteen, and had thought then nothing could ever hurt him more. But losing an only child was an agony altogether different. It had always been his understanding that mothers suffered such tragedies to a far greater extent than fathers, that men, never knowing the bond women formed with their children during pregnancy and childbirth, could not feel what a woman felt when death robbed her of a child. But Michael knew better now. Burying his son Adrian had destroyed him no less than it had the boy's mother, and eight months later he was still trying to go a whole day without some thought of Adrian cutting his legs out from under him.

Still, he considered himself far better off than Diane. She continued to cling to their son's ghost like a lifeline. Michael might heal in time, unencumbered by any hope he could ever again be as happy as he had been before Adrian died, but Diane was doomed to suffer forever. Whereas Michael had stopped asking God for something He would never grant, Diane continued to start each day and end each night on her knees before the Lord, pleading for the impossible. And not simply because she needed her prayers to be answered; she did it because she believed they would be.

Maybe if Michael had been able to convince her to join him in this cold new world that would never again have Adrian in it, they would still be together. Their marriage might only be a shell of what it had been, but they wouldn't be alone. They'd have a partner with whom to share their grief, to help carry the weight of their infinite loneliness.

But Diane would not be moved. As Michael's faith in miracles drained slowly away, Diane's went on and on, impervious to the enduring evidence of its impotence. In the weeks immediately following the accident, Michael was both willing and able to match his wife's devotion, prayer for desperate prayer. He'd been raised a good Catholic and remained one. He wasn't ashamed to confess a firm belief in a caring, loving God for whom all things were possible. But Michael had never had to put this belief to any real test. The things he had asked for—and, more often than not, received—resided squarely in the realm of reason, requiring no great stretch of credulity to accept. After the accident, however, what he sought from God—to have it all be a dream from which he could simply awake—was nothing short of an impossibility, the kind of event that only happened in the Bible. And what he came to discover, much to his horror, was that his faith did not—could not—extend that far. So his prayers became smaller and more infrequent as time wore on. Instead of miracles, he asked for a respite from his pain. When that didn't come fast enough, he prayed only for sleep. Nothing he wanted was ever granted to his satisfaction.

Meanwhile, Diane continued to ask God for one thing and one thing only: that her son be returned to her, by any means necessary. Michael went from being in awe of her resolve to finding it absurd, before finally resenting Diane for it. Her tirelessness made him feel inadequate, like his love for Adrian was inferior to hers. She made him feel guilty for giving up on something only he could see was pointless.

He'd needed to get out before he lost his mind. He had to try to piece what was left of his life back together, even if he had to do it alone.

Diane had let him go with almost no argument. She had shed all the tears she could on his behalf. She claimed to love Michael still, as he did her, but she no longer wanted her invocations diluted by her husband's increasing lack of faith. The morning he moved out, on an unseasonably cold, gray Saturday in August, she barely graced him with a glance.

They'd become little more than friends since. They spoke on the phone once or twice a month but said little of substance to each other. Sometimes Michael stopped by the house to get some mail that had been delivered there by mistake. They'd gone to dinner together once, in September, but could not bring themselves to do it again, afraid of being drawn back into a relationship that remained untenable. The subject of divorce was never broached, and they avoided the mention of Adrian at all times.

It had come as a surprise to Michael, then, when Diane called him that afternoon to ask for a meeting that night. He would have been alarmed had it not been for the sound of her voice. It rang with something he hadn't heard from her in a very long time, something he would have taken for happiness had he thought it remotely possible. Whatever it was, it would remain a mystery until they met at the house at ten o'clock.

"Why so late?" he'd asked. He got off work at six, he could be at the house by a quarter to seven. But Diane had ignored the question and hung up without offering him a single clue as to what the hell was going on.

When she opened the door to greet him now, he nearly gasped. Neatly dressed, hair combed, a touch of makeup. And she was smiling. His first thought: She had finally crashed and burned. Reality had set in and her response was to find it funny.

"Michael. Something wonderful has happened," she said. Not with the wide-eyed stare of a crazy woman, but with the measured delivery of someone overcome by an act of great kindness.

Before he could form a reply, Diane pulled the door all the way open and ushered him inside.

"We have to sit down. Come." She took him by the hand and led him into the living room, where she lowered herself onto the couch and, patting the cushion beside her, urged him to do the same. He sat on the opposing easy chair instead.

"What is it, Diane?" He was already feeling the itch to cut and run.

"I need you to do something for me. I need you to keep an open mind." She was keeping her voice down, treating the house like a movie theater that demanded their silence. "To remember the things you used to believe in before Adrian died and try—just *try*—to believe in them again."

Their son's name immediately set him on edge. "I don't understand."

Diane inhaled deeply. "He's back, Michael. Our son." Her eyes filled with tears. "He's on our bed right now. Asleep." She stood and started out of the room. "Come."

Michael couldn't move. His tongue was thick in his mouth and he was having trouble swallowing. He had feared this moment would come, certain it was the only possible outcome of his wife's unshakable resolve to pray their son out of the grave. Now that it was here, he didn't know how to handle it, what to say or do that wouldn't push her farther off the edge of sanity than she had already slipped.

"Diane. . . ."

"Come. See for yourself." She headed to the bedroom without him, leaving him no choice but to flee or obey. He chose to obey.

He found her waiting for him in the hallway at the open bedroom door. As he approached, he could see the room was dimly lit, the way it might've been for a child who disliked total darkness, as Adrian had. The thought of what he might find in the room terrified him. He didn't want to know just how far gone Diane's mind had drifted off, what kind of props she may have set up in the bed she and Michael once shared to make Adrian feel real to her again. But Michael couldn't stop himself from going in.

He could see right away that the bed was occupied. Something or someone lay under the covers on the right side, the side that had been Michael's. The shape wasn't big enough to be an adult. Michael inched closer, willing himself forward against every instinct to do otherwise. He saw the side of a small face pressed into a pillow. A boy's face. The hair above it, short and brown but unruly enough to obscure an eye, was something Michael had seen in hundreds of photographs, most of which he had taken himself. His breath caught in his chest. He stopped beside the bed and turned the head of the nightstand lamp to remove all doubt.

The next thing he knew, he was in his car.

Driving somewhere, anywhere, both hands frozen on the wheel. He didn't know what street he was on until he checked the signs. His apartment was miles away in the opposite direction. He knew he should stop and turn around but couldn't bring himself to do either, the impulse to run too strong to be denied.

What he'd seen at the house was a trick. An illusion manufactured by a mad woman. It had to be. He couldn't fathom what exactly Diane had done, or how she had done it, but he wasn't going back until he could.

His son was dead.

His son was dead.

SEVEN

MILTON TRIED FOR ALMOST two hours before giving up. Tonight, for some reason, no online search within his limited powers as a computer user would turn up a single thing pertaining to his killing of Adrian Edwards.

Stories he had viewed dozens of times, articles and postings he could find with his eyes closed, simply did not appear. It was as if the internet itself had been wiped clean of any mention of the tragedy.

Strange.

Milton went to bed cursing his luck. Tomorrow he would have to start looking for a new laptop, because the problem *had* to be his ancient computer. One more expense he didn't need.

He pulled the bed covers up to his chin and fell asleep not only immediately, but more soundly than he had in a very long time. He dreamt, as he sometimes did, though not of the usual things. Tonight, he did not dream about the taste of liquor in his mouth, or the pain in his knee he no longer had. Or the wife of thirty-eight years he had finally come to miss so desperately.

Tonight, he dreamt of something he never had before.

The funeral.

It was odd because he hadn't been there. He hadn't dared to even consider going. And yet, here he was in his dream, in a strange Christian cemetery, standing on the wet grass far from the grave site, spying on those in attendance. From his vantage point, through a steady drizzle, he could see neither faces or the casket clearly, but he knew who the people were and whom they had come to see buried. The children left no doubt.

There were half a dozen of them, at least, dressed in black like everyone else, clinging to the skirt or pants leg of one adult or another. All were silent and motionless, until one little girl broke away and ran off, her grief too great to bear standing in one place. No one tried to stop her. She ran past Milton, almost close enough for him to touch, and didn't stop.

Milton was about to call after her when the dream ground to a halt.

* * *

Diane did not second-guess herself. She had done the right thing.

Michael had reacted to the news of their son's return exactly as she'd feared he might, but things could have been much worse. Had she called him to the house earlier in the evening, while Adrian was still awake, Michael's rejection of the boy could have been devastating, for Adrian as well as Diane. Being treated like a ghoul by the man he loved most in the world would have crushed Adrian beyond words, and perhaps even. . . .

Diane dared not think about the *perhaps*.

As it was, she was gravely disappointed. She had hoped Michael would let the evidence speak for itself, encouraged by the power he once possessed to believe the unbelievable. Instead, he had fled, racing past her on his way out of the house without uttering a single word. What she had seen in his eyes, for the brief moment they had flashed in her direction, had spoken volumes. He thought she was crazy and, perhaps even more than that, dangerous.

She had called him three times in the hour since he'd left but he wasn't answering his phone. The one voicemail message she had left for him had gone unreturned. Diane didn't know what she would say when she reached him, but she felt compelled to keep trying. Sooner or later, Michael would have to accept what had happened, the incredible gift they'd both been given. The longer Michael lived in denial of it, the less he and Diane would appear to be deserving of it. He had to find his faith again and soon, lest God begin to question the wisdom of His blessing.

Diane finally went to bed, with her son right beside her. She would let Michael come to her.

He would have to eventually, after having laid eyes on a miracle.

EIGHT

"I'M THINKING ABOUT lying on this one," Allison said.

"What kind of lie?"

"Well, an MFA from NYU sounds better than a BA from Chapman, doesn't it?"

Flo gave her a look and a thin smile. "You aren't serious."

"No. But if I were, could you blame me? People do it all the time and get away with it. Telling the truth on these things is like playing baseball clean. It might be honorable but it's the juicers who get paid."

Flo shook her head and turned back to her iPad screen, leaving Allison to return her attention to her laptop. It was like this every night with the two of them now, using the time right before turning in not to talk or make love but to peck away at their individual devices, each on her side of the bed. Allison couldn't pinpoint when exactly this drift toward indifference had started, but if she had to guess, she'd say it began just over a year ago, on the heels of her losing the last steady job she'd been able to find in ages.

Allison Hope was a journalist, which was a more dignified description than forty-one-year-old unemployed writer who once worked for a number of now-defunct newspapers. Her partner, Florence Davenport, younger by six years, was an assistant professor of environmental sciences at the University of Washington Bothell. To say the two women were on different career paths would have been to understate the obvious. Flo was thriving and Allison was barely treading water, and it had been this way going on half a decade.

When they met nine years earlier, and for the first four years of their partnership, they had been equals. Allison was a regular columnist for the *Seattle Weekly*, writing for both the physical paper and its online iteration, and she was shopping a first novel to agents that Flo and the only two friends Allison had trusted enough to read it thought would become an instant bestseller. Instead, the book earned her nothing but apologetic rejections from agents and editors alike, and her job at the *Weekly* went away, never to be replaced by anything as remotely, or consistently, lucrative. She had patched together a decent living for a while, throwing herself into the lion's den of freelance writing, but little by little that work dried up, too, until she was left with no choice but to accept any form of employment she could get just to pay her share of the mortgage on Flo's home.

Teaching was the most obvious fit, and she'd tried it for almost two years, working as a tenth-grade substitute for the local school district. The hours were long and the work was grueling, and sometimes she came home convinced that no battlefield in the history of man could have been as dehumanizing as her assigned campus of the moment. But teaching was an honorable profession and the challenges were often intellectually stimulating, and the money paid almost all her bills. If it wasn't her true calling, it was at least a vocation versus a mere job, and she would have been happy to continue doing it had the state budget not gone into a death spiral last spring, taking the funds for her salary down with it.

Clerical assistant, grocery store cashier, coffee shop barista—she'd done it all since, inching her way through the writing of a second novel as she waited for something momentous to happen that might resuscitate her writing career.

It was a hope Flo had seemed willing to share without complaint in the beginning. She had thrown her lot in with a writer, with her liquid brown eyes wide open, fully aware Allison's good times could be countered by a stretch of bad at any moment. But a year of career instability was one thing and five was another. The money was a problem, but the more serious issue for Flo lately was the growing disparity between the Allison she had fallen in love with and the one she was committed to now. The former had been vibrant and full of promise while the latter was fragile and unsure. The relationship was an experiment that, if Flo's history was any indication, would probably not show the results necessary to keep both Flo's libido and affections alive.

And God knew Flo was all about results. That was one of the many things about her Allison had always found attractive. What Flo wanted or needed to happen, she made and followed a plan to realize. Excuses were for losers and quitters. Allison had initially thought her race—Flo was African American—was at the heart of this killer attitude; black people, it was often said, had to work three times as hard as their white counterparts to achieve the same level of success. But Flo attributed her unremitting work ethic solely to her father, the late Reverend George B. Davenport. She had watched him toil away at the church he built from the ground up—First Glory Baptist in Atlanta, Georgia—fifteen hours a day, every day, until he keeled over and died of liver cancer at the age of sixty-one. Flo had been nine years old.

"'When the Lord wants somethin' done, the fool asks why while the wise man's figurin' out how,'" Flo liked to say, repeating a lesson the reverend had instilled in her as indelibly as his own DNA.

Allison was confident her partner didn't consider her a fool, at least not yet, but Flo was losing faith fast that Allison could ever again be confused for someone wise.

Such was the sorry state of their love tonight, two people moving toward disparate ends of the universe despite sitting only inches apart. Neither wanted to call it quits, but only one believed they weren't delaying the inevitable. Allison was still in love, helplessly so, and losing Flo was no more an option for her than walking into the sea. She understood Flo's unhappiness, her diminishing respect for a partner so prone to failure, but Allison continued to embrace the hope she could turn things around by reclaiming her best self. Land a permanent job, write something she couldn't help but sell, put some real money into their joint checking account, and give them both reason to expect she could go on doing so for a long time.

It was what Allison prayed for every day.

Her faith in God wasn't much, just the detritus left behind by a lifetime of spiritual hunting and pecking, but it was more than Flo had. The reverend's daughter had grown up to be a woman beholden only to science, as proudly closed to the idea of a divine being as it was possible for any atheist to be. Allison knew all of her praying served no purpose other than to give Flo one more reason to question their relationship.

Allison kept on praying anyway.

"Wow. That's crazy," Flo said now.

"What's crazy?"

Her eyes still on her tablet, Flo said, "This Facebook friend of a friend—Betty Marx, she's apparently a vice principal at some elementary school here in Seattle—just posted about something that happened on campus today."

"Okay."

"Well, she says this young second-grade teacher just went nuts in her classroom this morning. Broke down in complete hysterics over this student she claims—get this—has been dead for eight months."

Allison had to grin. "What?"

"I said it was crazy. But Marx says the teacher was insistent. She told everyone the boy died in a car accident last March, she was able to describe where it all happened and how. She even claimed to have attended the child's funeral with everyone else on the school staff, including Marx herself. Naturally, they all say they have no idea what this poor woman's talking about."

"Can I see?"

Allison took the iPad, scanned the Facebook post and most of the comments. It was just as her partner had said.

"Henry Yesler Elementary. Do you believe her?"

"Marx? Well, I don't know her personally. She's a friend of a friend, like I said, and she's a bit of a gossip, to be sure." Flo took the tablet back, not bothering to ask if Allison was done with it. "But why would anyone make up such an outrageous story if it weren't true?"

"I don't know. I just. . ." Allison shrugged. "What could have made this teacher go off like that?"

"In a word?" Flo laughed. "Drugs. Psychotropics. What some kids drive a teacher to do these days just to keep from wringing their necks. What, have you forgotten so soon?"

She was talking about Allison's four-month stint at Franklin High, when she'd come home from school some nights and smoke half a key in front of something dead-stupid on television lest she go insane.

"Yeah, but those were high school kids," Allison said. "This lady teaches the second grade. How bad can that be?"

"Bad enough, apparently. Sounds like she scared those poor children to death."

Flo went back to her reading, the obligation to converse with Allison fulfilled for another night. Allison tried to return her own attention to revising her resume, but found herself unable to concentrate. Her mind kept drifting back to Betty Marx's anonymous schoolteacher, and the little boy the woman was convinced had risen from the dead.

Allison turned to Flo again. "Do you think this Betty Marx would give you the teacher's name if you asked?"

Flo barely registered the question. "What?"

"I'd like the teacher's name. Do you think you could get Marx to give it to you?"

Flo addressed her with a frown that was becoming all too familiar. "No. And why on earth would I ask her to, Ally?"

Ally. She used to call Allison *babe*.

"I don't know. Because I'm still a reporter at heart, I guess. It sounds like a possible story to me. Maybe something I could turn into a feature for *The Times* or—"

Flo raised an eyebrow. "*The Seattle Times?*" The idea clearly struck her as outlandish.

"Can you ask her for me, please?"

"Ally. . . ."

"It's important to me, Flo. Seriously. No one will ever know I got the info from her, I swear."

Flo's annoyance did a slow thaw. Allison didn't ask for very much these days, and this was an attempt to do something potentially profitable.

"Okay. I'll ask. But don't expect her to say yes, I'm practically a stranger to her and she's probably posted more on the subject than the school district would prefer, as it is."

"Fair enough. Thanks, babe."

Allison leaned in for a kiss, received one in return, Flo actually taking it on the lips for a change rather than deflecting it to a cheek. Encouraging.

But from there, they went their separate ways again, Flo tapping out the promised request to Betty Marx while Allison went back to her resume, newly energized. She had a feeling she was on to something. Something big. The story of an elementary school teacher experiencing a psychotic episode in front of a roomful of second-graders didn't sound like much on the surface, but Allison sensed there was more at play than that.

Had someone asked her why she thought so, she would have had no ready answer. She couldn't remember her instincts as a journalist, as good as they often were, ever affecting her quite this way. She only knew the teacher's story was a potentially huge one. More importantly, Allison was sure of something else.

It was her story, and hers alone, to write.

WEDNESDAY

NINE

IT WAS SHORTLY AFTER six a.m. when Michael called Diane. He hadn't gone home at all the night before. He'd simply grown tired of driving in circles and parked the car, indifferent to where he was, and fallen asleep as soon as his racing mind allowed.

"What did you do, Diane?" he asked when he heard her voice on the line. "The truth."

His wife answered with the tranquility of a nun. "I didn't do anything, Michael. All I did was pray."

"Bullshit! I said I want the truth!"

"I'm telling you the truth. You saw it for yourself last night."

"No. No." Standing outside the car, his clothes a wrinkled mess that felt like a rain-soaked blanket against his body, he ran a hand through his hair. "What I saw was a little boy or. . .something made up to *look* like a little boy. But—"

"It was Adrian, Michael."

"No. It wasn't. That's impossible and you know it."

"You used to believe in the impossible once, remember?"

"What I remember is asking for something that I never received. Because I was asking it of someone who either doesn't care or doesn't exist. That's what I remember."

"He does exist," Diane said. It seemed there was nothing Michael could say to dislodge her from a state of infuriating calm. "And the proof is still in our bed, right where you saw him last night. I'll have to wake him for school in about an hour. Did I tell you he went yesterday?"

"Stop it. Just stop it! Don't you hear what you're saying? Don't you know what you sound like?"

"I don't care what I sound like. All I care about is our son. He needs you, Michael. I need you. We've been given the chance to become a family again. All of us."

"Christ." Michael shook his head for the benefit of no one. "You really are insane."

"No, I'm not. Adrian's teacher will tell you. Miss Laura. No one besides us remembers, but she does."

"Remembers? Remembers what?"

"The accident. Adrian's death. No one else at his school has any recollection of any of it, but Miss Laura does. I'm not sure why."

Michael's head was spinning. What was she saying? That she'd sent some child who resembled their dead son—or whatever it was he'd seen in their bed eight hours ago—to Adrian's school yesterday? Causing one teacher, at least, to think their son had been returned to life? Was Diane really as mad as that?

"I have to go," he said, completely spent. "I can't hear any more of this."

"Don't hang up! Please."

"Diane. . . ."

"If what you've seen with your own eyes can't convince you, there is one thing I know that will. Forest Glade."

The cemetery where Adrian was buried.

"Go there. Right now. Look for Adrian's grave. I promise you it won't be there."

She hung up.

Michael considered calling her back, only to realize there would be no point. Diane had lost her mind. That much at least had just been firmly established.

He checked his watch, saw it wasn't yet six-thirty. There wasn't time to go home first for a shower and a shave, or a badly needed change of clothes, but he could still get to the recording studio by eight if he got a move on. He jumped in the car and started out.

He didn't really believe he was going to Forest Glade instead until he was following the curve of the freeway off-ramp that would take him there.

* * *

Laura woke shortly after seven with no intention of going to work. Elliott seemed relieved.

"I can't," she said.

Nothing had changed. *Nothing.* She had drifted into unconsciousness the previous night clinging to one faint, desperate hope: that the dawn would bring an end to the nightmare she was having. But the nightmare was not only still in force, it wasn't a nightmare at all. What had happened yesterday at school was real—Elliott's delivery of her principal's phone message was proof of that—and so the new day was nothing but an extension of the last. A little boy she knew to be dead and buried had walked into her classroom, as alive and healthy as she could ever remember him being, and she was the only one in the entire world who seemed aware of it.

How could she go back to school?

They would ask her the same questions they'd asked her yesterday, and all her answers would be the same. Even if she wanted to recant everything she'd said about Adrian Edwards, she'd never be able to do so convincingly. She still believed every word to be true. And if Adrian was there in her classroom waiting for her, the sight of him would terrify her no less now than it had then. As it was, the very thought of him chilled her to the bone. She could imagine no circumstance under which she could ever share a school campus—let alone a classroom—with the boy again. Or, more accurately, the boy's ghost. Because he *was* a ghost, whether or not anyone besides Laura recognized him as such.

"What are you going to do?" Elliott asked. He was dressed for work, travel mug of coffee in hand, itching to get out the door.

"I'm not going to do anything. I'm going to stay right here in bed until"—she searched for an end to the sentence—"until I understand."

"Understand what?"

"Why this is happening. What it means."

"We talked about that last night. It simply means—"

"I am *not* overworked. This is not a nervous breakdown."

Elliott let a beat pass before speaking again. Treading lightly. "Don't you think we should let a doctor determine that? I mean, that's what doctors are for, isn't it?"

"I don't need a doctor."

"The man said you've got to see one before you can go back to work, Laura. Whether you think you need one or not. I think—"

"I know what you think. You think what Howard thinks, and everyone else at school. That I'm crazy or something. Well, I'm not. Adrian Edwards is dead. He's *dead*, Elliott. An old man ran him over in a park last March and killed him. I don't know who or what that was at school yesterday but. . .it couldn't have been Adrian. It couldn't have been."

Elliott just looked at her, finding the restraint somewhere to keep what he wanted to say to himself.

"I'm all right," Laura said. "Go to work and leave me alone. I'll be okay."

"To hell with work. I'll stay home if you want me to. Just say the word."

"No. Go. Get out. Please."

He wasn't a man so easily dismissed. At times like this, he was prone to ignoring all her protestations to show her some affection: a hug, a kiss, a hand gently stroking the hair away from her face.

But not today.

After he was gone, Laura did exactly as she'd promised—lie in bed with no intention of moving until she had some understanding of what in God's name was going on. But it was hopeless. The minutes went by without changing a thing. Her memories of Adrian's death, and all the days that had followed, remained as undeniable as ever. She could neither drive them from her mind nor reconcile them with all the evidence she had that they weren't real.

Her cell phone rang around eight-thirty. Howard Alberts, checking up on her. She didn't answer.

Eventually Laura had to face the truth, the only one that held up under scrutiny: she was sick. Elliott was right. Her great affection for a special child in her class had spun out of control somehow, driven her to fixate on him to the point of inventing a false history for him, complete with death and resurrection. It didn't matter how genuine this false history felt to Laura; it had to be imaginary. What else could it be?

The district psychologist, a woman named Karen Nakashimi, had given Laura a referral for an independent doctor in town. Laura left the bed only long enough to dig the doctor's card from the bottom of her purse and retrieve her phone. She forced herself to make the call and schedule an appointment: the next day at three, the earliest the doctor had available.

She turned the television on and did her best to forget everything else.

* * *

Howard Alberts's phone was ringing off the hook. As he had expected, the second graders in Laura Carrillo's class had gone home the day before and told their parents about her breakdown in far greater detail than Alberts and the school staff had offered, and now those parents were flooding the principal's office with calls.

He did what he could to reassure them, giving his word Laura would not be allowed anywhere near their children again until he was satisfied she posed no threat to them, but not everyone was buying it. Several of Laura's students had been traumatized by her actions and their parents weren't happy about it. Almost half the children in Laura's class were being kept home, some indefinitely.

It was almost laughable. If these people knew the part of the story Alberts wasn't telling—that Laura Carrillo had gone berserk because she thought a boy in her class was a dead child walking—they'd probably never send their children back to Yesler. The way Laura had looked, the conviction with which she'd repeated over and over the same fantastic explanation for her behavior, would have convinced these parents she was unfit to be a teacher, at Yesler or anywhere else, and that any principal who had failed to recognize this fact earlier had no business being a principal in their school district. Alberts would have felt exactly the same way had their positions been reversed.

He had tried to reach Laura hours ago, to confirm she'd received the message he'd left with her fiancé, but she wasn›t answering her phone. The last thing Alberts wanted was for her to show up at school today, determined to teach her class. It seemed safe to assume that wasn't going to happen now—it was well after eight o'clock—but the idea still made him uneasy. He'd feel better if he could talk to her, hear her say she understood and would follow his orders to go see a district-approved doctor.

But that wasn't the only reason he'd been hoping to talk to her.

Nagging curiosity was the other. Could Laura have woken this morning in the same delusional state she'd been in yesterday? Did she still believe all that insanity she'd spouted about Adrian Edwards? Alberts hoped to God it wasn't true. Because one isolated incident of mental instability was something Laura's young career as an educator could probably survive; Alberts had known of teachers who'd suffered similar lapses and remained in the classroom for many years. But an extended detachment from reality would brand Laura a safety risk for all time. If she persisted in this talk of Adrian's death and resurrection, even for only another day or two, Alberts would be hard-pressed to justify any decision to return her to active duty at Yesler.

He wondered if he should feel similarly uncertain about Adrian. Not about the boy having died, of course, but whether he knew more about what had happened yesterday than he'd admitted. Ironically, unlike some of his classmates, Adrian was in school today. Alberts had seen his mother drop him off in the carport and had rushed out to greet them before Diane Edwards could drive away.

"How is he?" he'd asked her after Adrian had hurried off to class.

She spoke through her open window, the car's engine running. "He's fine. A little confused, but fine. Thank you for asking." She added, "How is Miss Laura?"

"I can't really say. I haven't spoken to her yet today. Naturally, she's taking some time off."

"Yes. I'm sure that's very wise."

Alberts found it interesting that she'd brought Adrian to school without asking about Laura first. If anyone could have been expected to keep their child at home until Laura's actions could be fully explained, it was Diane Edwards.

"Did you ask Adrian about what happened yesterday?"

"Of course."

"Do you mind if I ask what he said?"

"Not very much. He said Miss Laura just started screaming. I asked him if he knew why and he said no."

"Does he still think she was screaming at him?"

"No. We talked about that and he understands now that she couldn't have been."

Alberts considered that a curious choice of words. "Couldn't?"

Diane Edwards shrugged. "Well, I can't imagine why she might have been screaming at Adrian. Can you?"

Without sharing Laura's reasons for her outburst, Alberts had to admit he couldn't. He thanked Adrian's mother for her time and wished her a good day.

He had already decided to check in on Laura's students later in the day. They were with a substitute who was likely to be their teacher for some time. He hadn't planned to pay particular attention to any one of them; they all bore watching for indications of fallout from their harrowing experience the day before. But Alberts had just changed his mind.

He went back to his office, committed to having another talk with Adrian Edwards during the lunch break.

TEN

IT WASN'T THERE.

Michael had visited his son's grave dozens of times. He knew the names on the markers to the left and the right, behind and in front of it. He recognized the cedar tree at the crest of the hill above, and the hard cement bench with a crack down the middle that sat in its shade. Everything that should have been there was there.

Except for Adrian's grave.

The entire plot was gone. The familiar markers that used to encircle it were now crammed together with nothing but old grass in between.

Michael stood at the site for a small eternity, trying to believe what his eyes were telling him. The obvious conclusion demanded his acceptance, but even now he couldn't bring himself to acquiesce. Finally, he jumped in his car and drove down to the cemetery's main office, where he blew through the doors and marched to the service counter.

"What have you done with my son? Where the fuck is his grave?"

He heard the words come out of his mouth, knew what they sounded like, but he was powerless to stop himself.

Perhaps because they dealt with distraught, grieving people all the time, the two women behind the counter did not panic. The older of the pair, gray-haired and plump as a Thanksgiving turkey, wound Michael down until she could understand his ramblings, then tried to assure him no one by the name of Adrian Edwards had ever been laid to rest at Forest Glade. He must have the wrong cemetery. He ordered her to check her records again and again, cursing her refusal to believe what he was telling her, and she humored him for a while. But all the data at her disposal told the same story, and that story wasn't going to change no matter how many times Michael rejected it. Eventually he gave the woman no choice but to threaten a call to security.

Michael crashed out of the office the same way he had bulled his way into it.

He went out to his car and shut himself inside. He tried to clear his head but couldn't. He was locked in battle between what he knew to be impossible and what he now wanted with every fiber of his being to be true. His son was alive again. The world had been remade so that his death had never happened, just as Diane had said. All Michael had to do to make it real was join his wife in believing it. Find the faith in God he used to have before that terrible day last March, when the sight of Adrian's broken and bloodstained body had stripped Michael bare and cold and left him sick of living himself.

It was a devil's bargain: risk madness to have his old life back, or risk nothing and keep his present one, which was almost no life at all.

* * *

"I need a new computer."

Lisa didn't catch her father's comment. "What?"

"I said I need a new computer. Mine doesn't work anymore."

"Doesn't work how?"

"What do you mean, how? It doesn't work. I tried to use it last night and nothing happened."

"You mean the screen didn't turn on?"

"No, no, no. The screen is fine." Milton put down his toast, waited to stop chewing before continuing. "It's that search thing. What do they call it? The Google?"

"Google, yes. It's a search engine, Daddy."

"Well, that. That's what's wrong with it, the Google engine. It doesn't work anymore."

"You searched for something and couldn't find it. Is that what you mean?"

"Yes. That's it, precisely. I need a new computer."

Lisa laughed. "No, you don't."

The two of them did breakfast together like this every Wednesday, taking the same table in the back corner at Sherman's, his favorite deli. Lisa ordered according to her mood, but Milton was happy to have three boiled eggs and toast every time. Janet had an open invitation to join them whenever she wanted but she almost never did. She liked to use work as an excuse, but both Lisa and Milton knew Janet just wasn't interested in blocking out a regular space in her calendar for them. Her father was too aggravating and her sister far too cheerful.

"I don't? Why don't I? You think you can fix it?"

"It doesn't need to be fixed, Daddy. Just because you can't find something when you google it, that doesn't mean your computer's broken. Sometimes, what you're looking for just isn't there."

"Not there? Of course it's there. It's always there. But last night, it wasn't."

"What wasn't? What were you looking for?"

Milton suddenly realized his mistake. He hadn't meant for the conversation to turn in this direction. Neither of his daughters knew about his habit of revisiting the past and he wasn't ready to tell Lisa about it now. She had more patience than Janet did for talk of how he'd killed that little boy, but even she wouldn't understand his need to keep the memory fresh in his mind.

"Nothing," he said, biting into another egg in the hope of closing the subject.

Lisa studied him. She took a sip of her coffee, set the cup down gently. "What was it, Daddy? Tell me."

Milton kept chewing.

She waited.

"I was looking for a story in the paper. What time is it?"

"Don't worry about the time. I've got all morning and so do you. What kind of story?"

He wiped his mouth with a napkin, one last effort to put her off, but he could see it was useless. She wasn't going to let him leave their table until he'd answered the question.

"About the accident," he said. "And I don't want to talk about why so don't ask me. I have my reasons, that's all you need to know."

"Accident? What accident?"

"The accident in the park. What else?"

"The park?"

"Yes, the park. Of course the park. Why are you acting like you don't know what I'm talking about?"

His daughter's eyes grew big. "Oh, my God. You had an accident in your car at the park? When? Was anybody hurt?"

Milton tried to decide if she was playing some kind of cruel joke.

"I don't want to talk about this anymore. I'm ready to go. Where's the check?"

"Daddy, you have to tell me. If you had an accident and somebody got hurt—"

"Hurt? *Hurt?*" Milton couldn't hold back his anger any longer. "I killed that little boy! I ran him over and killed him! You know what I did as well as I do!"

All color drained from Lisa's face. "You killed. . .oh, my God. Oh, my God!"

Milton realized now she wasn't faking it; she really didn't know what he was talking about. The more she questioned him, the more obvious this became.

His agitation turned to fear. Clearly, one of them had lost their hold on reality and common sense said it wasn't the one who was only thirty-eight years old. The prospect of growing senile had always terrified Milton. His brother Stuart, three years younger, had died from complications of Alzheimer's six years earlier, and what Milton had seen of him near the end was horrifying.

"Take me home," he ordered Lisa, pushing away from their table. "I want to go home!"

She tried to continue grilling him on the drive back to his apartment but Milton was all done talking. As she let him out of the car, he could tell they had both arrived at the same conclusion, one Milton knew she would relay to Janet before the day was out.

The old man's mind was slipping.

ELEVEN

MICHAEL WANTED TO SEE the boy Diane insisted was Adrian again, but at some distance and without his wife around, so he drove out to Yesler Elementary. He timed his arrival for the ten o'clock recess, when all the children would be out in the yard, playing and having a snack.

He went straight to the main office. By rights, asking to see his son should earn him some strange looks and a few questions about how he was feeling. They would sit him down somewhere with a glass of water and shake their heads and wonder who they should call, too concerned for his wellbeing, the poor devil, to trust him to get home safely on his own.

But that was not the treatment he was expecting.

Based on all he had experienced over the last twelve hours, he anticipated a brief exchange between himself and the clerk, and maybe the principal, Howard Alberts, if he was around. Everyone cordial and polite, no one acting as if anything was amiss. Just a parent asking to see a student to deliver a personal message. That the parent was Michael Edwards and the student Adrian would raise not a single eyebrow.

And that was precisely how things transpired.

He had been to the office only twice before that he could recall, once to deliver a forgotten lunch and, on another occasion, to pick up Adrian after he'd fallen ill and Diane's car had failed to start. But Michael used to do morning drop-offs with some regularity, so he was known by sight to most if not all of the staff.

The office clerk, Edna or Edie, smiled warmly when he entered, and reacted to his request to see Adrian as if it were routine.

"This doesn't have anything to do with what happened yesterday, does it?" she asked, lowering her voice, presumably so that no one behind the closed office doors behind her could hear.

"No," Michael said. "It's just a small family matter, nothing at all serious."

And there it was. *What happened yesterday.* What else could she be referring to but the epic scene Diane had said Adrian's teacher caused upon laying eyes on him? Michael hadn't come here looking for additional confirmation of his wife's claims about their son—what he'd seen at Forest Glade Cemetery had been confirmation enough—but now there could be no doubt. Everything Diane had told him was true. Time itself had been rolled backward to undo not only Adrian's death but any record of it.

Still, for all the reasons he had to believe, Michael needed one more: Adrian himself. Michael had to see him again, to watch him move and hear him laugh, to see him do all the things little boys do, to finally be sure he was Michael's son. The child he had thought he'd lost forever, returned to him by the grace of God.

Edie (or Edna) offered to have Adrian brought into the office but Michael declined. He asked instead if he could go find his son in the yard; Adrian was in recess, wasn't he? The clerk hesitated—technically, parents weren't supposed to be given free rein of the campus—then decided to let him go. She had Michael sign in, gave him a name badge, and sent him on his way.

He found Adrian almost immediately. His son was watching a group of children play kickball on the tarmac, happy as always to coach and counsel rather than take part in the game himself. Adults had often mistaken Adrian for a snob, a child who held himself in too high esteem to behave like one, but that wasn't Adrian at all. It wasn't contempt he felt for his peers but empathy; the desire to help, to facilitate the joy of others, drove him more than anything else. Michael used to worry about him, unable to understand how a seven-year-old boy could be happy observing fun rather than having it, but eventually he realized Adrian was content. The boy's isolation was not indicative of insecurity, but of uncommon comfort in his own skin.

Michael watched him from a distance, behind a corner of the cafeteria where his son couldn't easily spot him. Adrian and another boy were engaged in a discussion that seemed to revolve around kicking motions. Adrian was no doubt imparting a lesson on the most efficient, and when Adrian began to laugh, amused by the other kid's inability to mimic his example, Michael had to do the same. The sound of the boy's laughter was dim but unmistakable. When the tears came, Michael knew he'd seen and heard enough. The child he had been watching was no apparition or facsimile.

He was Michael's only son.

* * *

Milton definitely needed a new computer now.

He'd come home from his breakfast with Lisa and immediately gone back to his laptop to try again. Over and over he entered *Adrian Edwards* in the Google engine box, and every time the results were the same as they'd been the night before: nothing. No articles, no blog posts, no photos. Everything on his screen referred to some other, adult Adrian Edwards, or had no connection to the name that Milton could discern. After an hour he'd lost his temper, ripped the mouse thing right out of its socket and flung it across the room, then pounded his fists on the keyboard until it was in pieces and keycaps were all over his desk and the floor.

He couldn't understand it. An old man needed to be able to trust his memory. In order to function like a normal person, he had to be able to recognize what was real and what wasn't. When confidence in that ability was shaken, fear took hold, visions of hospitals and nursing homes, faces that all looked strange and unfamiliar. And in Milton's case, the lure of drink would reassert itself. Milton would kill himself before he slipped that far.

The problem was his computer. It had to be.

He had killed a little boy last March. Adrian Edwards, seven years old, in Lakeridge Park. His foot had slipped on the brake and hit the accelerator. The proof was out there, it had always been out there, and Milton needed to find it again to stave off the notion dementia was written in the cards for him.

Milton went to the library. It had computers and they were free to use. He would run his search on one of them and put his fears to bed.

He tried three different machines before he surrendered to the unthinkable. His agitation eventually drew a librarian to his side, but she was of no help. He wanted her to explain how pages and pages of content pertaining to a given subject could be on the internet one day only to be gone the next, and naturally she had no answers for him.

Milton realized the young woman was starting to talk to him like he was one of the homeless people there who had nowhere else to go, so he left before his shame could turn into something more volatile.

TWELVE

MICHAEL COULDN'T BRING HIMSELF to go into the studio so he went home. He was in a daze, halfway between euphoria and delirium.

He went straight to the bathroom and took a shower, setting the water temperature hot enough to make a sauna of the room. For a long time, he just stood there under the showerhead, eyes closed and face upturned to the spray, not moving a single muscle. Waiting to be cleansed, for the last of his doubt—or his sanity?—to be rinsed down the drain.

He left the shower and fell onto his bed, naked and exhausted. His mind had been churning at a breakneck pace for over fourteen hours, ever since he'd fled the sight of his son curled up in Diane's bed the night before, and his body craved sleep.

He found it the moment his head hit the pillow.

* * *

Diane went to answer the doorbell thinking she was doing it for Michael, but it was Adrian's teacher, Laura Carrillo, standing on the porch. The young woman looked haggard and shaken, her clothing seemingly tossed on, and Diane couldn't help but feel a pang of guilt, knowing her son's role in his teacher's sad condition.

"I need to talk to you, Mrs. Edwards. Please," Carrillo said.

"Miss Laura. Of course, come in."

Carrillo didn't move. "Is Adrian. . .?"

"No. He's at school."

They settled in the kitchen at the breakfast table, Diane using every minute beforehand to ponder what she would say and how she should say it. She'd known this meeting would happen sooner or later and had prayed for the wisdom to deal with it appropriately. She was still guessing as to God's true intentions and feared one wrong word from her would prove disastrous.

"How are you?" she asked after Carrillo had declined all offers of food and drink. "I heard about what happened yesterday. Are you okay?"

Carrillo shrugged. "I don't know. I'm still trying to make sense of it, I guess."

"Howard Alberts said you had some kind of panic attack."

Diane waited to let Carrillo do with that what she would. She would speak the truth only when the younger woman led their conversation to a place where nothing but the truth would do.

"That's not what it was," Carrillo said. "And I came here this morning because I think you know that."

"Me?"

"It may very well be that I'm insane. That all this"—she glanced about the room—"is just a figment of my imagination. I've been trying to convince myself since yesterday morning that that's what's going on. I called and made an appointment today to see a psychiatrist because they won't let me return to school until I do. But I don't believe I need a psychiatrist. If I haven't lost my mind and you and I are really sitting here, in this house, at this table, then yes, Mrs. Edwards, I think you know exactly what happened to me yesterday, and why." She fixed her eyes on Diane's. "Don't you?"

After a brief hesitation, Diane nodded.

The confession seemed to take Carrillo's breath away. She inhaled deeply and said, "Oh, thank God." Her eyes welled with tears and she wiped them away with the palms of both hands. "I knew it. I knew it was all some kind of trick. It had to be."

"It wasn't a trick. This is all very real."

Carrillo blinked at her. "But you just said—"

"That you didn't just have a nervous breakdown yesterday."

"So, what are you saying? That the accident in the park, Adrian's death. . . ."

"All really happened. Yes. That's what I'm saying."

"But how?"

"I'm afraid there's only one word that fits: it's a miracle. God performed a miracle. I know that sounds ridiculous, but there's really no other way to describe it. I'm sorry."

"A miracle?"

Diane told her the way it was and how it had been. Her recital of the same prayer every morning and every night since the accident, her faith ebbing and flowing as the weeks and months passed. Michael's eventual loss of his own faith and the disintegration of their marriage. And finally, finding Adrian back in his bed three nights ago, in every respect the same little boy he had always been. *Her* little boy.

"It isn't possible," Carrillo said, shaking her head.

"But it is. Adrian is living proof." Diane smiled, letting her contentment serve as all the additional evidence necessary.

"I don't believe it."

"You don't believe in God."

"No. Frankly, I don't. But even if I did—"

"Did you ever?"

"Oh, sure. Once. Before I knew better."

"I see. So what do you believe in now, if not God?"

Carrillo had to think about it. "I'm not sure. Love? Death?" She found a smile of her own. "Taxes?"

"That's not much to live on."

"No. But I've been getting by on it. At least, I was until yesterday."

"You believe me, then?"

"No. Of course not. I still don't fully understand what's going on, but I know it's not what you're describing."

Diane got up to put some fresh coffee on and to let a moment pass before asking, "So, what are you going to do?"

"Me? I'm not going to do anything. Now that you've admitted the truth—"

"Miss Laura, God didn't just bring Adrian back to me. He changed things—everything, as near as I can tell—so that to everyone but the two of us and my husband, his death never happened. Surely you've noticed that by now?"

"I've noticed that it appears that way, yes," Carrillo said, turning all the way around in her chair to face Diane again. "That's why they all think I'm crazy. Howard, Betty, Edie, even Elliott. My fiancé. No one seems to remember anything about the accident, the funeral. . . ."

"And they never will. That's what you need to understand. If you go on trying to make them remember something that never happened—"

"But it did happen! You just admitted it!"

"No." Diane shook her head. "I'm sorry."

"You're *sorry?*"

Diane only looked at her.

"But you have to tell them the truth! If you don't—"

"If I don't, what? The world will go on exactly as it is. Which is precisely the way I want it, now that I have my son back." Diane had no desire to be cruel, but Carrillo needed to understand how things were. "I didn't ask for it to be this way, Miss Laura. I didn't care how He made it happen, I just wanted it to happen. And it has. It's the Lord's miracle, not mine, and I'm not going to do anything to undo it."

"Undo it?"

"That's right. What God can do He can just as easily undo, if He chooses."

"But what about me? What am I supposed to do with this 'miracle' of yours, now that I know about it? Pretend that I don't? Act like I'm not aware that it's occurred?"

"You don't have any other choice. That's what I'm trying to tell you. There's nothing you or I or Michael could ever do to convince people that Adrian was dead three days ago and now he's not, and it would be completely pointless to try."

Carrillo fell silent, letting the weight of Diane's words sink in.

"Let me show you something," Diane said, softening. "Please."

* * *

Diane Edwards left the kitchen, came back a few minutes later to set a short stack of disparate-sized and colored papers on the table in front of Laura. Laura saw it was a sampling of Adrian's schoolwork—paintings and drawings, illustrated writing assignments—and a pair of progress reports.

"I found these yesterday, in the drawer in my bedroom where I've always kept Adrian's things from school. I'd never seen any of it before. Have you?"

Laura sifted through the stack, one piece after another, her heart rising into her throat. She recognized the origins of each piece, yes, because she had assigned the work and seen many other papers exactly like it. Some of these had been graded and stamped with a comment in her own hand: *Great work! Nice job!* But every page here was new to her, and all bore the name and distinctively mature scrawl of Adrian Edwards.

"Look at the dates," Diane Edwards said.

They ran from March right up to last Thursday. Six days ago. Laura's signature was on the two progress reports that had been mailed to parents during that same eight-month period.

"Do you see? If I have these here, what do you think they have on file for him at school? If you were to check your own records, what would you find? It's all been changed, Miss Laura. Anywhere you'd care to look, or have someone else look for you, you'd see the same thing. Adrian never died. He's been with us all along. *That's* the only truth anyone besides us will ever believe now."

Laura could think of no way to go on denying it. She had the sense if she tried, if she inspected her own cache of student classwork, the result would be exactly as Adrian's mother was predicting.

"I know it's incredible. That it defies all earthly logic and reason. But God is real and so is this. What He's done is a beautiful thing, a wonderful thing. Accept it. Be thankful for it. Or else. . . ."

Edwards stopped herself from completing the thought.

Laura glared at her. "Or else what? Lose everything I love? My job and my career—is that what you were going to say?"

"I shouldn't have to say it. I think you've seen what your life will be like if you don't let this go. They'll never believe you. They'll weigh your word against all the physical evidence to the contrary and choose the latter. Because that's exactly what you'd do in their place. Isn't it?"

Laura fell silent, suddenly feeling as if she lacked the strength to stay upright in her chair. It had finally come down to this, a choice between two equally terrifying options: belief in something she could never hope to understand, or capitulation to the idea—probability?—that she was insane.

"What about Adrian?" she heard herself ask.

Edwards sat back down in front of her. "What about him?"

"What does he say? Or remember? Does he talk about. . .?"

"Death? No." Adrian's mother was smiling again. "He's like everyone else. For him, it's like the accident never happened."

"Then he can't tell us anything about. . .what it's like. On the other side, I mean."

"Oh, no." Edwards laughed. "I've talked to him some, of course. Just to see what he does know. But he doesn't seem to know anything he didn't know before. He hasn't changed. He's the same little boy I've always known and loved. That *you* used to know and love." She met Laura's gaze. "You don't have to be afraid of him, Miss Laura."

It wasn't a declaration as much as a plea. She was asking for Laura's acceptance of her son. Not so long ago, the boy had held a special place in Laura's heart, after all.

"I have to go," Laura said, rising.

She started for the door and Diane Edwards rushed to follow. "What are you going to do?" she asked again.

Laura kept walking. "I don't know yet. I can't think straight. I need some sleep, and some time. To think and. . . ."

Edwards opened the door for her. "Pray?"

Laura hurried off without answering the question.

THIRTEEN

BETTY MARX WOULDN'T give up the teacher's name.

Flo had made a gallant attempt to sell Allison's promises of confidentiality, but they fell on deaf ears, the vice principal at Yesler Elementary probably realizing she had made a terrible mistake that could cost her her job. The story of a young teacher under Marx's charge insisting she'd seen a seven-year-old ghost in her classroom should have been kept in-house, not made the subject of public conjecture on Facebook.

Allison was unfazed.

Yesler was a post-modern spread of single-story bungalows nestled deep into the Seattle foothills near Lake Washington. Allison pulled into the parking lot out front just before noon, in the hour-long space she had between her household duties and her latest dead-end job as an Uber driver. The sound of laughing children, emanating from the far reaches of the campus where the playground was situated, was a feather on the air as she entered the main office, where she was greeted like an old friend by the black woman behind the counter.

"Hi, there. Can I help you?"

Allison had visited the school's website before leaving the house, so she knew this was Edie Brown, Yesler's office administrator.

"I was hoping to see your principal, Mr. Alberts. Is he in?" She thought it safe to assume Betty Marx wouldn't talk to her, and doubted Laura Carrillo would be back at work only a day after suffering what Marx had practically diagnosed as a psychotic break.

"I'm sorry, no," Brown said. There were no antenna visible on her head, but Allison could sense Brown's were up all the same. "Mr. Alberts is out of the office and I can't say when he'll be back. What is this regarding?"

"I understand you had a bit of excitement here yesterday. Paramedics were called out to see a teacher of yours. I think her name is Laura Carrillo?"

The name earned a flinch. "I don't think—"

"I'm considering writing a piece on the incident and I thought I'd get a statement from Mr. Alberts to start."

"A 'piece'? Are you a reporter?"

"What's going on, Edie?"

Roused by the tone of their conversation, someone had emerged from one of the two offices at the rear. Not the principal, but a woman Allison recognized as Betty Marx.

"This young woman is asking to see Mr. Alberts, Ms. Marx." Brown gave the vice principal a look only Marx was supposed to see. "About that fainting spell Laura had in class yesterday. I think she's a reporter."

The look of horror came over Marx's face for only an instant, but it was long enough for Allison to catch it.

"A reporter?"

"That's right. You're the vice principal here, aren't you? Betty Marx?"

"That's right, Miss. . . ."

"Hope. Allison Hope." Allison held her hand out for Marx to shake but the vice principal wouldn't oblige her.

"Well, listen, Ms. Hope. What happened to Miss Carrillo here yesterday was nothing I or anyone else would call newsworthy. Like Edie says, she grew faint in class and was sent home after the paramedics examined her. That's all there was to it."

"I see. Then the information I have is incorrect."

"What information is that?" Brown asked.

"Well," Allison said, cutting a side-eye in Marx's direction, "I have it from a reliable source on social media that Miss Carrillo's breakdown was in reaction to a specific child in her class. A boy she seemed to believe had been—"

"Let's not talk about this out here. Come into my office, please," Marx said.

Brown started to complain. "But Mr. Alberts—"

"It's all right, Edie. There's no need to bother Howard with this. I'll handle it."

Marx opened the counter gate for Allison and escorted her into the rear office she had emerged from. She closed the door behind them, directed Allison to a chair, and sat down at her desk. The room was dark and cool, the blinds in the windows deflecting all outside light. Marx cleared space for her elbows on the blotter, then entwined the fingers of both hands in front of her with great precision.

"You're Florence Davenport's friend. The one she emailed me about."

"Yes." Allison couldn't see any point in denying it.

"I told Florence I had no interest in speaking to you, and neither will Mr. Alberts. What happened to Miss Carrillo here yesterday is a private matter I should never have made public, and I'm not going to make a bad mistake worse by discussing it now with a reporter. Do you understand, Ms...? I'm sorry, but I've already forgotten your name."

"Hope. Exactly what did happen to Miss Carrillo yesterday?"

"You aren't listening to me. I'm not going to comment on that, and neither will anyone else here at Yesler. Not Howard Alberts, not me, not anyone. So you've made this trip for nothing, I'm afraid."

"Oh, I wouldn't say that. If nothing else, you've removed any doubt that there's a story here. Otherwise, why would you be so anxious to put me off it?"

Allison smiled. Marx deflated before her eyes.

"Ms. Hope, please. Let this matter drop. Nothing good can come from your writing about it, I promise you."

"You mean you could lose your job if anyone found out you've been posting about it online."

"No. I mean...." She stopped, tried again. "Yes. It would be personally embarrassing to me, and possibly worse. But it's not me I'm worried about. It's Laura. If what happened to her yesterday became public, I doubt she'd be allowed in a classroom ever again."

"It was that serious?"

"No. It wasn't. But perception is everything, and a teacher who is perceived as a potential danger to her children is a liability few school districts will employ."

"Your post said she became hysterical in the middle of class. Over a student she claimed was dead."

Marx said nothing.

"That isn't true?"

"What's true is that she had a breakdown of some kind and frightened her children. She said some things that were nonsensical by way of explanation. More than that, I'm not prepared to say."

"Look, I'm not looking to hurt Miss Carrillo or anyone else. I'm just trying to do my job. A second-grade teacher has a meltdown in the middle of class because she thinks one of her students has risen from the grave. I'm sorry, Ms. Marx, but that's a story people will want to read about."

"What people? Who do you work for? If it's some sensationalist rag like the *Star* or the *Enquirer*—"

Allison thought about lying. Admitting to freelance status was often akin to confessing to rank amateurism. But realizing her independence might be a point in her favor for once, she said, "I don't work for anyone. I'm a freelancer writing this on spec. Which means I can approach it any way I see fit. I can write it as an exploitative piece of trash or an honest piece of journalism. It all depends on you."

"Me?"

"With your cooperation, I can write a story that treats everyone involved honestly and fairly. But without it. . . ."

Allison shrugged, her inference clear.

The vice principal grew quiet again.

"I don't want anything I tell you to be directly attributed to me," Marx finally said.

"No problem."

"And I won't give you his name. The student Laura says. . . ." She corrected herself. "The one who set her off yesterday."

This last condition wasn't to Allison's liking, but she nodded, started the recorder app going on her phone, and set the instrument down atop Marx's desk. She could always get the boy's name from someone else later.

Marx proceeded to offer her version of the previous morning's events, showing great care to avoid identifying the student who had triggered Laura Carrillo's outburst. It was a heavily redacted account but Allison didn't care. Even in such abbreviated form, Allison found the tale compelling.

What could have led a bright, young, but otherwise unremarkable teacher to suffer such a bizarre delusion about one child in her class? And why was this delusion so multidimensional, replete with false memories of events that everyone but Carrillo agreed could not have possibly ever happened?

"We really don't know," Marx said when Allison put these questions to her. "Drugs, perhaps?"

She caught the look on Allison's face and added, "Oh, I don't mean the illegal kind, of course. I mean prescription medication. Take the wrong combination by accident and a person is liable to experience all sorts of hallucinations."

"Was she on prescription meds?"

"Not that we're aware of."

"What about the boy? Could he have said or done something to upset her?"

"No. Were we talking about any other child, that would have been my first thought. But Adrian—" Marx caught herself too late. She glanced forlornly at the cell phone laying on the desk in front of her before continuing. "He's the exact opposite of a problem child. That's one of the things I find most baffling about all this."

"What does he say about it?"

"Nothing. He seems as confused by Laura's behavior as the rest of us."

"So what happens to Miss Carrillo now?"

"She'll be put on paid leave until we and the district are satisfied she's safe to return to the classroom. Which I'm sure will be very soon, providing the incident is kept private. Laura is a fine teacher, Ms. Hope. Whatever happened to her yesterday, I have every confidence it was something we won't ever see from her again. Far stranger things have happened in other classrooms, at other schools, I can assure you."

She sat back in her chair. "So you see? It's like I told you at the start—there's no story for you here to write. One of our teachers suffered a brief, essentially harmless emotional breakdown and was sent home strictly as a precautionary measure, in accordance with district guidelines. No one was hurt, and no one will be"—she sat upright again, to better look Allison straight in the eye—"as long as you behave in a professional manner and forget this whole thing, just as Laura herself is hoping to, I'm sure."

Allison smiled and took up her cell phone again. "I'd like to thank you for speaking with me, Ms. Marx. You've been very kind."

She stood to show herself out, with Marx fast on her heels. "Wait! I need to know what you're going to do."

"I'm not sure yet. I'm going to have to think about it. Have a good day."

Allison hurried past Edie Brown, through the gate in the service counter and out the main office door, Marx racing after her like a crazed fan before finally letting her go.

FOURTEEN

IT HAD BEEN A LONG time since Laura was last inside a church, but she went to one today. St. John the Baptist Episcopal was only blocks from the apartment she and Elliott shared in West Seattle.

She had no idea what she expected to gain from the experience. This wasn't something she'd thought about beforehand. She was driving by on her way home from seeing Diane Edwards and had turned into the church's parking lot before she knew what she was doing. She got out of the car and tested the front doors, then slipped inside when she found them unlocked. She sat down in a pew at the back and waited for something to happen, something that might give her reason to believe she wasn't going insane.

For over an hour she sat there in the lovely little church, alone, save for a single priest who flitted in and out, disrupting Laura's solitude with nothing more intrusive than a smile. Laura wondered when she'd last been inside a church and realized that, ironically, it had been the day of Adrian Edwards's funeral service at St. Bernadette's. Before that? It might have been a wedding she'd attended at a nameless house of worship in Phoenix during her junior year at Arizona State.

She couldn't remember devoting a moment's thought to God on either occasion.

But she was making the effort today. Her visit with Adrian Edwards's mother earlier had given her little choice. To accept what Diane Edwards had told her as the truth required a complete reevaluation of Laura's attitudes toward religion and faith. How could she leave the Judeo-Christian ideal of God out of any concession that Adrian Edwards had in fact been brought back from the dead? Laura's long-standing adherence to the belief that random chance was the only guiding force in the universe could not explain such a phenomenon.

And yet. . . .

Her feeble attempts at prayer here were yielding her nothing. She'd never been good at praying, having been left to her own devices as a child to learn what the word even meant. There'd been no open prayer in her home, short of the occasional saying of grace over a holiday meal, and she'd received no formal instruction in how prayer was properly done. What did one say to God at a time like this, under these circumstances? What could one ask for that did not sound ridiculous? She wanted an end to her confusion, certainly, but she feared the cost. If she were granted the gift of belief, if she were suddenly shed of all her doubts, her life would be changed forever. The lens through which she viewed the world would cast everything in a wholly different light: her work, her friends and family. . .and Elliott. The man she was engaged to marry, the man upon whom she'd hung all her hopes and dreams for the future.

How could she explain such an abrupt embrace of faith—something neither of them had ever found much need to discuss, let alone share—to a committed atheist like Elliott without losing him? What words could she use that wouldn't make her sound like a lunatic both beyond his help and unworthy of his love?

Such words did not exist. If nothing else became crystal clear to Laura in this hushed, immaculate little church on California Avenue, that much did. For all the reasons Diane Edwards had laid out for Laura to accept that Diane had asked her Christian god for a miracle and actually received one, Laura had one reason to do exactly the opposite, and it trumped all the others: Elliott.

She couldn't risk losing Elliott.

This was not the great epiphany she had come here halfway hoping to experience. This hour had been God's chance to speak to her, to turn aside all her skepticism with a sign she could not ignore. And no such sign had come. She had entered this house unconvinced of God's existence, had all but dared Him to show Himself to her face, and His response had been to do nothing. She was just as bewildered now as she had been at the door. What more proof did she need that the God of Diane Edwards was only a myth?

She went to her car and drove home. She didn't know what was happening or how any of it was possible, but she was more resigned than ever to make sense of it all without resorting to the smoke and mirrors of blind faith. She would talk to Elliott tonight, tell him everything she had seen and heard at Diane Edwards's home. Elliott would know what to make of it. Elliott understood things she did not.

Even things that seemed beyond all explanation.

* * *

Allison had been too excited to go to work. She passed on a driving assignment Uber tried to give her and went to a coffee shop to transcribe her recorded interview with Betty Marx. She wanted to start writing while everything was still fresh in her mind.

It had all happened, apparently, exactly the way Marx had described it on Facebook. The teacher had gone batshit in a classroom filled with second graders because she believed one of them was a dead boy she'd seen buried at Forest Glade Cemetery.

It would have been funny were it not so sad. Carrillo's poor students must have been horrified by the experience and Carrillo herself, depending on what the cause of her breakdown turned out to be, might never teach at Yesler again. If the frantic scene Carrillo had created in her classroom wasn't proof enough that she needed professional help, the crazy story she told everyone afterward, of car accidents and funerals that only existed in her own mind, surely did.

Oh, yes. There was a story here.

The teacher was the most obvious choice for Allison to interview next, but something about Marx's description of the child—she'd used the words *serene* and *imperturbable*—piqued Allison's interest more than everything else. According to Marx, the boy had said very little about what happened, and Allison had no idea why he would say anything more about it to her. But she was compelled to talk to him nevertheless. All she had to do was find him, with nothing but a first name to go on.

Another driving assignment came in for her while she was still at the coffee shop, and she didn't dare decline two in a row. Flo was already running out of patience with Allison's propensity for squandering what little employment she could scrounge up, and Allison wasn't anxious to give her partner anything more to grouse about.

For an hour or so at least, solving the mystery of little Adrian's last name would have to wait.

* * *

Betty Marx regretted talking to Allison Hope almost immediately.

She had thought she was being smart, undoing the mindless mistake of sharing Laura Carrillo's breakdown online by putting Hope off a story that could ruin Marx and Carrillo both, but instead, she had probably only made things worse.

She had told the writer too much. Her plan had been to say very little, to admit there had been an incident in Laura Carrillo's class yesterday but make it sound unworthy of anyone's attention. But as her interview went on, she'd gotten caught up in the story all over again, just as she had the night before, posting to Facebook with too many glasses of wine in her. What happened yesterday was fascinating, and not as easily explained away for Hope's benefit as Marx had wanted to make it. Drug use was often explanation enough for all kinds of bizarre behavior, but the more she thought about it, the less she could see drugs being the sole cause of Laura's state of mind the day before. Try as she might, Marx couldn't make a convincing case for the reporter to leave the story alone.

Now she was looking for ways to cover her ass.

The first step had been to tell Howard Alberts what she'd done before Edie could beat her to it. The office administrator hadn't said anything to her face, but she'd made it known with a frown how unwise she thought Marx had been to speak to Hope at all. Edie was puppy dog loyal to Alberts and could always be counted on to keep him informed of things she felt he needed to know, especially any act committed by a member of his staff that could be viewed as an attempt to usurp his authority.

Practically dogging Alberts's steps into his office as soon as he returned from his lunchtime campus rounds, Marx offered the principal a brief summation of the conversation she'd had with Hope, painting the writer as a shrewd interrogator who had tricked her into revealing more about Laura Carrillo's breakdown yesterday than she had intended.

"Did she say who put her on to the story in the first place? Somebody here must have talked to her."

"I asked, but she wouldn't say. Citing confidential sources and all that."

Which was exactly what Marx was praying Hope would do, should Alberts ever pose the question to the reporter.

"We have to warn her."

"Laura?"

"Yes, of course. This Hope woman will be trying to talk to her next. And if Laura isn't ready for her. . . ."

"You don't really think she'd talk to her?"

Alberts gave her a get-serious look. "*You* did, didn't you?"

"Yes, but," Marx tried not to stammer. "I was trying to protect the school."

"And Laura will want to protect herself. She isn't likely to agree with your account of things, Betty. She'll want to set the record straight where she feels it's warranted, and that will be a mistake, for her and for everyone else. The best thing she can do in her own defense is turn this writer away at the door and not talk to her at all."

Marx nodded.

"You said Hope doesn't know Adrian's name. Is that right?"

"Yes." It was a half-truth at best, but Marx wasn't overly concerned about it. She'd let slip only the boy's first name, and as long as no one else at the school spoke to Hope, Marx doubted the reporter could discover Adrian's full identity on her own.

"Okay. I'll give Laura a call right now," Alberts said. "In the meantime, you start making the rounds and let the rest of the staff know this reporter's been snooping around and we don't want anybody talking to her. Right now, if you could."

"All right." She was about to offer him yet another apology, but he already had his phone to his ear.

FIFTEEN

MICHAEL OPENED HIS EYES again after what felt to him like only minutes, but the alarm clock on his nightstand told a different story: he'd been asleep for almost two hours. He didn't know what had awakened him, but he was glad for it. His sleep had been restless and fragile, perforated by bits and pieces of a dream that was joyful one minute and disquieting the next. In it, he made love to Diane and spat insults in her face, watched Adrian being born and lowered into the grave. He saw things both real and unreal. He heard Diane's voice as she said the rosary and gave him the news: *"He's back, Michael. Our son."*

He lay on the bed, in no hurry to go anywhere. His eyes took in the bedroom as he asked himself the same question he'd been asking for many hours now: What did he believe? What faith in God—any god—did he have left?

For the majority of his life, he had considered himself a good Catholic. It was what his grandmother Emma, more than anyone else, had raised him to be. He bought in to all the rituals and doctrine of the religion because of her, and even after Emma died, he'd kept on believing. Not without question, but with the resignation of a man who'd weighed all his other options and decided none of them fit him as well as the belief system he already had. He went to Mass when he felt the need, confessed his sins and asked for forgiveness, and dealt with proclamations out of the Vatican with either respect or derision, depending on how well each aligned with his conscience.

This was who he was that day eight months ago when he'd taken the frantic, almost unintelligible phone call from Diane that would burn his world to the ground in the space of an instant.

He'd been grateful to have his faith in the immediate aftermath of Adrian's death. How else could he have hoped to survive it but with the knowledge he could call on an all-powerful, loving God to grant him more strength than he could muster on his own? Alone he was helpless, hurtling down a chasm of grief without end, but with the mercy and grace of God, maybe he could save himself. Maybe this day or the next, he'd find a reason to go on living.

Michael had yet to find that reason, but he'd gone on living anyway. If peace had come in response to his prayers, it had not come fast enough. Though he had never said the words—*I don't believe in you anymore*—his faith had withered in tandem with his marriage, so that now he barely knew how much of it still remained. He still went to Mass occasionally, and sometimes walked out afterward feeling something he hadn't felt going in. But he had no idea why. Once he would have said it was the grace of the Holy Spirit he was feeling.

Now?

Pondering the question, Michael let the minutes roll past, his gaze assessing the minutiae of his bedroom. He was drifting off to sleep again when something caught and held his attention: a pair of brightly colored objects on top of his dresser, nestled among a cluster of cologne bottles and the remote control to his television.

Superhero action figures. Spider-Man and the Incredible Hulk.

Michael didn't leave the bed until he was sure he wasn't imagining them. He made his way to the dresser and took the figures into his hands, brought each in turn right up to his face for a close inspection.

The familiar burn mark on Spider-Man's right calf was there. A memento from the night just over a year ago that Adrian had left the poor devil too close to the stove while Diane was making dinner.

But the Hulk. . . . To the best of Michael's recollection, Adrian had never owned a figure of the Hulk. And this one looked relatively new, devoid of all the scars and bruises the boy's toys generally bore after only a week in his possession.

Michael moved to the bathroom, superheroes still in hand, and only now spotted the extra toothbrush on the counter near the sink, and the tube of fruit-flavored toothpaste resting beside it. He'd been too much in a fog to notice them before, the shower the only thing in the room he cared to see. Now that he was taking the time to look for them, however, clues to Adrian's presence were sprouting up everywhere.

In the bathroom, a blue bathrobe hanging on the back of the door; on the floor in the bedroom, on the far side of the bed, a coloring book and a box of crayons; in the kitchen, Adrian's favorite foods and drinks in the cabinets and refrigerator. The second bedroom Michael had never used as such was exactly that now: a bedroom. Adrian's bedroom. Michael's desk and computer, his bookshelves and filing cabinet, had all been shuffled around to make space for a small bed strewn with his son's pajamas, a nightstand, and a dresser.

Of course, in the scheme of Michael's new reality, it all made sense. He didn't know how often he had custody of his son—he didn't even know why he and Diane had decided to separate, now that they didn't have Adrian's death to blame—but it was clear this was now Adrian's home as much as Michael's. From the look and smell, the *feel* of things, it had been that way for a while.

He went back to his bedroom and quickly got dressed. It was a few minutes after two; he still had time. He found his cell phone and called Diane, told her he'd like to pick their son up from school today and bring him home to her.

"I think that would make him very happy," Diane said.

* * *

A reporter. Allison Hope, Howard Alberts had said her name was.

Laura had finally answered one of the principal's phone calls twenty minutes ago, and she received the news of Hope's visit to Yesler with abject terror. Someone at the school had betrayed her; Alberts claimed to have no idea who. It had been mortifying enough to become what she was certain was a laughingstock at Yesler, among parents and staff alike, and now the whole world was about to hear of what she'd done yesterday. One reporter would inevitably turn into two, then three. . . . The school district might have ultimately forgiven her, left to handle her "nervous breakdown" on its own terms behind closed doors. But once the media got hold of the story, the district would feel compelled to let Laura go, citing the safety of the children and sending a clear signal to other potential employers that she was too high a risk to ever trust in an elementary school classroom again.

Only after some time had passed did Laura's sense of outrage and impending doom begin to give way to more mixed emotions. On one hand, the idea of being thrust into the public eye scared Laura to death, but on the other—who better to help her uncover the truth than a reporter? Alone, Laura was getting nowhere trying to piece together the events of the last twenty-four hours in a way that made any sense. Maybe if she spoke to this Allison Hope, wrested control over her own story while she still could, the two of them could get to the bottom of the hoax Diane Edwards was perpetrating. And oh, yes, this had to be a hoax, by any definition, because no other explanation better fit these bizarre circumstances.

Still, Howard Alberts had made himself very clear: Laura was not to say a word to Allison Hope should the reporter contact her. Nothing good could come of going public about what had transpired at Yesler the day before, he said, so the best policy for everyone was to withhold comment. He even suggested Laura's return to the classroom might be delayed or worse if she failed to adhere to such a policy.

An hour after talking to her principal, Laura still didn't know what she would do. It was damned if she did, and damned if she didn't. Everyone thought she was crazy; others at Yesler were bound to talk, oath of silence or no, and if theirs was the only version of events Hope got to hear, how else could the reporter portray Laura but as a loon? At least in an interview, Laura could prove herself to be sane and levelheaded, posing no threat to young children or anyone else.

In the end, she decided the question was yet another she'd be better off letting Elliott sort out for her, if he could.

Since he'd left for work, they had spoken only once, right before she'd turned into the driveway at St. John the Baptist, but beyond her repeatedly telling him she was fine, their conversation had been painfully brief. Now she couldn't wait to talk to him again, in the flesh. Another telephone call would not do.

Elliott got off work today at four. Returning to the shelter of her bed, Laura turned on the TV and settled in to wait.

* * *

"Daddy, are you okay?" Janet asked.

"Of course. I'm fine."

"Lisa told me—"

"I know what she told you. She thinks I'm getting senile. Or I'm drinking again. But she's wrong, and so are you for listening to her."

The minute Lisa had dropped him off at home after breakfast, Milton had known his older daughter would check up on him. The two compared notes about him with the thoroughness and zeal of Homeland Security agents. But he had hoped Janet would make do with a phone call. Instead, she'd left work early and shown up at his door around three, confronting him face-to-face so he would find it hard to lie to her. Janet was smart like that.

"She said you think you were involved in an accident. A car accident that killed a little boy, in March."

"I'm tired," Milton said, lowering himself onto his recliner. "I don't want to talk about this right now." And it was true. He was tired and didn't want to talk about the accident. Not now, maybe not ever again.

"Daddy, you have to tell me. Is that what you said? Is that what you really believe?"

He couldn't understand it. She was talking just like Lisa had, like somebody who didn't know what he'd done, like it was all just a story he'd made up in his head.

"I believe it because it's true. I don't know why you and your sister are acting like it didn't happen."

"Tell me about it. Tell me everything you told Lisa. Please."

She sat down on the couch across from him, leaned forward with her hands clasped in front of her like one of his doctors. When she set herself like this, there was no moving her, she was just like her late mother in that way, so he spared himself the wasted breath of further argument and gave her the short version, describing the accident and its ensuing impact on his life in only enough detail to make it clear it was real. It had happened.

"No, Daddy," Janet said, shaking her head. She was on the verge of tears.

"What? What do you mean, no?"

"I mean it didn't happen. None of it. I don't know where you got the idea it did, but it didn't, I swear to you."

"You're crazy. Both of you. You're both crazy!"

"Daddy, there is no little boy. You've never lost your driver's license. You drive yourself everywhere. To the bank, to the market, the dry cleaners. . . ."

"In what? My car was destroyed! How would I drive myself anywhere without a car?"

Milton knew Janet hadn't meant to wear her pity for him on her face; she wasn't that cruel. But it was there for Milton to see just the same. It occurred to him his daughter may have dreaded this moment as much as he. After all, what could be more devastating for a child than an elderly parent whose mind was unraveling? Or, perhaps even worse, had reverted to the irate, unrepentant alcoholic he once had been?

"Stop looking at me like that!"

"I can't help it. I don't know what you're talking about," Janet said. "Look in your wallet, Daddy. Go look at your keys. Your driver's license and car key are right there where they've always been. Your car's parked downstairs in the garage. Go ahead and look."

Milton had no intention of looking, the thought of what he might find chilling him to the bone. But he got up and went to the little table near the door, grabbed his wallet, and flipped it open.

There behind the clear plastic window, where nothing had resided for almost six months now, his own face stared back at him from a Washington State driver's license. It was a photo he'd always hated, his head tilted slightly left like a door off one hinge, his eyes nearly closed. He had been sick that day and could barely take a breath without sneezing.

He closed the wallet and glanced at the five keys on his chain. Five? One was for the lock on his front door and another for the deadbolt above it, one fit his mailbox and a fourth opened his safety deposit box at the bank. But the fifth was a key that shouldn't have been there: a Honda car key. Specifically, the Honda car key he had once used to unlock the doors and turn the ignition on his old silver 2007 Accord, before the car's mangled remains were towed out of Lakeridge Park to a police impound yard in Renton, never to be seen by Milton again.

He wondered how he could have missed the key before, until he remembered what a mess he'd been earlier in the day. His computer's lack of cooperation last night had put him in a foul mood, the expense of a new machine looming, and he'd headed out for his breakfast with Lisa in a dither. Who had time to pay attention to the keys on his chain? And when he'd come back from the diner, in far worse shape than he'd been when he left, it was all he could do to unlock his front door and let himself in without screaming for help. He would have missed a human skull hanging from his key chain then, let alone the key fob to an old Honda sedan.

"Daddy?"

Janet offered to walk Milton out to the garage so he could see the Honda for himself, but he had no interest and even less need. He knew the car would be there, just as she said.

There was nothing he could do now to get her to leave. He was crying and his distress had only intensified her own. She followed him from room to room, treating his pleas to be left alone with total disregard, bombarding him with questions he was disinclined to hear and ill-equipped to answer. She saw the wreckage of his laptop on the table in his bedroom and gasped, one hand flying to her mouth. She started to call his personal physician right then and there, but he clawed the phone away from her ear until she gave up the idea. Not for good, he knew, but for the time being.

"Daddy, you need help," Janet said, with more compassion than she generally showed him. "If you've started drinking again, it's not the end of the world. We can get you help."

"No! I haven't been drinking, goddamnit! Do you smell alcohol on my breath? Do you?"

"No, but—"

"I don't need anyone's help. I just. . . ." What? What did he need if not help? No answer came to him.

He had been to the boy's funeral. He had watched one of Adrian's classmates run from his grave, black pigtails flying behind her in the rain. Or. . .wait. No. That wasn't right. That was something he had dreamt the night before.

He dared not mention the dream to Janet.

"I'm going to stay with you here tonight," his daughter said. "I'm going to have Alan bring me over some things and we'll all have dinner together, and then I'm going to sleep in the guest bedroom. Don't bother arguing with me because I'm not going to change my mind."

He argued with her anyway. He liked her husband well enough; Alan was a short, barrel-bellied insurance salesman with a relaxed manner and an uncanny ability to tell jokes that were actually funny. But Milton didn't want to see him tonight. He didn't want to see anyone. He was confused and frightened and other people in the house would make him only more so.

Janet would not be swayed, however. There would be no peace for him tonight.

SIXTEEN

IT BECAME REAL for Michael only after he'd held Adrian in his arms.

The fear that it was something other, a fevered dream or extended lapse of sanity that was soon to pass, did not leave him until that moment. The boy had seen Michael standing in the carport, waiting, and taken off running toward him, wearing the wide grin Michael had seen in his sleep a thousand times since last March. With the reckless abandon he had always reserved for his father alone, Adrian threw himself into Michael's embrace and laughed. And that was when Michael knew. This was his son. This was Adrian.

When he could bring himself to let the boy go, Michael loaded him into the car and drove him home. During the drive, they talked about nothing important, just the usual trivialities they used to exchange regarding Adrian's day at school. Laura Carrillo's name didn't come up, nor did the subjects of death and the afterlife. If today was different from any the week before for Adrian, the indicators were lost on Michael.

Diane was waiting for them in the driveway when they pulled up. Michael stood back while she and Adrian shared a hug, then he went to her himself and pulled her close, burying his face in her hair as the tears came like rain. Neither of them said anything for a long time. They just stood there, holding on to each other as if for dear life, occasionally daring to laugh at something they imagined was relief.

Gratitude came later, after they'd gone inside and settled in the kitchen. Diane was starting dinner while Michael watched from the dining table, his attention divided between his wife and Adrian, who was stretched out on the floor of the living room reading a book. To Michael's eye, Diane looked like the woman he'd taken vows with almost nine years ago, her eyes full of light and her face aglow with serenity.

"I'm afraid to breathe," Michael said.

Diane peered over her shoulder at him. "Because you're afraid you'll wake up?"

"Yes."

"I know. I felt the same way at first." She turned back to the stove. "But it's okay to breathe. This isn't a dream."

"It isn't?"

"No."

"How can you be sure?"

"Because I've never been this happy in a dream."

Michael went to her, slipped both arms around her waist. They stood like that for a while, until Michael said, "There's a question I've been asking for hours now. I expect you've been wondering the same thing."

"Why us."

"Yes. Why us? Why *our* son, Diane? Why your prayers and not someone else's?"

Diane wriggled free from his grasp and resumed the business of putting dinner together. "I don't know. Does it matter?"

"Does it matter?" Michael asked, surprised. "Of course it matters."

"Why? What difference does it make why He did it? It should be enough for us that He did, Michael."

"Diane—"

"Questions are for people who need answers in order to believe. Is that what you're saying? That you still don't believe?"

"No. No! But—"

"But what?"

"But what happens now? What are we supposed to do? You and I were leading separate lives only yesterday. Do we just pick up now where we left off and pretend it's always been this way, without having any understanding whatsoever about the point of it all?"

"Yes. Why not? Would that be so hard? We aren't meant to understand everything. Some things we're just supposed to accept and be grateful for."

"I am grateful. I do accept it. I just. . . ." He went to the edge of the living room, fixed his eyes on their son. "I just want to know what we did to deserve this."

Diane slipped up alongside him and took his hand in hers. "We didn't do anything. We *don't* deserve it. We're no different from anyone else in the world and neither is our son. He just chose us, Michael. I don't care why and neither should you."

Michael turned to her, prepared to extend the argument. This wasn't as simple as she was making it sound. Belief in the incredible, and the impulse to question it, was not something you could turn on and off like a switch. But Michael held his tongue. He knew Diane was right: they were owed no explanations. They were owed none and would receive none. Faith was nothing if not a contract with God to accept what He willed to be, no matter how great or small, in relative silence.

Acknowledging his wife's wisdom with a smile, Michael leaned down to kiss her. Adrian, seeing them, laughed, and his laughter so delighted his parents, they were moved to laugh themselves.

* * *

By the time Elliott got home, Laura had grown tired of lying in bed. She wanted dinner out and she wanted some air, so she talked him into walking up to their favorite Thai restaurant on Genesee Street. She put off all his questions about her day until they were out the door and on their way.

"Now do you believe me?" she asked, after telling him about her visit with Diane Edwards.

"No. I don't believe any of it," Elliott said, exasperated.

"Excuse me?"

"Laura, what do you want me to say? The woman is obviously either insane or incredibly cruel, playing along with you like that. A miracle? Come on!"

"Playing along with me?"

"Well, what would you call it? You go over there talking about her son being dead and buried and she agrees with you?"

"She agreed with me because it's what she wants me to believe! All that business about a miracle is nonsense, I know that. But everything else she said proves I'm not imagining it. She really did fake Adrian's death. Or something."

"Or something?"

"I don't know what she did, Elliott. I've been trying to figure it out on my own, but I just can't."

"And you think I can?"

Laura stopped walking to turn to him. "You have to. You must. If I can't find a rational explanation for what's happening to me, I'll never be able to teach again. They won't let me."

"Laura, you already know what the rational explanation is. You had some kind of stress-related breakdown yesterday. You must be more tired and uptight than either of us realized and you simply broke down. Nothing Adrian's mother told you today changes that fact."

"No." Laura shook her head. "You aren't listening to me! She said—"

"Forget what she said. What did she *prove*? What evidence did she show you that Adrian died in a car accident, the way you insist he did?"

"The papers! She showed me all his papers, all his schoolwork from. . .from after. . . ."

"Exactly," Elliott said. "All she proved with those papers was something everyone but you and she seem to agree on—that her son's been in school, doing work for you in class, since last March, when you say he died."

He was right. Laura felt like a fool for not having realized it before. All Diane Edwards had done to corroborate Laura's memory of Adrian's death was talk, which was proof of nothing.

"Her husband. She said her husband knows the truth, too," Laura said. "We could talk to him. You and me, together."

"No," Elliott said. "No way." He started walking again, not appearing to care whether she followed or not.

She hurried after him. "Elliott, please!"

"This is crazy, Laura. I'm trying to help you, but you aren't being reasonable."

"All I'm asking is for you to be in the room when I talk to him. You won't have to say or do anything, just be there."

Elliott kept walking. Laura stopped.

"All right. I guess I'll have to talk to the reporter, then."

That brought her fiancé to a halt. He turned. "What are you talking about?"

"Some writer is doing a story about what happened at school yesterday. Howard called to warn me not to talk to her. I wasn't going to, but now I'm thinking maybe I should."

Elliott closed the gap between them. "You can't be serious."

"I'm not crazy, Elliott, and I didn't have a nervous breakdown yesterday." She was choking back tears. "I swear to you, I remember what I remember about Adrian Edwards because it happened, or appeared to happen. All of it. And I need you to help me prove it."

"Jesus...."

"I don't want to talk to that reporter but if no one else will listen to me—"

"All right. All right!" Elliott threw up his hands. "I'll go with you to talk to the father. But only on one condition."

Laura smiled, scraped the tears from her cheeks with the back of both hands. "Name it."

"If he tells us the same thing that I've been telling you—that this insane idea you have that a funeral was held for his son eight months ago is just that, insane—that'll be the end of it. You won't talk to any reporters, you won't talk to me, you won't talk to anybody else about this ever again except the doctors you need to see in order to go back to work. Is that understood?"

Laura nodded. "Understood. Can we go tonight?"

"Tonight?"

"To see Michael Edwards. Adrian's father. I'm sure I have an address for him somewhere. We could go after dinner."

She could see it was the last thing on earth Elliott wanted to do. This could not be the end of a long day at work he had hoped to forge. But he loved Laura and she was in trouble. Serious trouble.

"Okay."

They went on to the restaurant, walking hand in hand.

* * *

Milton went to bed early, right after dinner. Janet had made roast beef and scalloped potatoes, his favorites, but he barely touched a thing on his plate. The table had grown stone-cold silent after he finally lost his temper and screamed to be left alone. Janet and Alan had been peppering him with questions about Adrian Edwards and the accident from the moment Alan walked in the door, and Milton was sick of it. They didn't believe any part of what he had to say, especially his denials regarding drink, so what the hell was the point?

He went to his room without bothering to clear his dishes or say good night, and they let him go with nary a word of complaint. Milton knew why. Any other time, Janet would be pleading with him to stay up a little longer, take a seat with her on the couch in the living room while she watched one of her insipid reality shows on television. But not tonight. Tonight, she was happy to see him turn in early, because she and Alan had bourbon bottles to search for, and important things to talk about that they couldn't discuss with Milton around to hear them.

Next June, Milton would celebrate his seventieth birthday, but as he crawled into bed, he felt much older than that.

* * *

Alan Berger had always had a calming effect on his wife, but Janet was beyond his powers of influence tonight. She was certain that alcohol or the ravages of time, or some combination of the two, had finally laid claim to her father's mind, and she was already making plans to become his full-time caretaker. She started crying the minute Milton shuffled off to bed, and every effort Alan made to comfort her was for naught.

"I can't believe it," she said, shaking her head. "Just the other day, he was perfectly fine!"

"He's still perfectly fine," Alan said, with all the supreme confidence he could fake. "Poor guy's just a little confused, that's all."

"Confused? Did you hear him? He thinks he killed a little boy! He talks about it like something that really happened. Names, dates, locations...."

"Yes, I know, I heard the man. But maybe he talks about it that way because it *is* real. Or some of it is, anyway."

"What?"

"Maybe a little boy really was killed in that park last March, exactly the way he says. Only he just read about it, or saw it on television. I can't explain why he would want to hold himself responsible, but...."

"Momma. It's his guilt over the way he treated Momma." Janet nodded vigorously, embracing the idea. "Yes, that's it. That must be it. He's doing that thing they say people do when they have feelings about one person that they should really have about someone else."

"Transference," Alan said.

"Yes! Transference! He's transferring his guilt over Momma to this little boy who was killed in the park."

Alan smiled, happy to have given his wife some reason to believe her father was not on the brink of madness or—despite their having found no evidence to support such an idea—back in the clutches of his once raging alcoholism. And yet, Alan had his own doubts.

"Assuming there was such a little boy," he said.

"Assuming? But you just said—"

"I was thinking out loud, sweet. Maybe the boy's real and maybe he isn't. If he is, then our theory's sound. If not. . . ."

Janet glowered at him.

"It's possible he made the whole thing up. Which wouldn't make him crazy, of course, but it would suggest we're dealing with more than transference here."

And just like that, Janet was crying again. Alan felt like an idiot.

He watched her sob into a balled-up tissue and tried to think of a way to reverse the damage.

"He said the boy's name. Adrian something."

"Edwards." Janet nodded. "Adrian Edwards."

"That was it. And his mother's name was Diane, he said."

"Diane Edwards, yes. And the father's name was Michael. Why?"

Alan got his smartphone out, tapped a number with one hand while waving his wife off with the other. Into the phone, he said, "Seattle, Washington." Then, "Diane Edwards."

SEVENTEEN

MICHAEL WENT HOME SOON after they put Adrian to bed. Diane wanted him to stay the night—she would have been open to any sleeping arrangement satisfactory to him—but she knew better than to ask. Her husband had been given enough to absorb over the last twenty-four hours as it was. Trying to force reconciliation on him, too, even for only one night, would have been folly.

Despite the bravado she'd put on for Michael, she didn't know what she was supposed to do, how God did or did not want her to function from here on. It felt as if her every step held the potential for ruin. When your world was this close to perfect, the fear of doing anything to lose it was almost paralyzing.

She had been praying all day that she had dealt with Laura Carrillo properly. Telling the young woman the truth had seemed fraught with risk. Intellectually Diane understood Carrillo posed no threat; there was nothing Carrillo could do to prove Adrian had passed away eight months earlier, and that both his parents were fully aware of the fact. Still, Diane wondered just how complicated Carrillo could make their lives, now that Diane had given the teacher reason to go on speaking the truth in defense of her own sanity.

For all her uncertainty, there was still no question in Diane's mind that the miracle of Adrian's return was not meant to be widely known. God's scrubbing of the past to remove any reference to his death made that obvious. And yet, the evidence was equally clear that God had chosen to leave the eyes of some open to the truth. She and Michael for obvious reasons, and Laura Carrillo for no reason Diane could imagine.

Were they the only ones?

The question made Diane uneasy. It didn't seem possible that God had brought Adrian back to life just to receive glory and praise—or, in

Laura's case, scorn—from three people. Surely there were others. But who and how many? And why had they been chosen?

Diane only had to wait until the phone rang, minutes after her reunited family's first dinner together, to learn the answer.

* * *

"Hello, is this Diane Edwards?" Alan asked. He and Janet had agreed he should be the one to make the call, but now he wasn't so sure he could do this.

"Yes?"

"Adrian's mother?"

They had discussed exactly how this question should be phrased. If her child had indeed been killed, asking in the present tense if she had a son named Adrian might upset her, but so would using the past tense if her son was alive. This was the compromise they'd come up with.

The woman on the other end of the phone line hesitated before answering. "Yes, this is Adrian's mother. Who is this?"

There had been no trace of heartache in her voice. A good sign. "My name is Alan Berger, Ms. Edwards. I know this is going to sound ridiculous and I apologize beforehand, but my father-in-law seems to think. . . ." Alan had to stop, gather all his nerve to say the rest: "He seems to think Adrian was involved in an accident he witnessed some time ago and I'm just calling to make sure. . .well, I guess I'm calling to make sure your son's all right."

Again, Diane Edwards, whose number Alan had gotten from directory assistance, did not respond right away. "What kind of accident?"

"A car accident. Last March. That isn't possible, is it?"

"No. It isn't. What's your father-in-law's name, Mr. . .Berger, is it?"

"Yes. Alan Berger. My father-in-law's name is Milton Weisman. His daughter Janet is my wife. I understand you live in Lakeridge. Milton lives here in Skyway. Perhaps you or your son know him from somewhere?"

"No. I don't think so," Diane Edwards said, almost before Alan had finished the question.

"Lakeridge Park, maybe? Milton says that's where the accident occurred."

"We never go to Lakeridge Park. It's always too crowded there."

"I see. Then Adrian—"

"Has never been in a car accident. No, thank God, never."

"Good. Good. I'm so glad to hear that. Milton had my wife and I quite alarmed."

Diane Edwards didn't say anything.

"Though I must say we can't imagine where he would get such a story about a little boy he doesn't know. Are you sure the name's not familiar? Milton Weisman?"

"I'm quite sure."

"Is there any chance Adrian knows him from somewhere that you don't?"

The thought occurred to Alan this was a terrible thing to ask—it made Janet's father sound like a pedophile. But all Diane Edwards said was, "No, Mr. Berger, there isn't. His father and I make it a point to know all of Adrian's friends, especially the adults. Now, I'm sorry, but—"

"Of course. I've bothered you enough. Thank you for your patience and have a good night."

"Wait! Mr. Berger?"

"Yes?"

"Maybe I should talk to him."

"Excuse me?"

"Your father-in-law. Mr. Weisman. I'd like to talk to him. Would you mind?"

Alan couldn't hide his surprise. "I'm afraid he's gone to bed. Why—"

"Well, I'm curious now, just as you are. I'd like to know how he knows my son's name, and I'm sure my husband would, too. Maybe if I spoke to him, Mr. Weisman and I could figure it out together. And I could reassure him that Adrian is fine. Could you have him call me tomorrow sometime?"

This wasn't at all a turn Alan had thought their conversation would take. "I suppose so. I can ask him, anyway. But—"

"Please. I'd very much appreciate it. Good night."

She hung up before Alan could say anything more.

Standing right behind her husband in Milton's living room, close enough to be Alan's second skin, Janet said, "Well? What did she say?"

Alan told her.

"She wants to talk to him?"

"That's what she said."

"Do you think she was lying?"

"About wanting to talk to him?"

"No! About the boy being alive."

"No. Of course not. Why would she lie about something like that?"

"I don't know. I just. . . ." She started crying again. "Oh, my God, poor Daddy! What's happening to him?"

Alan put his arms around his wife, let her weep into his shoulder. He didn't know what to say. She had every right to be worried about her father. Sane people didn't imagine they'd run over the children of perfect strangers in the park. Especially children who were still alive. Some of Diane Edwards's responses to Alan's questions had seemed peculiar, if not dishonest, but there was one thing about her Alan could say with certainty.

She was not the mother of a dead little boy.

* * *

Milton Weisman. Of course.

Diane chided herself for not thinking of the old man before now. Who else would God have wanted to bless with the knowledge of her son's resurrection more than the man who had killed him?

It had taken Diane a long time to care about Milton Weisman's pain. Her own suffering had come first. She understood Weisman was sorry, and that his only crime was being old and slow and clumsy. She could see his shame and guilt were heartfelt, that his grief ran nearly as deep and wide as her own, but it was hard for her to give a damn. There had been nothing Milton Weisman could do to bring her son back, and that was the only form of recompense Diane had any interest in accepting from him.

Time, however, had dulled the blade of her anger. Eventually her lack of compassion for Weisman withered and waned, as had Michael's, the two of them unable to deny the old man their pity forever. They realized Weisman was also living with the loss of their son, only without any of the sympathy and support they had been showered with. It became impossible for Diane to go on hating someone upon whom others were heaping so much abuse in her name.

Once, before her change of heart, Weisman had shown up at the house unannounced. Only weeks had passed since the accident and Diane couldn't find it in herself to answer the door. Michael was at work, so the awkward business of talking to the old man couldn't be relegated to her husband. Peering out at Weisman through the narrow space between curtain and living room window, Diane let him ring the bell until he grew weary and walked away, never to return. Until this moment, the memory had given Diane no cause for regret. She knew what Weisman wanted to say and had spared him the trouble.

Now she wished she had heard him out.

If Milton Weisman called her tomorrow, it would be a day of second chances for them both.

* * *

Milton couldn't sleep.

He had tried for only several minutes before giving up. He went to the kitchen for a glass of water. Halfway down the hall, he stopped. Janet and Alan were talking about him in hushed tones. Milton stood there in the dark, stock still, and listened to them worry over the scope of his madness. Then he heard Alan call Adrian Edwards's mother on the phone.

Milton was privy to only half of their conversation, but he didn't need to overhear Alan tell Janet the other half afterward to know what Diane Edwards had said: Milton's name meant nothing to her. There had been no accident in the park.

Adrian was alive.

Milton returned to his room before they could catch him spying on them, climbed back into his bed as if he'd never left. He lay there in the dark and fought the urge to cry for what felt like the fifteenth time that day. He was tired of crying. But he was more tired of being afraid. What the hell was going on? How could a man, regardless of age, be perfectly sane one day and completely mad the next?

He had killed Adrian Edwards. He could see the view from his windshield as the Honda vaulted the parking-lot curb, engine screaming, and careened toward the play structure in the park, as if it were all only moments removed from the present. He could feel the steering wheel in his hands, its metal core threatening to bend beneath the death grip of his fingers. The little boy on the ladder of the slide vanishing below the car's hood, his mother's scream splitting the park's quiet, the Honda plunging into a tree. Every detail was as fresh in Milton's mind as his last thought, and each held the fine, intricate filigree that nothing dreamed or imagined could ever claim.

He had killed Adrian Edwards.

He had come to grips with this fact long ago. Milton didn't care what the boy's mother said. She was either a liar or insane herself. The loss of a child was a heartbreaking thing. If Adrian's death had driven his mother mad, she would hardly be the first mother to suffer such a fate. As for why Milton's daughters and his son-in-law seemed similarly deluded, or why all the goddamn computers in the world had chosen this moment to also forget the accident, Milton had no answers. His certainty went no further than this: he was not insane. He was not growing senile. Something was happening he couldn't explain, but it had nothing to do with a loss of his faculties.

He had heard Alan tell Janet that Diane Edwards wanted to talk to him. Alan didn't know why, but Milton thought he did. She wanted to tell Milton the truth about what was happening and why.

Tomorrow, against her better wishes, Janet would tell him what Adrian's mother had told Alan tonight, and much to his daughter's horror, Milton would call Diane Edwards right away. He would ask her for a meeting. He would send Janet off to work and go alone.

Driving the very same silver Honda Accord that had killed Diane Edwards's son.

EIGHTEEN

FLO DIDN'T COME HOME for dinner. This time her excuse was a lunch meeting that at the last minute had turned into one over dinner. It was becoming a habit with her, finding some reason not to come home until late, but beyond Flo's ever-growing indifference to Allison, she had done nothing yet to suggest her late nights were anything but business related.

Still, Allison wondered.

She was desperate to tell her partner about the day's events. They'd had a brief conversation over the phone late that afternoon, but that was all. Allison imagined Flo's reaction would be muted, slow as she always was to get excited about things that could not be easily explained. But all Allison needed Flo to do tonight was listen, to serve as a sounding board for all the thoughts and questions about Laura Carrillo that Allison had bottled up inside her.

Yet here she was alone, waiting.

She still needed a last name for Adrian, the little "dead" boy who had allegedly driven Carrillo over the edge. At the coffee shop this afternoon, Allison had revisited the Yesler Elementary website to search for Adrian's full name or photo. Neither was there. As Uber assignments had kept her busy the rest of the day and well into the evening, this was the first chance Allison had been given since leaving the coffee shop to try again.

Once in bed, she plugged *Adrian, car accident,* and *Lakeridge Park* into several different search engines and was mildly disappointed, if not at all surprised, to see no useful results. Mixing and matching other search terms with the original three proved equally unproductive, but combining *Yesler* with *Howard Alberts* finally brought one meaningful photograph to the fore.

It had run in the local Lakeridge newspaper more than a year earlier as part of a story on a field trip some Yesler staff and kids had taken to the Boeing Aircraft factory in Everett. It depicted Alberts—a tall, gawky man with a long forehead and authoritarian smile—squeezing himself into the simulated cockpit of a Boeing 787, where a pair of his young charges, a boy and a girl, were seated in the pilot's and copilot's chairs, respectively. The caption identified the school's principal, the first-grade girl (Angela Liggens), and her smaller classmate: Adrian Edwards. Alberts and Liggens were beaming for the camera, but not the boy. His smile was a quiet one, understated and serene.

The smile told Allison this was the Adrian she was looking for.

She sent a copy of the photo to the printer in the office and ran a search on *Adrian Edwards*. Nothing even remotely related to a seven-year-old boy from Seattle, Washington, turned up. She hadn't required any further convincing, but this was all the proof she needed to know that the accident Laura Carrillo claimed had taken the boy's life never happened.

Allison turned now to Carrillo.

Unlike Adrian Edwards, the teacher had an online presence, threadbare though it was. She had profiles on the more common social media sites—Facebook, LinkedIn, Twitter, etc.—and a handful of photographs, including a couple taken at Yesler. The starry-eyed countenance of a drug addict or overwrought professional on the verge of emotional collapse was nowhere to be seen. If anything, Carrillo consistently appeared happy and vibrant in the way young adults, especially women, were when their lives seemed to be going exactly as planned. Allison understood normalcy was often just a façade for some people, but she found herself doubting that Carrillo's blowup could be easily written off as stress or the side effects of prescription meds.

She spent most of the next hour perusing the online records of Carrillo's life, gathering a likely address and phone number for her in the process. Allison took a tour of Carrillo's social network pages and learned little of interest, besides what her boyfriend, Elliott Jeffries, looked like and how hopelessly devoted Carrillo was to him. Allison remained drawn to Adrian Edwards as a subject, even more so now that she'd seen his photograph, but could no longer deny the story she was preparing to write belonged not to him, but to Carrillo. This wasn't the true-life tale of a child who'd risen from the dead, but of a seemingly sane young woman who'd become convinced the child had done precisely that. Carrillo was the star of this drama, not Adrian, and Allison knew she'd be unwise to approach it any other way.

She decided to call Laura Carrillo first thing in the morning.

There might be no Pulitzer prize in the teacher's story, but Allison was confident she could get it published somewhere. Any published story with her byline on it held the potential of re-lending her some semblance of professional relevance, and right now, out of the game as she was, that was prize enough. All she had to do was work the piece from every angle and write it with some flair. She'd watched other writers spin gold from material far less intriguing than this, some even making a name for themselves in the process, and if writing Carrillo's story garnered her nothing more than a three-figure check and some online "shares," it wasn't going to be because she misplayed the opportunity.

She turned off her computer and watched television until right before midnight, when she finally understood waiting up for Flo was a fool's errand. She killed the lights and TV and curled up into a ball, drawing the covers up all around her.

Don't quit on me, yet, baby, she thought. *Hold on just a little while longer.*

* * *

Michael was peeved, but not greatly surprised, when Laura Carrillo and a man she introduced as her fiancé showed up at his door late Wednesday night.

Diane had told him over dinner how Carrillo had ambushed her that afternoon, and they both agreed Adrian's teacher was likely to seek Michael out next. Nothing Diane told her had seemed to comfort Carrillo, and Diane was sure she had left their meeting as determined as ever to find an explanation for Adrian's return that did not involve the benevolence of a supreme being. She had to be dissuaded from this undertaking, Diane said, for her own sake if no one else's, and the odds were it would be left to Michael to do it.

It struck him as a thankless and cruel task. He understood Carrillo's position perfectly, and felt more sympathy for the woman than Diane cared to invest. Only hours ago, all of Carrillo's confusion and fear had been his own. But Diane was right. Nothing good could come from Carrillo's continued refusal to accept the truth and let it be. Even if she couldn't derail the miracle that had brought Adrian back to life, as Diane feared, trying to convince the world that its history of events was just an elaborate falsehood of Michael and Diane's making would bring Carrillo nothing but ridicule and scorn. She would risk losing everything, personally and professionally.

Still, Michael couldn't imagine what he might say to Carrillo to appease her. Adrian's teacher was standing on his front porch now, less than an hour after he had left Diane's, and there was no time for Michael to decide what was or wasn't safe to say to her. She had brought her boyfriend along with her, so being completely honest with the woman was the very least of Michael's options.

"I guess you know why I'm here," Carrillo said, after offering Michael an insincere apology for this impromptu late-night visit.

"I think so," Michael said, glancing at the grim-faced young man standing beside her. Elliott, he'd said his name was. Heroically handsome and steeled with confidence, he was already reading Michael's eyes for the slightest hint of disingenuousness. "Diane told me you'd been by to see her today. How are you feeling?"

Carrillo went rigid. With a bitter smile, she said, "Frankly, I feel lousy. How do you think I feel?"

Michael said nothing.

"I've gone through hell since yesterday morning and things will only get worse if you don't help me."

"Me? How can I help?"

"By telling me the truth. With Elliott here as my witness. Adrian has been gone for almost a year and the three of us all know it: you, your wife, and me. You led everyone to believe he died in an accident at Lakeridge Park. I don't know how and I don't know why, but. . . ." Carrillo paused. "You did.

"Then yesterday, you sent him back to school like nothing ever happened, and of course I reacted as you would expect. I was terrified."

Michael offered no response.

"Are you going to deny it?"

"Deny what?"

"That you faked Adrian's death!"

Michael glanced at Carrillo's friend, to let him know how much sympathy he had for them both. "I'm afraid I have no choice."

"You have no *choice?*"

"I can't admit to something that's so obviously untrue, Miss Carrillo."

"Bullshit!"

The man named Elliott reached out to take her arm. "Laura—"

"No!" She jerked free of him. "He's lying. He knows he's lying!" She began to cry. To Michael, she said, "You want everyone to believe it's a 'miracle.' That Adrian was dead and now he's alive, just because God made it so. But it's a trick. A hoax. And I'm not leaving here tonight until I hear you say it!"

Michael fell silent again, the way he might have while arguing with a lunatic. He turned his attention once more to Elliott, whose growing discomfort was impossible to miss.

"My fiancé is not in the habit of making wild accusations, Mr. Edwards," Carrillo's boyfriend said. "And I don't believe she's suddenly lost her mind. I admit what she's describing sounds incredible, but if she says you and your wife know more about what happened to her at school yesterday than you're admitting, I've got to believe her."

Michael gave him an even look. "Are you saying you do believe her?"

Any hesitation on Jeffries's part would have been enough to answer the question, but that and his need to reset his jaw before speaking again left no doubt.

"Yes," he said, and Michael couldn't remember ever hearing a man tell a more courageous, and unconvincing, lie.

"You think Diane and I faked our son's death eight months ago, then just decided to send him back to school yesterday because. . .because what? What reason could we have possibly had to do such a thing?"

Of course, Elliott had no ready answer, leaving him to color with embarrassment as he wilted under Carrillo's withering gaze.

Michael turned back to Adrian's teacher. "And who else besides you remembers this accident at Lakeridge Park? If we did all the things you're accusing us of, how is it you're the only one complaining about it?"

"I don't know. If I knew all that, we wouldn't be here," Carrillo said, her anger dwindling. "Maybe you aren't alone in this. Maybe you've paid everyone at school to look the other way."

"No."

"You're religious fanatics. You have to be. You're looking for publicity, trying to bring glory to God, or some such nonsense, at my expense. But why? That's what I need to know. *Why?*"

"Miss Carrillo. I'm sorry about what happened to you at school yesterday, and so is my wife. Adrian and his classmates are very fond of you and we hope you'll be back at school very soon."

Carrillo turned to her fiancé. "Elliott!"

"But it's late and I don't know what else to tell you that I haven't already said." Michael took the door in his hand, directed a small nod at Jeffries. "Good night."

"Wait!" Elliott leapt forward at the last minute. "Just one more question. Please."

Michael waited.

"Miracles. Acts of God. People being healed and brought back from the dead. Do you believe such things are actually possible?"

It was meant to be a trap, a question that would incriminate Michael if he answered honestly. Jeffries and Carrillo studied him as if he were a fish wriggling on a hook, Adrian's teacher even showing a slight smile.

"Yes. I believe in all kinds of impossible things," Michael said, his gaze fixed on Carrillo. "Because I think this world would be a very sad and lonely place if I didn't."

* * *

Diane slept that night in Adrian's bed. Long after he'd fallen asleep, she'd crawled in under the covers and held him close, as she had when he was a toddler. She smelled his hair and listened to the steady rhythm of his breathing, and prayed for strength in the days to come.

Things were happening too fast. It seemed like every other hour, someone was turning up who remembered the accident and knew something incredible had happened to bring Adrian back to her. First Laura Carrillo, then Michael, and now Milton Weisman. Who would be next, and how many would there be in the end?

This wasn't the miracle she had prepared herself for. She had thought it would be hers and hers alone, a test of one woman's faith against that of all mankind. That was a fight she could win, a fight she could control. But this. . . .

She had no worries about Michael. The disbelief with which she had known he would greet Adrian's return had been mercifully short-lived. His faith had brought him through, and after their dinner tonight, Diane had no reason to think he would ever do anything to jeopardize the great gift they had been given. Carrillo and Milton Weisman, however, were a different story. Carrillo appeared to have no real faith to speak of, and Weisman, from what Diane could remember, was a secular Jew. If Diane and Michael couldn't convince them both to accept Adrian's resurrection as the act of a compassionate God, an act that didn't require their understanding or an explanation, what damage might Carrillo and Weisman do? Was Adrian's return unconditional, or only as permanent as the pair's skepticism would allow?

The sense it was the latter was growing stronger by the minute.

Still, Diane was not one to cave in to fear. If the little boy in her arms proved nothing, he proved she was not alone. God was with her. And if she had to fight to hold on to what she had, what she had lost and now regained, He would give her whatever she needed to prevail.

Diane was certain of it.

THURSDAY

NINETEEN

"WELL? WHAT DO YOU THINK?"

"What do I think? I think it's very sad, of course," Flo said.

"Sad?"

"Yes. That poor thing will never see the inside of another classroom as long as she lives. I don't care what Marx told you."

"Yes, but—"

"What? Was I supposed to say something different?"

Flo hadn't wanted to hear about any of it. Allison practically had to bar the kitchen door to get her to sit still for the ten minutes it had taken Allison to describe all she'd learned about the Laura Carrillo affair. Given her way, Flo would have grabbed her breakfast on the fly and left for work without any conversation whatsoever, but Allison wasn't putting up with that shit today. A few minutes at the breakfast table together before they both went their separate ways was not too much to ask, especially when Allison had something good to talk about for a change.

At least *she* thought the news was good. Obviously, Flo didn't agree.

"This isn't just about a teacher going postal in the classroom, Flo. This story is bigger than that."

"It is?"

"Yes. Think of all the themes it has the potential to touch upon. Mental illness. Drugs, maybe. The stress on public school teachers to perform, even at the grade-school level."

Flo shrugged. "Okay."

"My God. Are you telling me you aren't the least bit curious to know what could have caused this woman to suffer such an off-the-wall delusion? That a little boy in her class died, was buried, and has risen from the dead like Jesus fucking Christ?"

"Am I curious? Sure, I guess so. But you just ran down all the likely explanations yourself, Ally. Either she's crazy, on drugs, or the victim of some kind of stress-related nervous breakdown. And in any or all of those cases, it's a sad story, like I said, but hardly an earth-shattering one." Flo glanced at her watch. "Hey, I've really gotta go."

She pecked Allison on the cheek and got up.

Before she could get to the door, Allison blurted out, "What about the fourth possibility?"

Flo stopped, raised an eyebrow. "The fourth possibility?"

"That she's as sane and healthy as you or me and is simply telling the truth. The boy was dead but is alive again."

Flo smirked. "What?"

It had only been something to say to stop Flo from leaving. Now that she had to answer for it, Allison was just as struck by the inanity of it as Flo.

"Maybe that's the real theme to be explored here," she said, flying blind. "The viability of Old Testament miracles in modern times."

Whatever humor Allison's partner had found in their discussion to this point vanished. "Miracles have no viability," Flo said. "In modern times, or any other. Really, Ally."

She let the admonishment serve as a parting shot and walked out.

In the sudden quiet, Allison checked the time on her phone, saw it was only a few minutes after seven. Too early to call Laura Carrillo, whom she intended to interview to start her day. She finished her coffee, fighting to keep her loneliness at bay. With no other sound competing for her attention, she could hear her wristwatch counting off the seconds. She sat there for several minutes, fidgeting, then gave up and tried Carrillo at the number she'd found online.

Her call went through to voicemail. The woman who'd recorded the outgoing message didn't identify herself, but she sounded like a perfect match for the vivacious brunette in all the photos on the Yesler website. Allison left her a brief message, and wondered before she even hung up how many times she would have to duplicate the act before Carrillo returned her call. Assuming she ever would.

Allison had been planning to give the teacher a chance to connect by phone before forcing herself upon Carrillo at home, but she realized now she lacked the patience for such a passive approach. Flo's unflagging negativity had lit a fire under her, so that every minute spent doing nothing held the bitter aftertaste of failure. Her Uber driving assignments could start coming in at any moment, and she had to make whatever time she had between them as productive as possible.

She got up, dropped her coffee cup in the sink, and rushed out of the house.

* * *

For the second day in a row, Howard Alberts stopped Diane in the carport at Yesler as she was dropping Adrian off.

"There's something I think you ought to know," he said, looking even more grim than he had the day before. "That is, if you don't know already."

"What is it?"

"A reporter visited the school yesterday asking about Laura Carrillo. Somehow, she got wind of what happened in Laura's classroom and intends to write some kind of story about it."

"Oh, no."

"My feelings exactly. Ms. Marx spoke to her briefly but didn't tell her anything of substance, beyond letting her know we'd prefer she not write anything at all, for Laura's sake as well as Adrian's. Unfortunately, she seemed determined to go ahead with the story. I take it you haven't heard from her?"

"No."

"Well, so far, so good. But I'd bet even money you will eventually. Naturally, you're free to talk to her if you want. I can't stop you. But frankly, Laura's going to have a hard enough time getting through this thing as it is. If what happened to her here Tuesday goes public, regardless of what we determine were the reasons for it, I'm not sure she'll be able to survive it with her teaching credentials intact."

He was trying to guilt Diane into silence, surely more interested in protecting himself and Yesler than Laura Carrillo. But Diane knew he was right: any news story about Carrillo's breakdown could do both her and Adrian more harm than good.

But would Laura Carrillo see it that way? Or would she jump at the chance to tell her version of things to the world at large, regardless of the consequences? Diane feared it was the latter. Michael had called her this morning about Carrillo's visit to his apartment last night, and if they hadn't known before she would be trouble, they definitely knew it now. The teacher hadn't waited even a day to seek Michael out after bolting from Diane's home, apparently unmoved by Diane's arguments for accepting what had happened as the will of God.

From what Michael had said, it sounded like his conversation with Carrillo, and the fiancé she had brought along to bear witness to it, had left her more angry and humiliated than ever. Michael had rejected all her accusations as nonsense and shut her boyfriend's support of them down to a benign whimper. It wasn't hard for Diane to picture Carrillo today talking to this reporter for no other reason than to exact a measure of revenge.

"Does Miss Laura know?" she asked Alberts.

"Yes. I called her yesterday as soon as I found out myself. I made it clear to her that talking to anyone about the incident before the district has finished investigating it would probably not be in her best interests."

"And she agreed?"

"Of course." He seemed surprised by the question. "Why wouldn't she?"

Diane said, "If she comes back, you won't let her anywhere near Adrian, will you?"

"Who? The reporter?" Alberts shook his head. "Not a chance. You don't have to worry about that."

"What was her name? In case she calls us?"

"Hope. First name Allison. She didn't mention to Betty who she works for, so I assume she's just a freelancer."

"Allison Hope. I'll pass it along to Michael. Thank you for the warning, Mr. Alberts. If we hear from her, we'll be sure to let you know."

Diane drove off, suddenly in a great hurry to get home.

* * *

Laura was still in bed at nine a.m. Elliott had tried to rouse her before leaving for work but she had ignored him, too tired to take up the argument they had only dropped last night for the sake of sleep.

It was their worst fight ever. Some of the things they had said to each other cut right down to the marrow. Come the dawn, Elliott had been nearly as remorseful as he was angry, but Laura regretted nothing. As far as she was concerned, Elliott deserved every insult she had peppered him with, and more. He had failed her miserably.

She had wanted him by her side when she confronted Michael Edwards, thinking she could count on the man she loved—the man she planned to marry and build a family with—to defend her from any attack Edwards might make on her sanity or character. If he really loved her, Elliott should have been able to play that role easily. Gladly. But no. When Edwards had given him the opportunity to state his faith in Laura, Elliott had frozen. Muttered some weak response and gone mute.

He didn't believe her and he never would. His doubt was like a dagger to her heart, and throughout their ride home and well into the night, Laura had struck back, saying everything and anything she could to hurt and humiliate him the way he had humiliated her. She had woken this morning certain she would never be able to forgive Elliott, or care enough to try.

After he left, however, and she'd had some time to reassess matters alone, she realized the magnitude of her hubris. She loved Elliott and was not ready to lose him. Over the last two days, she had placed him in an impossible position, one that demanded he profess a belief in something she was still struggling to believe herself. She had given him every reason to think she was insane, yet was asking him to behave as if nothing she was telling him deserved his incredulity or scorn. It wasn't fair, and it wasn't reasonable. He was only reacting precisely how she would, were he the one talking about dead children walking the earth instead of her.

The only logical explanation for what was happening remained the most obvious: she was sick and needed help. No matter how real her "memories" of the past eight months seemed, there was no way to reconcile them with the collective memory of everyone else, with the possible exceptions of Adrian's parents. And they were only possible exceptions because of Diane Edwards's bizarre talk of miracle resurrections. Who was to say the woman wasn't completely deranged?

Laura didn't want to believe she herself was mad—the very idea of accepting such a prognosis continued to make her blood boil—but denying it had brought her nothing but grief and exhaustion. She couldn't eat and could barely sleep, and every time her phone rang, as it had once already today, she pretended not to notice, certain that anyone calling besides Elliott would have questions she had no desire to answer. Whatever this nightmare was, she needed it to be over, and if the only way to end it was to acquiesce to the probability the death of Adrian Edwards was all in her mind, she was finally ready to do so.

She had a three o'clock appointment with Noreen Ives, the psychiatrist she'd been referred to, and she was going to keep it. She had no idea what she was going to tell Ives, or how she was going to tell it. She only knew what she wanted the end result of their meeting to be: a clean bill of health. A report that would persuade the Renton School District and Howard Alberts she was fit to return to the classroom. If she had to lie to convince Ives such was the case, she would do it without hesitation. And then, once back at work, surrounded by the children she loved and was loved by, including Adrian Edwards, she would put this episode behind her and never think of it again.

That was Laura's plan, and she was certain it was a good one. It only fell apart at 9:17 a.m., when the doorbell rang and she decided to answer it.

TWENTY

MILTON DIDN'T WANT TO meet Diane Edwards at her home. He
wanted to meet her at the park.

He had called at her request, and yet she sounded surprised when
he gave her his name. Like maybe she hadn't really thought he would call,
or had expected at least a few days would pass before he found the nerve.
His name should've meant nothing to her before last night, but she knew
him, all right. Her pause had been too long. She had asked him to repeat
his name for appearance's sake only.

"Oh, yes. I spoke to your son-in-law last night. I'm glad you called,
Mr. Weisman."

He had heard her voice only once before, at the park the day of the
accident when, of course, she had sounded much different. But he was
certain this was the same voice.

"You are?" Milton asked.

"Yes. Your son-in-law—Alan, was it?—said you're under the im-
pression our son Adrian was hurt in some kind of accident, a car accident,
and that you were responsible. Is that correct?"

She knew it was, they both did, but he had made up his mind not to
lose his temper.

"Yes."

"Well, I'm glad you called because I wanted to assure you that Adrian is fine. You've got no reason to worry about him, or to feel guilty about
harming him in any way."

"He's fine?"

"Yes. He's perfectly fine."

"And the accident? I suppose you're going to tell me it never happened, too."

A moment passed before she spoke again. "Well, Mr. Weisman, I don't know what else I *can* tell you. Adrian's never been involved in a car accident in his life."

"How about the truth? You could try telling me the truth. I've suffered enough. I killed a little boy, your little boy, and I've been living with that for damn near a year. Don't you think I deserve to hear the truth now? From you, if from no one else?"

This time, her silence fell hard and long, leaving little doubt as to why. "What do you want me to say?" she asked finally.

"I want you to tell me what's happened. If the boy really is fine"— Milton found the words catching in his throat, pulled himself together before continuing—"if he really is alive, I want to understand. I want an explanation. That's all I want."

After another long pause, Diane Edwards said, "Well, I can't really tell you anything more than I already have, but if you'd like, we can talk further in person. Here at the house. When would you like to come?"

"Right now," Milton said, relief coursing through his veins like the old, familiar heat of alcohol. He wasn't crazy. He wasn't an old man losing his mind. She had practically proven as much by extending this conversation. "But not at your house. I want to talk at the park. Meet me at the park in thirty minutes. Can you do that?"

"The park?"

Milton continued to play along with her act. "Lakeridge Park."

"Oh. All right. I think I can do that. But—"

"I'll be alone. Of course I will."

Milton hung up. He sat on the edge of his bed and took a deep breath, on the verge of more goddamn tears. He listened for someone eavesdropping at the bedroom door, knowing he was just being paranoid. Alan had gone home late last night and Milton had sent Janet to work well over an hour ago, deflecting every argument she posed against her leaving him alone. With all the reluctance Milton had predicted, she had told him about Alan's conversation with Diane Edwards and given him the woman's number. She knew Milton would call and didn't like the idea, especially if she wasn't going to be around to police what he did afterward. She was as convinced as ever her father had started drinking again or was going senile. Milton had watched the street a full five minutes after his daughter drove off before he was satisfied she wasn't coming back.

Now, he was dressed and ready to go. The Honda was waiting for him in the garage and, yes—there was no denying it—the old temptation to have a drink was starting to make itself felt. But it had no hold on him. Not yet.

To hear Janet tell it, he had driven the Honda only days ago and had never stopped driving it, but in his mind, it had been months since he last sat behind the wheel. He didn't know if he could turn the key in the ignition, let alone drive the nine blocks from his home to Lakeridge Park. But he had to try. He wanted Diane Edwards to see the car, to remember it.

And to explain to him how it was that it didn't have a scratch on it.

* * *

Laura's first instinct was to slam her apartment door in Allison Hope's face. That was what Elliott would have wanted her to do, as well as Howard Alberts and the part of her that was thinking straight. But as the door began to close in her hand, she stopped it, and said something pointless and embarrassing instead.

"I'm not supposed to talk to you."

"You aren't? Why is that?"

Hope had a pleasant smile and an easygoing manner, which Laura hadn't been expecting at all. It made the task of sending her away much harder. "I meant I don't want to talk to you. Please leave me alone."

"I visited the school yesterday. I was told what happened to you Tuesday was probably the result of prescription drugs. Are you presently taking any prescribed medications?"

"No. *No!*" Laura was instantly furious. "Who told you that—" She caught herself before the word *lie* could form on her tongue, but her anger was unabated. Somebody at Yesler had betrayed her, and her guess was Betty Marx. Betty was good for mining the business of others for her own entertainment. "Whoever you spoke to doesn't know what she's talking about."

"I didn't think they did," Hope said, not taking the "she" bait. "That's why I came here to see you. To get the real story."

"The 'real' story? There is no story, real or otherwise."

"Well, I hate to disagree with you, Ms. Carrillo, but it sure sounds like a story to me. A little boy shows up at school eight months after his death. . . ." She waited for Laura's reaction.

"You don't really believe that's what happened," Laura said.

"I don't know what happened. Only you and Adrian know that, and possibly his parents. I was going to talk to them next. But if you'd rather not talk to me, I guess I'll have to hear their account of things first." She handed Laura a business card. "Have a nice day."

Laura watched her walk down the hall and exit the building, seemingly without an ounce of regret.

Laura closed her door and settled in the living room, feeling herself being pulled in a dozen different directions at once. She understood perfectly well what Hope was doing: pitting her need to remain silent against her desire to be heard. And Hope's play was not off the mark. The thought of a story brimming with speculation, half-truths, and outright lies about her did make Laura crazy. Even if Betty Marx and Howard Alberts and everyone else at Yesler withheld all comment from this point forward, Laura knew how Diane and Michael Edwards would answer Hope's questions. And the more she thought about it, the angrier she became. Because they would hang her out to dry. Express their sympathy for "poor Miss Laura" and deny any knowledge of what had caused her horrible "breakdown" at school Tuesday morning. There would be no acknowledgement of any accidents or funerals involving their son, and certainly no talk about miracles and/or resurrections. And to what end? What was the truth they were so willing to sacrifice Laura to hide?

Could Adrian Edwards really have been raised from the dead?

It was an idea Laura had finally become desperate enough to ponder seriously. No other possibility could have been more wonderful or more cruel. Because it would mean Adrian was alive again, that a prayer Laura might have said many times herself, had she possessed the faith, had actually been answered—but by a monster, not a god. For only a monster would throw Laura to the wolves this way, place all she held dear in jeopardy just so she could bear witness to its power. She loved Adrian, but he wasn't Laura's child, he was Diane Edwards's. What kind of "god" would lay the cost of his return at Laura's feet and not his mother's? This was the all-loving, all-merciful supreme being Diane Edwards was imploring Laura to accept and obey?

Laura couldn't bring herself to believe it.

It hardly mattered, in any case. What she believed or not had no bearing on the choice she had to make: capitulate or perish. Give in to the idea that she was a fragile, overworked educator who had temporarily lost sight of reality, or refuse and paint herself as something far worse. One course of action held some hope of redemption, the other did not.

It turned her stomach, but Laura decided not to go on fighting a battle she could never win.

She eyed the clock on the wall in the kitchen, saw it was only nine-thirty. Her appointment with Noreen Ives was over five hours away. If she could keep her pride and anger in check long enough to get to Ives's office, she would be okay. Seeing the psychiatrist would be galling, but it would satisfy the demands of her employers and fiancé and help her regain the normalcy she craved now more than anything.

She sat in the stillness of her living room and tried not to count the minutes as they ticked by. Her eyes settled on the business card on the table, turned away, then came back again. She picked up the card, examined the name and phone number on its face. She set the card back down and left it there.

Until she couldn't keep herself from reaching out for it one more time.

* * *

Diane found Milton Weisman waiting for her at the playground. The old man hadn't told her where specifically at Lakeridge Park he wanted to meet, but he hadn't needed to. This was where it had happened, after all, the seismic event that, until only days ago, had left a black stain upon both their lives. What more fitting place than this to acknowledge and celebrate the eradication of that stain?

Still, coming here had not been easy for Diane. In the aftermath of Adrian's death, she had visited the park only once, four months ago. The old playground had been demolished and a new wooden one erected, on the same small, grassy hill but several yards away, and Diane and Michael had been invited to attend the reopening ceremony. Park officials had named the new site in Adrian's honor, put a plaque down in the earth to memorialize their son's brief life, and unlike Michael, Diane hadn't been able to stay away. She had cut the ribbon, said a few words of thanks and left, intending to never return.

And yet, here she was.

She had known before she even left the house that the new playground would be gone, and it was. As was the plaque bearing her son's name and likeness. In their stead, the original play structure stood off to one side where it had been before the accident. An outdated yellow and blue construct of metal tubes and plastic bars, ladders and towers and fireman's poles, steering wheels and bridges—and a slide. *The* slide. Every piece scratched and scarred and weather-beaten, and, true to Diane's memory of it, crawling with children.

Milton Weisman was sitting on a bench nearby, watching the parking lot.

She recognized him immediately: broad-shouldered, head dusted with wisps of white hair, a face ill-suited to conveying much more than mild aggravation. It was the same man she had seen here eight months ago, dazed and frightened and mumbling useless excuses, and for days afterward on television, doing much the same for the sake of news reporters, and finally that afternoon at the house when she'd refused to acknowledge his presence on her front porch.

And yet, something about him had changed. Diane saw it the minute he pushed himself to his feet as she approached. It was a gesture of respect she would not have expected from the old man she remembered.

"You came. I wasn't sure you would," he said when Diane reached him. "Thank you."

They were both nervous, smiling like kids on a first date. Weisman looked like he'd been crying.

"Please. Sit," he said.

They took their places on the bench, Diane putting more distance between them than was necessary. She no longer had any reason to treat him so harshly, but this was a fact she needed some time to get used to.

"It's all back. Just the way I remember it," Weisman said, nodding toward the playground. And now Diane was certain: he *had* been crying.

"Back?"

She wasn't ready yet to speak the truth and Weisman's disappointment was palpable.

"The tree that stopped my car. The play structure that was here before the accident. The new one is gone, the wooden one they built over there." He pointed. "If you're going to tell me you don't remember, I'll just go and never bother you again. I'm not going to sit here and listen to you lie to me."

Diane studied his face. Voices on the playground filled the air. "What will you do? If I decide not to lie?"

"What will I do?"

"Yes. With this truth you think I'm hiding, I mean. Who will you share it with? How will you use it?"

"Use it? I don't want to use it. And who could I share it with? Who could I tell it to that would believe it, coming from me? I'm sixty-eight years old. To hell with sharing it!" He reined himself in, as if to hold another round of tears at bay. He looked straight into Diane's eyes and dared her to turn away. "I just want to know. I have the right to know."

Diane hesitated still, riding the razor's edge of a monumental decision.

Then she told him what he had come to the park to hear.

* * *

Allison sat in the car and waited, growing less confident by the second. Had she overplayed her hand?

It had been a bluff and nothing more, of course. Leaving Laura Carrillo without argument, tossing her a business card and driving off as if she were intent on talking to Adrian Edwards's parents in Carrillo's stead. Allison had driven all of two blocks from the teacher's apartment and parked in a shaded spot at the curb, expecting to be there only a minute or two before Carrillo folded and gave her a call.

Almost half an hour later, Allison's phone had yet to ring, and it was beginning to look as if she would have to come crawling back to Carrillo, not the other way around.

"Well, shit," she said.

Playing tough with the teacher was the kind of dumb stunt Flo would have expected from Allison. All bravado and no forethought. Allison could see her partner now, almost but not quite shaking her head, eyes filled with pity, a sigh suppressed only with great effort. Another misstep to add to all those that had come before, and all that were destined to come in the future.

Allison started the car and threw it in gear, so lost in thought as she pulled away that she almost didn't hear her ringing phone. She snatched it up off the passenger seat, brought it straight to her ear without checking the ID window.

"This is Allison," she said. Cool, calm, and without a hint of eagerness.

"I've changed my mind," Laura Carrillo said. "I'll talk to you."

* * *

Milton didn't ask Diane Edwards a single question. He just listened.

The story she told was every bit as incredible and unlikely as he had feared. God had answered her prayers and brought her son back to life, altering the very construct of time to remove all evidence of his death—save for the memories of only four people Edwards could name: She and her husband Michael, Adrian's teacher at school, and Milton. There could be others, Edwards said, but she doubted it. Why these four alone had been chosen, Edwards didn't know and didn't care. It was part of God's plan, she said, and she had no desire to question it.

Milton didn't know how to react. On the one hand, he was heartened by Edwards's account. If he had lost his mind, he wasn't alone; surely Adrian Edwards's mother was every bit as mad as he was, probably even more so. On the other hand, if they were both sane and what Edwards had told him was true, he was no better off now than he had been before, because Milton couldn't repeat anything he'd heard to anyone—Lisa, Janet, Alan—without solidifying their already firm belief he was no longer in possession of all his faculties.

Still, what troubled Milton most was not the outrageousness of Edwards's story, but how well it explained everything he had been experiencing over the last two days. It was contrary to every idea he had ever had about the existence of God and the relevance of faith, but in the context of all the inexplicable things Milton had seen and heard since Tuesday night, its logic was unassailable. What better way to make sense of the impossible than to lay it at the feet of God, the most impossible premise of all?

Diane Edwards waited a long time for Milton to speak. "Well? Say something, Mr. Weisman, please."

Milton shook his head. "I don't know what to say. I don't know what to believe. God did this thing? What God? Whose God? Yours, mine. . .?"

"*The* God," Edwards said.

"*The* God?" Milton almost laughed.

"I'm a Christian. So yes, I believe there's only one. But I don't think He belongs to anybody. Not the Christians, the Jews, the Muslims. . . ." She smiled with embarrassment. "I used to think that way, but not anymore. I think we give Him different names and worship Him in our own way, but we're all praying to the same god in the end."

"And this one god performed this 'miracle.' Turned the whole world upside down just to bring one dead child back to his mother. Why? I don't understand. Why one child, your child, when he could bring back a thousand children if he wanted? A million?"

"Maybe He has. Maybe Adrian's not the only one He's brought back like this. I don't know the answers to your questions, Mr. Weisman. I don't know anything more than what I've told you. I don't blame you for wondering. I would wonder, too, if I had any reason to care. But I told you: I *don't* care. Adrian is back, my son is alive again, and if I live to be a hundred without ever knowing why, that'll be just fine with me." She had changed before Milton's eyes, hardening like molten glass pulled from the fire. "Just as it should be with you."

"Me?"

"You ran my son down with your car. You crushed him like a doll and killed him, right there." She nodded toward the slide to their right. "You told me yourself—you've been living with the memory and the guilt of that ever since it happened, and you were going to go on living with it the rest of your life. Only now you don't have to. Your nightmare's over just like mine is. You're free."

Free. The word gave Milton pause. Having Adrian Edwards's death on his conscience had been almost more than he could bear. Ironically, it had somehow made him a better man, attuned him in a way he had never been attuned before to the damage he'd been doing to everyone around him. But killing a child was too high a price for such small benefit. Up until two days ago, he would have gladly traded his redemption for Adrian's life, without hesitation or regret.

But now? Now that such an impossible exchange seemed within his grasp, was the "freedom" Diane Edwards spoke of really what he wanted?

Milton knew the answer was yes.

"How do I know this isn't some kind of trick? That things won't go right back tomorrow to the way they were if. . .if. . . ."

"If you decide to believe me? You don't," Diane Edwards said. "And neither do I. Nobody can say what will happen tomorrow."

"And that doesn't frighten you? Not knowing?"

"When I stop to think about it. But I don't. I won't. I can't do anything about the future, Mr. Weisman. All I can do is deal with what life holds for me today, right now, and right now my son's alive and my husband's my husband again, and I have everything I'll ever want or need in this world. Everything."

Milton fell silent. It was too much. The woman didn't realize what she was asking, expecting an old man to suddenly believe in something he had written off as nonsense long ago. God? Even Milton's dead mother, who had wielded the Torah like a sword, had not possessed such faith. God for her had only been a prop to justify her authority, an excuse to get the last word in any argument. For Milton's father, the God of Moses had meant even less than that.

But now Milton was supposed to believe?

As he had gradually changed in the aftermath of that terrible day here at Lakeridge Park last March, giving up alcohol and fathering his daughters with a level of attention he had never demonstrated before, he came to believe none of it was of his own doing. His rehabilitation was neither a matter of choice nor a consequence of chance. He imagined it was part of God's grand scheme, but only because Milton didn't know who or what else to assign it to. God was still as preposterous an idea to him as leprechauns.

Milton shook his head, hands over his eyes. "I can't. I'm too old."

"Excuse me?"

"Yes! I'm too old. A man can't believe overnight in things he's never believed in before!" Finally he was angry. Not at Edwards alone, maybe not at Edwards at all, but no one else was there to take his abuse. "I've done without God for almost seventy years. I have no need for God! And now suddenly I have to accept His existence as fact. I have to believe that this god hears and answers prayers and brings little boys back from the dead, and makes everyone who knew them forget they were ever dead in the first place." He shook his head again. "I can't. I'm sorry."

"Then I'll ask you again: What will you do? Now that I've told you what you wanted to know? How do you intend to proceed from here, knowing what you do?"

Milton didn't answer.

"This isn't all in your head, Mr. Weisman. And you aren't dreaming. Surely I've managed to convince you of that much. But if you go on telling people what you remember, or worse, what we've just talked about here this morning, you know what will happen. You know what they'll think."

"They'll think what they already think. That I'm a senile old fool who's losing his mind."

"Yes. In the same way they think poor Laura Carrillo, Adrian's teacher, is either losing her mind or abusing drugs. It doesn't matter that she's forty years younger than you. What she's telling people sounds just as insane coming from her as it would from a seventy-year-old man."

"But she's telling them anyway."

"Yes. She has that right. I warned her not to. I told her how pointless it would be. But she wouldn't listen. She's going to lose her job and possibly her teaching career. Even her fiancé doubts her sanity. What's happened isn't meant for the world to know, Mr. Weisman. By now, that should be obvious to all of us. Trying to make people believe something God's gone to great pains to keep hidden is futile and ungrateful."

"Ungrateful?"

"Yes, ungrateful. Adrian's my child, having him back means more to his father and me than anyone else, of course. But we aren't the only ones who should be thankful. You and Miss Laura should be, too. You, for reasons we've already discussed. And Laura. . .she loved Adrian, she was inconsolable at his funeral. Regardless of how it happened, she should be ecstatic that he's alive again. Instead, all she can see fit to do is question it. Deny it. As if nothing would make her happier than to see Adrian back in his grave."

She smiled, and for the first time, Milton wondered if it was the devil and not God to whom this woman was beholden. "Well, he's not going back. I lost him once. I won't lose him again."

Milton frowned. "I don't follow you."

"What I'm saying," she said, "is that this is the way God must want it to be: for four people to be aware of what He's done, and no more. And if we can't accept that, if we refuse to accept it. . . ."

"He'll take the boy back?"

"I know that sounds contradictory. How could God be so generous one minute and so cruel the next? But it's a fear I have, Mr. Weisman, I'm sorry. And because I have it, I'm going to do everything in my power to keep what's happened to Adrian a secret, and I would strongly encourage you to do the same."

"You want me to shut up. Is that it?"

"You'll only be hurting yourself if you do anything else. Let it go. Accept what's happened as God's will and never speak of it again to anyone."

"'God's will,'" Milton scoffed despite himself. "What if 'God' had nothing to do with this? Have you thought about that? What if I decide to go on believing what I've always believed, that there is no such thing as God?"

"You can believe what you like. Tell yourself men from Mars brought Adrian back and erased every record of his death on Earth, if that's what you want. Just know that if you continue to talk about it, trying to convince people that what you remember really happened, Laura Carrillo will be the only one listening. And the only one willing to speak so much as a word in your defense."

Milton didn't need her to elaborate. The threat, like the steel in her eyes, was crystal clear.

"I want to see him," Milton said.

For a moment, he thought he would have to repeat it. "Adrian?"

"What, did you think I would do what you're asking me to do without seeing him for myself? I want to see him."

Edwards stared at him as if struck mute. Surely she had known he would ask. What fool wouldn't?

"Please," Milton said.

"He doesn't know anything. He's like everyone else. He doesn't remember what happened. So if you were planning to ask him what it was like to be dead—"

"I wasn't. I wouldn't. I just want to see him, that's all."

Edwards continued to stare at him in silence. Milton wondered if he'd demanded too much. Finally, she surrendered a nod. "All right. Tomorrow—"

"No. Today. I can't wait until tomorrow." He showed Edwards a steely glare of his own.

"Okay," Edwards said. "We'll meet again after I pick him up from school. But not here." She glanced about the park and shook her head. "Not here."

"I'll meet you anywhere you want."

"He likes the hamburgers at Kidd Valley, on Lake Washington. Do you know it?"

"Yes. I think so."

"We'll be there around three. But we won't stay long. We'll order our food to go and sit with you inside for five, ten minutes at the most. No more."

Milton nodded, satisfied. "Five minutes will be fine. I just want to see him for myself, that's all." And in saying the words again, he realized how true it was: he did want to see the boy. Breathing, laughing, moving. Alive again.

He wanted that more than anything else in the world.

TWENTY-ONE

UNLIKE MILTON WEISMAN, who around the same time was hearing much the same story from Diane Edwards at Lakeridge Park, Allison Hope peppered Laura with questions throughout her account of the last forty-eight hours. Questions were the journalist's stock in trade, but Laura could tell most of the ones Hope had were coming from personal curiosity, not professional necessity. Hope simply could not believe what she was being told.

"Is that it?" she asked when Laura had finished.

"Yes. That's all I know."

"You're saying—"

"I'm not 'saying' anything. I'm just telling you the truth. You asked for the truth and I gave it to you."

Hope looked over her handwritten notes and shook her head, with amazement or glee, Laura wasn't sure which. "True or not—and I'm not saying it isn't true, exactly—I don't suppose I have to tell you how unlikely this all sounds? Resurrection and mass amnesia. The boy's parents conspiring to cover it all up."

"Of course I know how it sounds. If it weren't all happening to me, I'd be just as skeptical as you are. More so, in fact. But it's all true nevertheless."

"And if I asked the mother—"

"She'd deny it. She'd say I was crazy, like everyone else. That's what she promised she'd do if I didn't keep quiet, and I believe her. She and her husband don't want anyone to know what really happened, and they're willing to sacrifice my life and career to keep it a secret."

"But why? That's the piece that doesn't fit. If she prayed for a miracle and got one, why would she not want anyone to know about it? I thought people like her were all about bringing glory to God by making things like miracles as widely known as possible."

"Look at your notes again. I told you, she's afraid. She thinks it's God's will that nobody knows, with the exception of herself, her husband, and me, and she's not going to do anything that could be perceived as running counter to His wishes."

"Because if she did, He might decide to take her son all over again?"

"She didn't say as much, but I imagine that's what worries her, yes." Laura smiled. "And yet I'm the one people are insisting seek psychiatric help."

Hope seemed about to say something, only to think better of it.

"I know: She's not the one talking openly about dead children rising from the grave. I am. And maybe I'm a complete idiot for doing so. But I don't care, Ms. Hope. I don't care because I know what I'm telling you is true, and nobody's going to make me pretend otherwise just because they think that's what their 'god' wants me to do."

"But what is the truth? That Adrian died in a car accident last spring—"

"And was raised from the dead exactly like his mother says. Precisely."

Hope was taken aback. "Sorry?"

"You don't believe such a thing is possible. Neither do I. So that leaves us with just one other explanation, doesn't it?"

Hope refused to bite.

"The accident never happened. They faked it. Adrian's death, his funeral, everything."

"His parents?"

"Not her. Him. Michael Edwards. I think Diane Edwards honestly believes everything she told me. For her, the accident is just as real as it is—or used to be—for me."

"You're saying her husband staged Adrian's death and resurrection for her benefit?"

"Not necessarily for her benefit alone. But yes, I think he staged it."

"But why? And how could he possibly pull off such a thing? There would have been witnesses to an accident like that in a public park. And what about the old man you say was driving the car?"

"He was a part of the ruse, too. Obviously."

"You said his name was"—Hope consulted her notes again—"Weinman?"

"Weinman or Wiseman, one or the other. I'm not sure."

"First name?"

"I can't remember that either. I'm sorry."

Laura had been trying to remember the old man's name for two days now without success. She could recall seeing him on television, and had read about him in the few stories about the accident she'd had the stomach to skim through, but the old man's full name continued to elude her.

"Even if Michael Edwards could do everything you say—fake the accident in the park, pay off Weinman and all the alleged witnesses, arrange for a fake funeral—that doesn't explain why no one remembers any of it now except you."

"No, it doesn't."

"Then. . .?"

"Look—I don't know. I don't have all the answers, I wish I did!" Laura couldn't contain her frustration any longer. "You're the reporter, not me. It's your job to explain it all, not mine!"

Hope gave her the same look Laura had been getting from Elliott for two days now. Laura leaned forward in her chair to get right up in the writer's face.

"Listen to me. Look at me. Ask me a question about anything else. Anything. Math, science, geography. World history, you name it. I'll give you an intelligent answer. A sane answer. Do you know why? Because I *am* sane. I'm not a drug abuser or the victim of a nervous breakdown. I'm neither deranged nor confused. I'm just afraid, Ms. Hope. I'm caught in the middle of something I don't understand, and if I don't find a way to understand it, to make sense of it to people like you, I'm going to lose everything I have. Everything."

Laura refused to cry. She wanted Hope to see how strong she was, not how weak. She sat back in her chair and let the reporter go on examining her like she was a slide under a microscope. Hope would see the truth eventually.

Laura was as sane as she was.

* * *

Allison was stunned. Carrillo was the most cogent crazy woman she had ever met.

That she *was* crazy seemed hardly worth questioning. She wasn't claiming Adrian Edwards had arisen from the dead, as Allison had halfway been hoping she would, but the conspiracy theory she was offering instead was almost equally outrageous. Diane and Michael Edwards were religious fanatics who wanted Carrillo to believe—but only Carrillo, no one else—that God had indeed brought their son back from the dead. To this end, they had faked his death and burial, kept him hidden away for eight months, and then sent him back to school, having bribed everyone at Yesler Elementary to pretend the child had never gone missing at all. As for the why of it—for any *part* of it—Carrillo had no idea.

It was impossible.

And yet, the young teacher's telling of it could not have sounded more credible. Her account was laden with fine details, about small, relatively unimportant things, things Allison had learned were usually products of memory, not imagination. If, to cite only one example, the funeral for Adrian Edwards Carrillo had just described had never taken place, it was the most fully realized delusion Allison had ever encountered.

The teacher's demeanor, too, was an ill fit for someone out of touch with reality. There were no hysterics, no wide-eyed stares, no sudden outbursts of fury or outrage. She had raised her voice only once, when Allison pressed her for an answer she didn't have. Aside from that moment, Carrillo had been calm and in control, as reasoned as a lawyer delivering her opening arguments.

This wasn't what Allison had been expecting at all.

She didn't believe Carrillo's story because it defied belief. She couldn't give any part of it the slightest benefit of doubt without calling her own sanity into question. But implausibility was the only basis Allison had on which to judge Carrillo an unreliable witness. Had she any faith whatsoever in the supernatural, Allison realized now in amazement, she would have been more inclined to think the teacher was telling the truth than not.

"Why did you change your mind?" she asked, finally breaking the uneasy silence that had made its way between them. "About talking to me, I mean."

"I was just sitting here wondering the exact same thing," Carrillo said. "Because you don't believe a word I've said to you, do you?"

"Well, you have to admit—"

"I changed my mind because you're my only hope of finding out what's really going on. Everyone else is either lying about it or doesn't care enough about the truth to look for it. If I do what everybody wants me to do and keep my mouth shut, act like everything I remember about the last eight months is just a figment of my imagination, then I really will lose my mind. Don't you see that?

Allison was too slow to answer to suit her.

"No. You don't. Of course you don't. I was a fool to think you might."

"Wait a minute," Allison said. "Cut me some slack here. This is a lot to absorb in one sitting and I could use a little time to think it all over.

"Besides," she went on, "I'm not sure I know what you're asking me to do. It's not my job to prove who's right or wrong in all this. It's just my job to report it, as honestly as I possibly can."

"Weeks or months from now. After you've done a thorough investigation."

That had been the one stipulation Carrillo had set on her agreement to talk to Allison: that she not write a story for immediate release. Carrillo's desperation to get back in the classroom was palpable, and she probably knew any rush job on Allison's part would do her far more harm than good. She would worry about the ramifications of what Allison eventually wrote about her later.

Allison had agreed to her terms, but only because she'd already decided the teacher's story was too big for the web or the dailies. There was far more to exploit here than that. It was a feature for a major periodical at the very least, one that would take weeks, if not months, to put together. Even a book was not out of the question. Allison wasn't going to piss that kind of potential away just to see her byline on a published piece sooner than was necessary.

"Yes," she answered Carrillo now.

"Then that's all I'm asking for. A fair shake. No one else has any interest in asking the questions I need answered. They're all content to believe I'm delusional and leave it at that. If you can't get to the bottom of what's really happening here, nobody ever will. And I'll be branded unfit to teach for the rest of my life."

That this last was true, Allison had no doubt. Whatever chance Carrillo had of salvaging her teaching career probably depended upon Allison, and whatever explanations she could find for the bizarre tale the teacher had just told that did not involve her needing years of psychiatric help.

It wasn't a burden Allison wanted to carry, and yet she found herself hoping she could. Laura Carrillo did not strike her as someone who deserved the sorry fate that had befallen her.

"I'm not going to write anything intended to hurt you," Allison said. "But more than that, I can't really promise."

* * *

Laura was looking for a greater commitment from Allison Hope than she'd just been given, but she could see she wasn't going to get it. She smiled, a small flag of surrender. "Thank you."

Hope stood to leave and Laura walked her to the door.

"Who will you talk to next? Diane Edwards, I expect?"

"Probably. Either her or her husband, I haven't decided."

"Both will only tell you the same thing. Assuming either will speak with you at all. I'd suggest you try to find Weinman instead. He knows what the truth is. At least, his part of it."

"If he still remembers it, you mean."

Laura couldn't tell whether or not Hope was trying to be funny, so she let the comment go. They reached the door and Hope stepped out into the hall. "Adrian's mother is a lovely woman," Laura said. "You'll find her quite charming. But don't be fooled. She's not the innocent she seems."

Hope took that in. "And Adrian? What about him?"

"I don't understand the question."

"Well, is he what he appeared to be at Yesler Tuesday? Can you say for certain the boy you saw really was Adrian Edwards?"

"Oh, yes. Yes, I can," Laura said, and now the tears she had refused to let Hope see could not be held back.

From the moment he had walked into her classroom two days ago, she had wondered if the child she saw could be anyone other than Adrian Edwards. Sending an uncanny double to school that day would not have been beyond the scope of the elaborate hoax she'd become certain the boy's parents were perpetrating. But no. It had been Adrian. He held a place in her heart no other student could claim. She knew how he walked and how he spoke, the way his eyes peered deeply into her own without the slightest hint of guile. Even in the few minutes they had been in her classroom together on Tuesday, Laura had seen all of this in the boy before her. He hadn't merely resembled Adrian—he *was* Adrian.

And therein lay the only semblance of joy Laura had been able to derive from the last forty-eight hours.

Adrian Edwards was alive again.

TWENTY-TWO

"YOU OKAY?"

It was Bud Levitt, the senior tech Michael was working with today. Michael had retreated to the little parking lot behind Mighty Dynamo recording studios to be alone, forgetting Levitt was a smoker who liked to come out here on his breaks.

"That obvious, is it?"

"Well, that last take was fucking awful and the six before that were worse. Not to be too blunt about it or anything."

Levitt was right. The takes had been shit. The band whose tracks they were laying down was no second coming of Nirvana, but neither their music nor their drunk, overbearing producer had been the problem. The problem had been Michael. He was working the board this morning like a driver asleep at the wheel. The controls felt heavy in his hands, and he seemed to miss half of everything that came over his headphones.

Diane was going to meet Milton Weisman at Lakeridge Park this morning, and it appeared Weisman remembered his running Adrian over there last March as clearly as Michael, Diane, and Laura Carrillo did. Weisman's son-in-law had called Diane last night, and today she'd heard from Weisman himself. When she'd called Michael at the studio a little over an hour ago to report she'd agreed to meet the old man at the park, Michael had tried to dissuade her. He couldn't see what good could possibly come from it. They needed the poor devil to keep his memories of Adrian's death to himself, and engaging with him would hardly encourage him to do so. But Diane was going to see him in spite of all this.

Worrying over how the meeting was going, Michael had been present in the booth in body only this morning. He could have directed the recording session by phone, from home, and been just as effective.

"Sorry," he told Levitt. "Guess my mind's been wandering a bit."

Levitt drew in a lungful of smoke, tilted his head back to blow it out. "Trouble at home?"

"No. Quite the contrary."

He watched Levitt smoke. The tech was a redhead in his mid-twenties who wore the beard of a lumberjack and the ponytail of an ingénue. Three years earlier, he'd come home to Seattle after two tours of duty in Afghanistan, missing none of his good humor but almost all of his right leg. His prosthetic was so good, Michael only heard him complain about it when something reminded Levitt of basketball and how well he used to play it.

"I have a question for you," Michael said, moving to where Levitt stood.

"Okay."

"Strictly hypothetical."

"Uh-oh. One of those."

"Think of something impossible but wonderful. Something you'd give anything to have happen that you know, intellectually, never could."

"Never?"

"Let's just say it would defy all the laws of the known universe if it did."

"Huh." Levitt thought about it, dragging his cigarette down to a nub. "Like if I could suddenly fly or something?"

"No." Michael searched for a delicate way to say what came next, decided there was none. "Like if you suddenly had your leg back. You woke up one morning and there it was and no one cared. Everyone acted as if you'd always had two legs because that's what they remember."

"When you say 'everyone'—"

"I mean everyone. Friends, family, the people you work with. Me. Everyone. No one would have any memory of your injury at all."

"Except me?"

"Except you."

Michael had Levitt's full attention now. The tech crushed his cigarette out with the boot on his prosthetic foot, said, "Okay. I've got it. Next question."

"How would you explain it? To yourself, I mean. What would you attribute it to?"

Levitt shrugged, as if the answer was obvious. "God, man. What else?"

"God?" Michael couldn't remember him ever using the word before.

"Hell, I got my right leg back, no strings attached. I didn't have to sell my soul to the devil or any shit like that. Right?"

"Right. But—"

"And I'm not dreaming."

"No."

"Well, what else is that but divine intervention? Blind luck? Mike, I miss my leg. I miss the things I used to be able to do with it. I've learned to live with this piece of shit instead"—he rapped on his artificial thigh with his knuckles—"but I miss my leg. And every now and then—on my bad days—I go to bed wishing like hell I still had it.

"So now you say I've got it back. This thing I've been wanting more than anything I've ever wanted in my life. One day it's gone and the next day it's there, like magic. What, I'm supposed to think that's just a wild coincidence?"

"Well, why not?"

"Because coincidence doesn't go to all that trouble just to answer one man's prayers, man. Sure, holes open up in the space-time continuum and change shit all the time, but the results are a lot more random and benign than what you're talking about. I get my leg back and everyone else has their memory wiped, and for what? So one man can have his greatest wish come true?" He shook his head. "That ain't coincidence."

"Okay. Maybe not. But God—"

"Is a mythical creature, I know. But you asked a hypothetical question and I gave you a hypothetical answer. The way I would explain something happening that was both wonderful and utterly impossible is, I'd give credit to the most wonderful and utterly impossible being there is: God." He gave another shrug.

"So you'd become a believer, just like that. You'd suddenly accept the existence of something you'd once thought 'utterly impossible.'"

"Hey, I didn't say that. I'm sure, over time, I'd figure out something else more rational. Ours suddenly merged with a nearly identical, parallel universe and. . .you know, some metaphysical voodoo like that. But would I consider the God option, too, at least for a minute? Hell, who wouldn't? Because what you're describing is a miracle, Mike. Old and New Testament stuff. Seas being parted and sight being returned to the blind. You show a man a miracle—his own private miracle—and he's got no choice but to wonder if God ain't real. Right?"

Michael nodded, satisfied with Levitt's answer.

"So, what's the deal, anyway? What's got you pondering such heavy questions so deeply this morning you can't set a damn mic level right? You didn't see one yourself?"

"See one?"

"A miracle. Water turned to wine, a dead man walking. . . ."

"No," Michael said. "Nothing like that." Levitt was waiting for him to elaborate. Michael wondered now how wise it had been to say anything to him at all. "Just something I came across online last night. Two people going back and forth in the comments section, arguing about faith and religion. I guess it got me thinking."

"Yeah. A good flame war can do that sometimes. But do me a favor, huh?"

"Stop thinking until this session is over?"

"Please." Levitt started up the steps to the studio's back door. "Those guys inside aren't too bad, but if I have to hear that song about—ashes and silk curtains, was it?—one more fucking time, I'm gonna overload the board and torch the whole studio, I swear to God."

* * *

Before he got back in the booth, Michael's cell phone rang. It was Diane.

"No," he said when she told him what she'd done. "No way."

"Michael, we have to. We can't say no."

"Yes. We can." He hunkered down in a remote corner of the studio's main hallway and lowered his voice. "Diane, we've already got enough trouble trying to keep Laura Carrillo quiet. Now you want to admit the truth to Weisman?"

"He already knows the truth. He remembers everything, Michael, and he's afraid. The poor man just needs some help making sense of it."

"The 'poor man'?"

"What he did to Adrian was an accident. It wasn't his fault. You used to understand that better than I did."

"I do understand it. But—"

"He deserves our forgiveness. He's a changed man; the accident did something to him. He's closer to God now than he's probably ever been in his life, and we can bring him closer."

"By letting him see Adrian."

"Yes. God brought Adrian back as much for him as for us. I can see that now. He wants to see proof that Adrian's alive, just as you did yesterday, and once he's seen it, he'll believe and be glad. And he'll go in peace. He gave me his word. We have to do this, Michael."

Michael's head was reeling. He didn't know what to say. One minute, they were hell-bent on denying everything to everyone, and the next. . . .

"I'll take him," Michael said.

"What?"

"I'll take Adrian to see him. I want to be there when they meet."

"Alone?"

"Yes. Alone."

Diane said, "I don't know."

"What? He already knows all there is to know, you said. There's nothing I can tell him that you haven't already."

"No, but—"

"I'll pick Adrian up after school and take him. The minute the meeting's over, I'll call you. Sorry, I've gotta go."

He hung up before his wife could object any further.

* * *

Right before recess, Howard Alberts decided to sit in on Laura Carrillo's class. The district substitute who had taken over for Laura was Naeema Peele, an olive-skinned brunette in her mid-thirties nearly as tall as Alberts. Peele had subbed at Yesler only twice before, and for a single day on each occasion, so Alberts didn't know her well. But it wasn't the teacher Alberts wanted to observe today. It was Adrian Edwards.

For two days now, he had been studying the boy from afar, looking for anything to suggest he was in some way different this week than in weeks or months past. More sullen, perhaps, or less willing to participate in class. Did he sound the same? Run and play the same? Was this the way he had always smiled, or. . .?

Alberts had even taken the boy aside yesterday for a brief chat, to see how he would respond to a few general questions. How was it going? Did he like Ms. Peele? Had he and his parents talked to him about the incident at school on Tuesday? Adrian's answers were succinct and uninformative, seemingly proving the boy was suffering no great ill effects from Laura Carrillo's breakdown.

If Adrian had done something to provoke that breakdown, something mischievous at best or cruel at worst, it would have marked a behavioral shift of epic proportion. Alberts's trained eye could always detect clues signaling problem students in the making. And yet, Alberts could see nothing in this Adrian Edwards that had not been there before. The boy seemed as warm, bright, and eerily mature as ever.

When the bell sounded for recess, Alberts watched the children pile out of the classroom. He exchanged greetings with some and a silent nod with Adrian, then left his position at the back of the room to confer with Peele, who stood beside her desk waiting for him with what looked like mild apprehension.

"How are they doing?" Alberts asked. Peele hadn't been given any specifics about the scene Laura Carrillo had caused in her class two days ago, but Peele understood it had been traumatic.

"Fine. I've seen nothing from any of them to be concerned about so far."

"Including Adrian?"

"Yes. I've been keeping a careful eye on him as you advised, and he seems perfectly normal, and lovely, to me."

"Good."

"And Ms. Carrillo? Have you heard how she's been doing?"

Alberts wondered how far her curiosity went, considering how little he and Betty Marx had told her about the teacher for whom she was subbing.

"I understand she's feeling much better." In a rush to change the subject, he smiled and added, "Don't tell me you're anxious to have her back already?"

She laughed. It was a full, lighthearted laugh that Alberts recognized as the kind so many teachers started out with, only to lose as time wore on. "No. It's not like that." Peele turned serious. "I just hope she's going to be okay."

And now Alberts saw it, the glint in her eyes that signified Peele knew more about Laura's suspension than he would have preferred.

"I'm sure she's going to be fine," he said.

"I don't know him that well, of course. I've only been with him today and yesterday. But I think I feel comfortable saying, whatever happened here Tuesday, Adrian didn't do anything to precipitate it. He isn't that kind of child."

"No? What kind of child would you say he is?"

"Good. Decent. He's no angel, no child ever is, but he's empathetic. If he'd done something to upset Ms. Carrillo, I'm sure he would have admitted it to someone by now."

This was the opinion Alberts himself had formed of Adrian after years of observing the boy at Yesler. If Peele could reach the same conclusion in only two days, there had to be something to it.

Still, all he said was, "You're doing a great job under difficult circumstances. Keep it up."

"Thank you. I'll try."

* * *

The first thing Milton did upon returning home from Lakeridge Park was call his daughter Lisa. Janet had already left three cell phone messages for him this morning, meeting his every expectation, but he wasn't ready to talk to her yet. He was tired, almost too tired to breathe, and unlike Janet, Lisa would let him complete a whole sentence without ranting or wailing like he'd done something to break her heart in two.

"Daddy, where have you been?" Lisa asked. "Janet's—"

"Please. I don't want to talk to your sister right now. You call her for me and tell her I'm okay. Tell her I'm at home and I'm fine and I'm taking a nap. I'll call her myself later."

"But are you okay? She told me what happened last night. All those things you said about that little boy."

"That was a mistake. I shouldn't have said it."

"Did you call the mother? Janet said you were supposed to call the boy's mother."

"Yes, I called her. I called her!" Milton stopped to calm himself, determined to stick to the plan he had devised.

"And she told you he's all right. That this accident—"

"Was all in my head. Yes. I told you: I made a mistake. I understand that now. I got confused, but I'm all right now, Lisa. You don't have to worry about me. I'm going to lie down and take a nap, and when I wake up, I'll call Janet. Okay? Tell her that for me, please. I'm fine."

Lisa let him go shortly thereafter. Not because she was convinced, but because she wasn't Janet, who would have never given up so easily.

Milton did want to take a nap, a long one, and he got all the way to his bedroom before he chose to do something else. Teetering on his haunches at the edge of his bed, shoes kicked off and feet off the floor, he made another phone call, this one to a man he had last had a substantive conversation with four years earlier, days after Milton lost his wife, Shauna, to the ravages of cancer.

"Hello?"

"Rabbi," Milton said, "I need to see you. Right away."

TWENTY-THREE

FOLLOWING HER INTERVIEW of Laura Carrillo, Allison took only one Uber assignment—transporting a pair of chatty, surgically enhanced women from Bellevue to Laurelhurst—before calling it a day. It was only noon, but Carrillo's story was already writing itself in Allison's head and she was loath to lose a word.

She went home to work, eschewing the frenzy and expense of the coffee shop. Once she was at her desk, headphones on and laptop open, Allison rarely ever moved again until sleep or the dawn forced the issue. Today, it would have taken a team of mules to draw her from her chair.

Listening to her recording and hearing Laura Carrillo's answers all over again, Allison was once more filled with amazement and euphoria. Amazement because Carrillo's account remained astonishing, and euphoria because it held the potential to breathe some life back into Allison's writing career.

The hoax Carrillo was accusing Michael and Diane Edwards of perpetrating could not have any basis in fact. People did not fake the deaths of their children, for financial gain or otherwise, only to reenter them later into the very same social circles from which they had been removed. And even if such people did exist, they would lack the power to make everyone of their acquaintance, with a singular exception, oblivious to their deception.

As for the small matter of motive: What reason could the parents of Adrian Edwards have had to perform such a convoluted feat of subterfuge and magic? Laura Carrillo didn't know, and had made little effort to speculate.

Until she met them, Allison could only assume the Edwardses were innocent victims of Carrillo's unhinged imagination. To think otherwise would lead farther down the rabbit hole than Carrillo had already taken her. For instance, if Diane Edwards had indeed told Carrillo her son died eight months ago but was alive again today by the grace of God, Allison would be left to draw only one of three conclusions, each more incredible than the last: Edwards was no saner than Carrillo; she and her husband were gaslighting the teacher to destroy her; or she had told Carrillo the truth.

The first was a remote possibility, the second, one even more remote, and the third was simply out of the question. Or was it?

For the first time since she'd heard the name Laura Carrillo, Allison gave the idea of miracles more than a passing thought. Did she believe in such things? As scriptural signposts that went part and parcel with her faith in a Judeo-Christian god, she had to say yes, of course she did. What fool would believe in a god that lacked either the power or the will to do the impossible when answering their most desperate prayer often required nothing less? But buying into miracles in concept and believing God performed them now, thousands of years after the death of Christ, were not the same thing. Allison did not give God that much credit anymore. She offered prayers to Him, yes, but the things she hoped for in return were relatively minor, in keeping with her low expectations for intervention. If God took a hand in the affairs of men and women at all these days, it was almost imperceptible. His handiwork was so slight as to be easily mistaken for good fortune.

Resurrecting Adrian Edwards from the dead would not have been God's style.

Which brought Allison back to the most likely assumption of the three from which she had to choose: Laura Carrillo was psychologically disturbed. She'd had the out of claiming the incident at Yesler had been an aberration, the result of stress or an unwise combination of prescription meds, and she hadn't taken it. She'd recited a fairy tale, instead. Allison would have been hard-pressed to create a story that sounded more insane than the one Carrillo had told.

So why, Allison wondered, was she finding it so difficult to write Carrillo off as just another crazy in a world filled with them? How could it be that the longer she listened to the woman's interview, playing and replaying some parts over and over again, the more convinced she became there was a layer of truth in it?

Listen to me. Look at me. Ask me a question about anything else. . . . I'll give you an intelligent answer. A sane answer. Do you know why? Because

I am sane. *I'm not a drug abuser or the victim of a nervous breakdown. I'm neither deranged nor confused. I'm just afraid, Ms. Hope.*

Afraid. Wouldn't that be the proper reaction to the waking nightmare she was describing? Wouldn't Allison herself be terrified were she caught in such a trap, between a past she knew to be true and a present that disavowed it?

It dawned on Allison she'd just stumbled upon the ideal hook for her piece: the almost hypnotic way in which Carrillo embraced her madness. This was a story not so much about an emotionally disturbed young woman who'd gone berserk in the workplace as it was the effect she had on people who dared approach her with an open mind. Her investment in a bizarre delusion that was as alluring as it was tragic.

If Allison had had the luxury of heeding her conscience, she might have thought twice about writing Carrillo's story at all. The likely consequences for Carrillo of Allison's piece appearing in print, especially on the nationwide scale Allison was hoping for, were easy to predict. But Allison was in no position to sympathize. She was in a fight for her own professional life, a fight she felt closer to losing every day, and there was a very real chance this story was her last ticket to salvation. If she failed to write and sell it, to turn it into something both profitable and worthy of widespread attention, she might finally have to concede that every doubt Flo had about her was justified.

This last thought hung over her head as she worked, until she was moved to stop and leave her desk, distracted. She made a fresh pot of coffee to busy herself, then wandered the house with a cup in her hand, trying to refocus. Lately, once her thoughts turned to her and Flo, there was no turning back, and today was no exception. She was holding on to the woman she loved by a slender thread. Flo was holding on, too, but with less enthusiasm every day and for the worst possible reasons. Loyalty. Logistics. Sympathy.

Sympathy was a poor substitute for love, and no substitute at all for desire. Allison took her coffee cup into their bedroom and tried to remember the last time they had made love, the way two people did when both were equally starving for it and neither was doing the other a kindness. She gazed at their bed, imagined the covers thrown back and pillows scattered, and decided it had been six months earlier, after one of those alumni dinners at the university she and Flo were occasionally obliged to attend. This particular dinner had been more boring than most, but it was coming on the heels of Allison's last great professional high, the receipt of a glowing letter from a prospective agent in New York who'd read her novel and all but guaranteed he could find a fast home for it. Allison had charged through the evening like a star in the making. She was bold and confident, funny as hell, and Flo had had little choice but to fall under her spell. By the time they got home that night, intoxicated and giddy, what they would do to each other in the privacy of their own bedroom was a foregone conclusion.

Standing in that same room now, Allison slipped a hand inside her shirt and let the memory come.

The magic had been short-lived. The agent with the big promises had failed to deliver and Allison's manuscript had once more been relegated to its place among all her other unsold current work. She and Flo deflated to their previous inertia, Flo almost instantaneously. But for that one night, with both of them drunk on the hope the long drought for Allison was over, Flo believed again, as much as Allison did, that both Allison and their relationship had a future. Hungry and brazen, anxious to touch and be touched, their hands and mouths expressed this belief in ways words alone could not.

And now? Only Allison was in love, and the hand at her breast was her own. Allison snatched it away. So this was what loneliness had reduced her to, making porno movies out of memories just to feel alive again, even if only for a moment. She felt dirty and small. Pathetic.

She fled the bedroom and went back to her desk. She sat down and started typing, words that amounted to nothing. She gave up, dropped her head into both hands, and as she let go of the grief and fear she could no longer suppress, something began to spill out of her. Something she hadn't heard spoken in her own voice, with any degree of sincerity, for a long time.

"Dear God," she said, *"please. . . ."*

* * *

Laura kept her appointment with Dr. Noreen Ives.

She arrived on time, smartly dressed and composed, and prepared to lie to the psychiatrist's face every minute of their scheduled hour together. Sharing the truth with Allison Hope had been risky enough; if she brought Ives into her confidence, too, Laura knew what would happen.

Ives's report to the district would strike the death knell to Laura's teaching career.

The deception wasn't easy for her. Short, petite, and quick to laugh, Ives was not the clinical, cold fish Laura had been expecting, and her questions were straightforward, without overt subtext. She seemed almost old enough to be Laura's mother, and had her mother's same disarming way of saying things. The urge to trust her was almost too great for Laura to overcome.

But overcome it Laura did, because she knew one truthful answer would lead to two, and then three, and three would lead to all the rest of it, in a rush she would be helpless to stop. So she lied and lied again, painting the image of herself she had composed hours before, one of an overworked teacher who'd allowed stress and perfectionism to push her to the breaking point. Yes, she *was* taken by Adrian Edwards, and yes, perhaps enough so that his becoming the focus of all her pent-up anxiety made sense. But no, she couldn't imagine where she'd gotten the idea he had died, and as much as she could recall, nothing she'd told the staff at Yesler about the eight months following his "passing" was rooted in reality. The whole episode embarrassed her now, and she couldn't wait to put it behind her.

Naturally, Ives did not accept this all-too convenient insight from Laura without some pushback. Among more straightforward inquiries, Ives asked questions for which there were no simple "correct" answers.

Why do you suppose you chose eight months ago for Adrian's fatal accident? What was going on in your life at that time?

Have you ever had an abortion? Or a miscarriage?

What are your feelings about death in general?

And:

What do you think of Adrian's parents?

Laura had to hesitate before answering that last one. Had she said what immediately came to mind, the game she was playing with Ives would have been over. Her contempt for Diane and Michael Edwards—Diane, in particular—was only barely within her powers to conceal. Regardless of their motives, the Edwardses were attempting to foist upon the world a colossal lie that had ground Laura's life to pulp. She was but a means to their end, whatever that was, and she despised them for treating her with such gross disregard.

What she said to Ives, however, was:

"I've always admired them both tremendously."

Which, irony of all ironies, would have been well within the truth only four days earlier. She *had* admired Diane Edwards, and to a lesser degree, her husband. They had seemingly lost a child and shown little sign of becoming bitter and resentful, as Laura would have if Adrian had been her son. The reasons for Diane Edwards's uncanny grace in the face of tragedy were clear now, but at the time Laura had found it impressive.

Whether Ives was as taken in now by Laura's acting performance, Laura couldn't tell. Ives was impossible to read. All Laura could do was hope the psychiatrist was buying it.

If talking to Ives had been a mistake, Laura would find out soon enough.

*   *   *

Milton's synagogue was Temple Beth Isaiah on Rainier Avenue. Before her death, Shauna had dragged him to services here with the determination of an angry mule, ensuring his attendance for all High Holy Days as if it were her standing with God at stake and not Milton's. When she passed, he had buried with her all pretense of his religious devotion and stopped coming to synagogue, despite the efforts of his daughters to assume their mother's role as his living conscience.

Since the accident last March, he had been no less a stranger to Temple Beth Isaiah, but twice had come close to attending shul entirely of his own accord, without his daughters' knowledge. He had gotten as far as his apartment door, in his best black suit and tie, before changing his mind on both occasions. He didn't know why he'd felt moved to go; he imagined it was some odd manifestation of his love for Shauna and how much he missed her. But now, sitting in Rabbi Ira Kramer's office at the temple, Milton gave fresh consideration to an alternative explanation: he had been *called* to come.

Rabbi Kramer was many years Milton's junior, slim and robust and as handsome as an aging movie star, and Milton should have found it impossible to talk to him. What could they have in common? But Kramer was unlike any man of God Milton had ever met. He treated everyone, Jew and gentile alike, with the same level of respect, showing no one the slightest hint of condescension, and he met his obligations as a teacher and confessor with a feather-like touch. Shauna had adored him, Janet and Lisa were in his thrall, and Milton, despite his best efforts to feel different, trusted Rabbi Kramer implicitly.

Still, what Milton had to tell him today could not have been more difficult to share. The rabbi's opinion mattered to Milton, and if Kramer showed him the same look of pity and disbelief Janet had, Milton wasn't sure he could bear it.

He needn't have worried.

After the customary preamble of greetings and courtesies, the rabbi let Milton speak and kept his expression neutral, his attention unwavering. The few questions Kramer asked were short and direct, so Milton's train of thought was rarely if ever derailed.

When at last Milton was done, the rabbi sighed and said, "Well. Needless to say, Milton, that's an incredible story."

"It's not a story. It's the truth," Milton said, irritated.

"And forgive me for asking this, but—"

"No. I told you. I have not been drinking. This has nothing to do with drink."

Kramer sat there for a moment. "All right. In that case, I'm sure it all feels like the truth to you. Perhaps because it *is* your truth."

"*My* truth? I don't understand."

"What I'm saying is, the truth is a moving target, and it's unique to every one of us. We all have and adhere to our own version of it, whether we realize it or not. In your version, you had this terrible accident and killed this little boy. In my version, or Janet's, you didn't. That doesn't necessarily mean it didn't happen. It just means our versions of the truth do not happen to agree."

Milton shook his head. "No. No! It's not the truth because I *think* it is. It *is* the truth! Not my truth or your truth. *The* truth."

"I wonder," Kramer said.

"Why? Why do you wonder?"

"Simply put? Because God is not a bellhop."

"What?"

"It's an expression we clergymen use. It means God does not answer prayers on command. He's not a bellhop who hears our requests and meets our every need. Raising a child from the dead in answer to his mother's prayers is not beyond God's powers, of course, but neither is it the sort of thing He does. At least, not anymore."

"Then you're telling me I'm crazy."

"No. I'm merely suggesting there are other, perhaps more likely explanations for what you are describing than the intervention of God. For instance. . . ." The rabbi pulled himself forward in his chair, leaned across his desk toward Milton. "You're a man who could be feeling a great deal of guilt about the way you once treated your wife and children. You may recall briefly expressing such feelings to me when Shauna died."

Milton did.

"Often," Kramer went on, "what we do with guilt that can't be relieved any other way is, we redirect it. We attach it to something altogether different from what we're actually feeling guilty about and punish ourselves accordingly. In your case—"

"I killed a little boy in my car."

"Yes. That's one theory that could explain what's going on here."

"Except that it doesn't explain why the boy's mother remembers his death, too. If it's *my* delusion—"

"Without having heard what she said to you myself, I would venture to guess she was humoring you. Telling you what you wanted to hear in order to set your mind at ease. If you seemed as convinced to her that this accident really happened as you do to me, I can see how she might have thought it better to indulge you than argue with you."

Milton rewound his conversation with Diane Edwards, checking this last suggestion for merit before flatly dismissing it. "No. She wasn't indulging me. She wasn't pretending to remember. She *does* remember."

"In that case—there's one more possible explanation for what you're experiencing. No less far-fetched than the others, perhaps, but no more so, either: the nonlinear nature of time." Seeing Milton's confusion, Kramer quickly added, "That is, the idea that time does not run along one single, uninterrupted path, but is comprised of many paths that may on rare occasions intersect. In other words, maybe what's happened to you is that your life was once moving along a timeline in which you killed this little boy—Adrian Edwards—and now it's moving along another in which you didn't. Does that make sense?"

"No," Milton said angrily, thinking, *This was a mistake.* He had come to his synagogue to speak to his rabbi about a *spiritual* matter, and for all the Talmudic insight Kramer was bringing to the table, Milton might as well have consulted his mail carrier.

"I'm sorry. I'm not trying to confuse you," Kramer said.

"Well, you are. I came here to get some answers, Rabbi, and all I'm getting from you are more questions!"

"All right. Let's start over," Kramer said, the incongruity of his singularly secular outlook having perhaps become conspicuous even to him. "Let's assume for a moment that God did do these things. Raised the boy from the dead, left only four people in the world to remember his death, and all the rest. Yes?"

Milton didn't say anything, waiting for the rabbi to go on.

"What is your question for me, Milton? How can I help you?"

"You can tell me what to do. How to go on with my life knowing what's happened, that God has performed this. . .this. . . ."

He couldn't say the word.

"Miracle," Kramer said.

"Yes. This miracle. If it's true, it's a wonderful thing. A beautiful thing. Isn't it? This little boy is in the world again. His parents have their son back and I. . .I can finally forget that terrible day in the park. I can *allow* myself to forget."

"Yes."

"But his mother says no one should know. That we should all just keep quiet about what's happened and be glad."

"And she's right. Obviously."

"Obviously?"

"If He wanted the world to know, it would know. That only four people do know seems proof enough that such is God's will."

Milton thought this over. "So if I were to tell anyone else about it—Lisa or Janet—"

"You'd be operating in opposition to that will. Exactly."

Milton let Kramer's words sink in. "And you? I've just told you."

"Like I said when you first asked, the things I hear in this room never leave this room. It's all held in the strictest confidence. So your secret—and God's—is safe with me, I promise you."

Milton nodded, satisfied. Kramer was a good and honest man, and he would have had nothing to gain by sharing Milton's confession with others.

"Look at it this way, Milton," he said. "Whether what you're dealing with is truly a miracle or not, your responsibility for Adrian's death is now and forever moot. You've been absolved, either by the love of God or your own subconscious. And that is something to be grateful for, in and of itself. Right?"

"Yes," Milton said, nodding again. It was true.

"You said you were going to see the boy later today."

"Yes."

"Have you thought about what you might say to him? What questions you might ask?"

The glimmer in Kramer's eyes gave away his own curiosity on the subject.

"No. I'm not sure I'll say anything to him. His mother says he doesn't remember anything anyway. I want to see him, that's all. Seeing him will be enough."

"And then?"

"And then I'll do as you suggest and leave it alone."

Kramer smiled. "Do you think you'll be able to do that?"

"I don't know." Milton shrugged and returned the rabbi's smile with a small one of his own. "But I'm going to try."

* * *

Like Milton, all Allison wanted to do was see Adrian Edwards.

There were other things on her to-do list—talking to the boy's parents, for one, and giving the old man Weinman a first name, if she could, for another—but what she found herself most anxious to do Thursday afternoon was get a good, hard look at Adrian. He was the epicenter of the storm she was writing about, after all, and she wanted to find out if there was anything remarkable about him that photographs alone did not convey.

She drove to Yesler Elementary, intending to park some distance from the campus and use the binoculars from her trunk to try to catch sight of the boy out on the yard. Eventually, she would have to go back to the office to seek an interview with the school's principal, but so soon after her interview with Betty Marx, Allison could guess what that would buy her: a polite *no comment* and an escort to the door. Today, she would stay off school grounds and hope Adrian Edwards showed himself.

Only when she arrived did Allison give any thought to the time: just after three. Kids were pouring out of Yesler's front entrance in a swarm, the end of their school day at hand. Allison feared her chance to see Adrian had already come and gone. But before she could park the car, she spotted her quarry in the crowd across the street, walking down the steps to the buzzing carport.

He hustled straight to a green, late-model Acura sedan and climbed into the front seat. The big, squinty-eyed man behind the wheel leaned over, either to plant a kiss on the boy's head or ruffle his hair—Allison couldn't tell which through the glare of the car's windshield—and then the Acura was on the move. It paused briefly at the carport exit, waiting for traffic to clear, before turning right onto 76th Avenue and cruising away.

Somebody behind Allison hit their horn, reminding her she was blocking the street, and reflexively she hit the gas and sped off, taking care to keep the green Acura ahead of her just close enough to follow.

TWENTY-FOUR

MICHAEL RECOGNIZED MILTON Weisman immediately. For obvious reasons, the old man's face had been scored into his memory like a razor-cut tattoo. His hair was thinner and he'd lost some weight, but other than that, he looked to be the same pathetic creature Michael had seen on television, being hounded by reporters outside the man's front door days after the accident. Today, as Michael and Adrian entered the burger restaurant, Weisman was sitting in a booth at the back, watching the door with all the anticipation of a dog awaiting its master.

Spotting them, he started to stand, but Michael discreetly shook him off, tilting his head to one side to indicate he and the boy would order their food before joining Weisman at his table. The old man sat back down but his eyes never left them. Michael didn't need to see him to know it; Weisman's gaze was like a knife at his back.

Michael still wasn't sure he could do this. He had never been able to show Weisman the modicum of empathy Diane had come to grant him, and even now, with his offense against them null and void, Michael still felt entitled to view the man who had killed their son as a bumbling old fool. But Diane was right: it wasn't their place to deny him this meeting with Adrian. Like Diane, Laura Carrillo, and Michael himself, Weisman had been given open eyes with which to see the great miracle God had in all His mercy performed, and whatever peace of mind it would bring him to sit in Adrian's presence, if only for a minute or two, was surely his due.

Michael guided Adrian over to Weisman's booth, carrying their food tray, and once more the old man rose to acknowledge them, smiling through his obvious unease. Adrian smiled back. Michael had told his son on the way over they were going to dine with a friend, but he hadn't said who the friend would be. Adrian had no reason to recognize the old man, other than as someone he may have seen at the park, and Michael was curious to learn what his reaction to Weisman would be.

"I'm sorry, but my wife couldn't make it," Michael said. "I hope you don't mind that I came instead."

Weisman shook his head, then returned his gaze to Adrian. "This must be Adrian." He was shaking.

"Yes." Michael set their tray down. "Adrian, this is Mr. Weisman. He's the friend I told you about."

Adrian offered Weisman his hand, as he would have upon being introduced to any other stranger. "Pleased to meet you."

Weisman shook his hand, wobbling on his feet, and Michael thought he might collapse at any moment.

"Let's sit down and get this over with, shall we?"

Michael waited for the old man to do as he suggested, then slid alongside his son into the opposite side of the booth.

"Call me Milton," Weisman said to Adrian. For all the attention he was showing the boy, Michael might as well have stayed in the car.

Adrian nodded.

"We can't stay long," Michael said. He wanted Weisman to know up-front this meeting had been his wife's idea, not his own . "We're going to have to eat and run, I'm afraid."

"Okay," Weisman said.

"Are you crying?" Adrian asked.

Much to Michael's chagrin, the poor devil was.

"Yes. I am."

"Why?"

"Oh, I don't know. Because I'm old, I guess. And because it's so good to—" Weisman stopped, catching a mistake before he could make it. "Because it's so good to finally meet you. Your parents have told me a lot about you."

"They have?"

"Yes, they have."

"Like what?"

Caught in a trap of his own making, Weisman had no choice but to laugh.

* * *

Weinman, Allison thought. The old man who'd allegedly run Adrian Edwards over with his car at Lakeridge Park last March.

She sat alone at a table at the opposite end of the restaurant, having followed Adrian and the man she assumed was his father here, careful to keep a safe distance. None of the three people at the booth she was watching would have recognized her, but she wasn't taking any chances.

Laura Carrillo had suggested Weinman was a participant in the death hoax she believed the Edwardses were playing on the world, and if this old man was him, this meeting seemed to lend credence to that idea. Allison couldn't hear their conversation, however, so she couldn't confirm who the old man was or what he and Michael Edwards were discussing.

Still, she had a hunch this was Weinman (or Weisler?). His hangdog look, and the interminable handshake he'd just shared with Adrian, seemed to suggest the kind of weariness that often made older people careless, sometimes fatally so. This man may have never caused a serious accident, in or out of a car, but portraying one who had would not have been out of his reach.

The temptation to approach the trio's table was almost too much for Allison to resist. Three of the central players in the story she was working on were right there, all but begging her to ask the questions she was dying to pose. She might not get such a chance again. But she forced herself to stay put and bide her time, fearing she could lose all hope of talking to any of them if she set upon them in a group and things went sour. She liked her chances of getting something useful out of Weinman or Adrian in a one-on-one encounter, but Michael Edwards's reluctance to speak with her, in any setting, was a message she could read from his body language alone. For now, Allison would only watch, to determine as best she could how these people were related and what nature of business had brought them here.

Later, when they went their separate ways, she would choose a target and make her move.

* * *

Milton kept thinking about the handshake.

The little boy's right hand had felt like lamb's wool: soft and supple, and warm. It had been all Milton could do to let it go. When the boy entered with his father, all need for further proof had left Milton in an instant. This was Adrian Edwards, the child whose life he had taken last

March. Milton had seen him at the park only half a dozen times or so prior to that horrific day, and always at some distance, but there was no doubt in his mind. Adrian Edwards was alive again.

All that followed the handshake, then, was superfluous. Milton had come here to be convinced the miracle was real, that the God Milton had barely acknowledged as a remote possibility all his life was in fact far more than that, and he'd just been given all the evidence of both he would ever need. The small talk he was making with Adrian and his father now, alluding to a working relationship with Michael Edwards that didn't exist for the benefit of his son, was only to fill time. It was awkward and comically pointless.

Still, Milton went along with the charade, maintaining his part of the artificial repartee ("So, how do you like school?" "And work is good for you, Michael?"). He watched Adrian and his father eat, only sipping coffee himself, and felt the last vestiges of a guilt he'd thought he would carry to his grave melt away. He still had questions, many questions, but he no longer felt the need to have them answered. Ignorance of things he could never understand anyway seemed a small price to pay for four lives drawn from the abyss.

Eventually Adrian and his father cleared their plates and finished off their drinks. Michael Edwards, even more uncomfortable in Milton's company than Milton had been in his, said, "Well, we have to take off. It was good seeing you, Milton." And that was it. He and the boy started sliding out of the booth.

Milton got to his feet and held out his hand, this time to Adrian's father. More tears were coming but he held them at bay for now. He shook the man's hand and said, "Thank you."

Edwards nodded, and perhaps—or perhaps not—softened a little.

Milton turned to the boy, and the two shook hands again, no doubt for the last time. "It was a pleasure meeting you, Adrian. Tell your mother I said good-bye, will you?"

"Good-bye?"

It had been a poor choice of words. Milton and Michael Edwards exchanged a look. "I have to go away for a while and I probably won't be back."

Adrian nodded and, much to the adults' relief, asked no further questions.

* * *

Allison looked up from the plate of fries she was lathering with ketchup just in time to see Michael and Adrian Edwards leave the old man's table. They headed for the door and the critical choice she'd deferred was suddenly upon her: Weinman or the boy and his father? In the ten seconds she had to decide, her instincts chose the old man. It was a safe bet that Edwards, ambushed in a public place by a woman he didn't know, would refuse to talk to her and deny her any access to his son, no matter how she represented—or *mis*represented herself. But Weinman was likely an easier nut to crack. Not only because of his age, but because he struck Allison as vulnerable. Throughout his brief meeting with Adrian and his father, he had appeared to weep at least once, and the affection he had for the boy never left his face. Nothing about him had been consistent with Allison's idea of a co-conspirator to a massive fraud, unless he was in it for love and not money. He looked frail and shaken, and people like that were often as easy for a good reporter to pry open as the cap on an aspirin bottle.

Allison left her table and started toward Weinman's.

* * *

"Mr. Weinman?"

Milton looked up to see a middle-aged blonde woman peering down at him. He'd been looking out the window, following Michael and Adrian Edwards's path through the parking lot to their car, and hadn't noticed the stranger's approach.

"Weisman," he said, not yet stopping to wonder how this woman might almost know his name.

"Excuse me?"

"It's Weisman with an S. Not Weinman. Milton *Weis*man."

"Oh. Of course." The stranger turned up the smile she was already wearing, and Milton wasn't sure he liked the look of either version. "I'm sorry."

"Do I know you?"

"My name is Allison Hope. We've never met but. . . ." She looked around as if checking for eavesdroppers. "I think we should talk." She gestured at the empty side of his booth. "May I?"

She sat down before he could answer.

"What do we have to talk about?" Milton asked, not yet afraid but inching in that direction.

"The two people who were just here. Michael and Adrian Edwards. That *was* Adrian, wasn't it?"

Milton stared at her, confusion growing.

"I thought so. It's wonderful to see him looking so well, isn't it? Considering the accident and all?"

"The accident?" Milton didn't know how he'd gotten his mouth to move.

The woman who had identified herself as Allison Hope raised an eyebrow. "You, your car, Lakeridge Park. Last March."

"You know about the accident?"

Hope nodded.

"I don't understand. I thought. . .we were the only ones."

"The only ones?"

"The only ones who remembered."

Hope seemed taken aback.

"His mother told me no one else knew." Milton's mind was reeling now. "It was just the four of us. Her and her husband, me and. . . ." An idea occurred to him. "Wait. The teacher. Are you the boy's teacher?"

"You mean Laura Carrillo?"

Milton nodded, realizing that this was indeed the name Diane Edwards had given him for Adrian's teacher: Laura Carrillo. Not Allison Hope. Suddenly he was able to recall seeing news video of Carrillo at the boy's funeral. She was a willowy brunette, not this blonde with rounded hips and light eyes.

Now Milton was afraid.

* * *

Michael was almost out of the parking lot when he saw the woman sitting in Weisman's booth.

His work bag had toppled over in the car's backseat as he steered the Acura toward the nearest exit, spilling sheets of music to the floor. Having stopped to prop the bag up again, he'd caught sight of the pair through the sedan's rear window. He couldn't be sure from this distance, but he didn't think he knew the woman, and he doubted Weisman did. There was something almost predatory about the way she was leaning across the table toward the old man, as if she were trying to sell him something he didn't want to buy.

Michael re-parked the car, lowered the windows to let some air in, and said to Adrian, "Stay here, son. Daddy will be right back."

* * *

Allison's heart was in her stomach. Weisman was flipping the script she'd had in her head, saying things that didn't align with anything rational. He was supposed to be talking about the "accident" in Lakeridge Park like it was part of a plot, not an actual event. Insinuating Laura Carrillo remembered it made him sound more like a dupe to Diane and Michael Edwards's hoax than an active participant in it.

"Mr. Weisman, what do you remember about the accident? Tell me, please."

"But you said—"

"I know what I said. And I do know about it. But only part of it, and I was hoping to learn the rest from you."

The old man still seemed confused.

"How did it happen? Did something distract you, or were you going too fast, maybe?" Another thought came to her: "Were you drunk?"

"No! I lost control of the car! My foot slipped. The boy was on the slide. Why—"

"Who are you?" someone said before Weisman could go on.

Michael Edwards had come back.

Allison didn't answer.

"She said her name was Allison Hope," Weisman said. "She knows about the accident."

"No. She doesn't," Edwards said, glaring at Allison. "She doesn't know anything." He turned to Weisman. "She's a reporter, Milton. She's writing a story about Adrian's teacher."

Weisman's face fell. "A reporter?"

"He's right. I am a reporter," Allison admitted. "Or a journalist, to be more precise. And I *am* writing a story about Laura Carrillo. But—"

"We don't care about the *but*," Edwards said. "We've got nothing to say to you. Get the hell out of here and leave us alone." He reached for her arm, intending to lift her out of the booth, but Allison pulled away.

"Waitaminute! All I'm trying to do is follow up on a statement I got from Ms. Carrillo this morning."

"Statement? What statement?"

"She claims you and your wife have been trying to convince her your son's been raised from the dead. That you and Mr. Weisman here are all working together to pawn some kind of phony miracle off on the public." She turned. "Is that true, Mr. Weisman?"

"No. No! It's not a phony—"

"It's all right, Milton," Edwards said. "I'll handle this." To Allison, he said, "Laura Carrillo's a fine teacher, Ms. Hope, but it's obvious she's not well. These things you say she's told you about us are completely ridiculous. Insulting, in fact."

"I see. And she's chosen to say these insulting things about the four of you because of what, exactly, Mr. Edwards? Help me to understand, please."

"I wish I could. But I can't. I barely know the woman."

"And yet she knows your friend Mr. Weisman here."

"Milton *is* a friend. He and my father grew up together in Trenton. We brought him along to an open house at the school last year and Laura met him then. Why she's decided to involve him in this perverse fantasy of hers is beyond me. I'll ask you again: Go away and leave us in peace. Mr. Weisman and I have nothing else to say to you."

Allison didn't budge. "I don't get it. If Ms. Carrillo's story is as devoid of fact as you say it is, why are you all so reluctant to comment on it? What are you people so afraid I'll find out?"

This time, when Edwards reached for her, Allison couldn't evade his grasp. He pulled her from the booth, stood her up so he could bring his face to within an inch of her own. "We aren't afraid of anything. We just don't want to help you destroy a good teacher's career, publishing a piece of 'journalism' full of lies and nonsense."

Allison jerked her arm free, suddenly aware she'd become the house entertainment. Even the cook behind the order window stood stock still, watching her exchange with Edwards. She dug a pair of business cards from her purse. "I'm not looking to destroy anybody's career. I'm just trying to report the truth. If either of you would like to help me do *that*, I'd love to talk to you further."

She offered a card to Weisman, who took it because he clearly didn't know what else to do. The other she held out to Edwards until his refusal to even acknowledge it made the gesture a waste of her time.

Cheeks burning, Allison walked out.

In the parking lot en route to her car, she glanced over at Adrian, sitting behind the open windows of his father's sedan, and for a moment she entertained the idea of approaching him. But she quickly extinguished the thought, figuring she had tried Michael Edwards's patience enough for one day.

* * *

Michael watched Hope go to her car and drive off. As he'd expected, she'd given Adrian a look as she passed, but that was all. Which was good. If she'd taken two steps toward his son, in the state she'd left him in, Michael didn't know how far he would have spun out of control.

Milton Weisman was still sitting there in the booth, clearly afraid to move a muscle. His eyes had tracked Hope's departure, too, but unlike Michael, Weisman didn't seem to have noticed she was gone. His gaze remained fixed on the parking lot.

"Are you all right?" Michael asked.

Weisman's head snapped around. "What?"

"I asked if you're okay. You look pretty shaken up."

"She told me she knew. I thought. . . ."

"It doesn't matter now. Stay here a moment, will you? Please."

The old man nodded and Michael hurried out to the car. His son was engrossed in drawing a picture, making use of the pad of paper and crayons Michael always kept in the Acura to occupy him in a pinch. From all appearances, Adrian was as aware of the scene his father had caused in the restaurant as he would have been had Michael locked him up in the trunk.

Michael slipped behind the wheel but left the door ajar. "How are you doing, A? You okay?"

"Yeah." Adrian nodded without looking up.

"I have to talk to Milton again for just a few more minutes. Do you mind?"

"I don't mind."

"Great. I'll be right back." He waited for the boy to look his way but it wasn't going to happen. Giving up, he kissed his son on the top of the head and caught a good look at the drawing that was monopolizing all his attention. "Who's that?"

"Who's what?"

It was a portrait of a little girl, her brown face bloated and features—eyes, mouth, pigtailed hair—blown all out of proportion, the way details often were in the work of seven-year-old artists.

"The girl you're drawing. Friend of yours?"

Adrian just shrugged and kept sketching away.

Michael wanted to question the boy further, but Milton Weisman was waiting for him. With some hesitation, he climbed out of the car and went back into the restaurant.

* * *

Milton didn't want to wait for Adrian's father to return. He wanted to go home. His mouth felt dry in that old, familiar way and his mind was a cage filled with butterflies and bees. He needed time alone to clear it, to determine if he'd said anything to this woman Allison Hope that would prove to have terrible consequences. He stared at her business card and, before he could find the nerve to place it in his pocket and flee, Michael Edwards returned to take his seat across from him in the booth.

"I need to know what you told that reporter, Mr. Weisman," Edwards said. His voice made the gravity of the matter impossible to miss. "What did she ask you and how did you answer? Try to remember, please."

"I didn't tell her anything." Milton tried to reassemble the conversation in his head. "She knew who we were. She knew our names. She knew where the accident happened, and when. I said. . . ." What he'd said came to Milton then, but he couldn't make himself confess to it.

"What did you say?"

"I said I thought we were the only ones who remembered. You and your wife. The boy's teacher and me."

"You used that word? 'Remembered'?"

Milton nodded. And there it was: his grave error.

Edwards turned his head to one side, likely suppressing an expletive, and Milton rushed to defend himself. "What else was I supposed to think? If she knew all the rest—"

"No, Mr. Weisman. She didn't know anything. She was only repeating what Laura Carrillo told her."

"The teacher?"

"Yes, the teacher. You heard what Hope said. Laura thinks this is all some kind of hoax Diane and I are trying to pull off, and that you're a part of it somehow. It's crazy, but to her, I guess, it makes more sense than the truth. If Adrian weren't my son, I'd probably feel much the same."

Milton knew he was right. Edwards's wife had told Milton at the park that she had warned the teacher to keep quiet, just as she'd warned Milton, but clearly Carrillo hadn't listened.

"So what do we do now?" Milton asked. "Now that this woman *does* know everything, thanks to me—"

"Now we do what we were always going to do: nothing. So you used the word *remembered*. What of it? That doesn't prove a thing. Hope still only has Laura Carrillo's word for what really happened and I think it's a safe bet she doesn't believe her. Even now."

"Yes, but—"

"Listen. None of what Laura told her can be proven. *None of it.* So all Hope's got right now is the story of a teacher who's suffering massive delusions about one of her students, his parents, and you, and as long as this is the last time you or I or Diane speak to her, that's all she's ever going to have. Right?"

He held his hand out for Hope's business card.

Milton thought it over, nodded, and gave Edwards the card.

Adrian's father glanced out the window at his son, still sitting alone in the car.

"I have to go. Are you sure you're all right? Would you like us to drop you somewhere?"

"No. I'm fine."

"If Hope comes back—"

"I won't say a word to her. Not another word." He'd said it so that Edwards would have no doubt.

"Good-bye, then, Mr. Weisman. Milton." Adrian's father held out his hand one more time, smiling with unexpected warmth, and Milton shook it. "This should probably be the last time we see each other. Hope's likely to be watching us all now, and the more she sees us together, the more reason she'll have to believe Laura might not be as crazy as she sounds."

Milton nodded again, though with less conviction this time.

Suddenly, he felt very alone.

TWENTY-FIVE

FLO WASN'T ANSWERING her phone, so Allison went out to UW Bothell to try to catch her in her office. She wasn't going home to wait hours for Flo to show up today. The encounter she'd had with Michael Edwards and Milton Weisman was too important not to share with her partner immediately, Flo's indifference be damned.

Allison's piece was starting to shapeshift in ways she had never expected, and she needed Flo's help putting it in some kind of reasonable order. Everyone she spoke to about Carrillo's classroom meltdown offered one contradiction after another, each more confounding and incredible than the last, and Allison was getting lost in the mix. What she had initially thought was a simple but intriguing saga of a young woman falling victim to the pressures and imperfections of the American educational system had become a mess of a mystery, tinged with elements of religious fanaticism and fraud. Carrillo was deeply disturbed, without a doubt, but the evidence was mounting that not everything she'd told Allison could be written off as paranoia. Michael Edwards and Milton Weisman had proven that much.

Remembered, Weisman had said. *"The only ones who remembered."*

Why had he used that word?

If Weisman wasn't who Carrillo said he was—an accessory to some as-yet motiveless, dead-child scam—who the hell was he? Judging from the way he'd behaved at the restaurant, frightened and disoriented one minute, angry and defensive the next, Allison would have guessed he was a guilt-ridden old man who had in fact lost control of his car and killed a seven-year-old boy last spring. And not somebody merely portraying such a person, either.

As for Edwards, he and his wife were definitely hiding something they didn't want Allison to know about. But what? By Carrillo's account, the answer was the faked death of their son, but that didn't add up for any number of reasons, the most obvious being that no one other than Carrillo—and Weisman?—had any recollection of Adrian Edwards being missing or dead. Even if everyone at Yesler was faking ignorance, paid off by Michael Edwards to do so as Carrillo had theorized, it was impossible to imagine how Edwards hoped to profit from a death he was now adamant had never occurred. Insurance fraud didn't function so ass-backwards.

Flo might not know the answer to these conundrums, or any of the others Allison was struggling to unravel, but she could probably point Allison in the right direction to answer them on her own.

Flo's office was on the second floor of Founders Hall, a postmodern stack of red brick and dark glass nestled deep in the southwestern corner of the campus. Allison was far from a regular visitor, but she'd been there enough times to know how to find the room she was looking for without having to ask for help. On her way from the distant lot where she'd parked, she tried to call her partner one last time, feeling obligated to warn her she was coming, but again, Flo didn't answer. Allison assumed she was with a student, this being within the boundaries of time Flo set aside every Thursday for such meetings.

But Flo wasn't in when Allison reached her office. Allison knocked three times, called out her name, and received nothing but silence. According to the small sign beside her door, Flo was indeed supposed to be there for her students, though only for another ten minutes.

"Damn."

Allison turned away and started back down the hall, barely aware of the handful of students passing her on both sides. She was at the stairs when a peal of laughter stopped her cold. It had come from within an office there at the end of the hall, and though it was a flavor of laughter Allison hadn't heard from her partner in some time, she recognized it as Flo's just the same.

She went to the door. The plaque beside it read PROF. PATRICIA AVERSON. Allison leaned in close, too caught up to give any thought to discretion, and heard two voices, Flo's and a younger female's, both enjoying the punchline of a seemingly risqué joke. Her throat suddenly dry, Allison let the pair exchange another word or two before she put her fist to the door and knocked.

"Yes?"

Allison cracked the door, saw Averson sitting behind a desk, and Flo sitting on the corner of it beside her. Averson—presumably—was a petite brunette, with almond skin and short, wavy hair, who looked to be in her early thirties.

"Ally?" Flo got to her feet, too flustered not to show it.

"I'm sorry. I didn't mean to interrupt. But I heard your voice as I was leaving and. . . ." Allison tried to think of the best way to end the sentence. "And I had something important to talk to you about. Forgive me."

She turned to leave.

"No, no! Patti and I were just trading a little department gossip, that's all. Come on in."

Allison stopped, but could take no more than a half step back into the room.

"Patti, this is my partner, Allison Hope," Flo said.

"Very nice to meet you," Averson said, smiling with teeth far too perfect for Allison's tastes.

"It's a pleasure," Allison said, fooling no one.

"And Ally, this is Patricia Averson. Professor Averson teaches geomicrobiology here at UDub, among other things. She was just telling me about something one of our more misogynistic male colleagues said to her this morning. Unreal."

An awkward silence chose this moment to rear its ugly head, but Flo turned to Averson to make short work of it. "I'll have to get the rest of the story from you later. It sounds like a good one."

"It is," Averson said. To Allison: "Goodbye."

"Bye."

Flo ushered Allison out of the room and down the hall toward her office. "You should have called ahead, Ally. I still have a few minutes to give you if you want them, but if I'd known you were coming—"

"I tried calling first. But you weren't answering your phone. And like I said, this is important." As Flo unlocked her door, Allison tossed a backward glance in the direction of Averson's office, adding, "Though maybe not quite as important as your staying on top of the latest office gossip."

They stepped into Flo's office and she closed the door behind them. "Please. Don't be ridiculous."

"Ridiculous? I don't see anything ridiculous about it."

"You don't see anything, period, because there's nothing for you to see. The woman's a colleague, Ally, that's all. Jesus." Flo threw herself down in the chair behind her desk. "Now, what is it you wanted to talk to me about? Not your wacked-out teacher story again, I hope."

Allison had a difficult choice to make: Act like she didn't know that Flo was trying to divert her attention from Averson, and say what she'd come here to say, or pursue an argument over something that probably—hopefully?—amounted to nothing more than a harmless, if vexing, flirtation. The latter felt more urgent at the moment, but if she missed this chance to find out if Flo could see a pattern in her "wacked-out teacher story" that she could not, Allison might not get another one until late tonight, if not the next day.

Allison chose to leave "Patti" Averson alone for the time being and told Flo about her day.

She started with her interview of Laura Carrillo and ended with the brief meeting she'd had with Michael Edwards and Milton Weisman. To her credit, Flo listened attentively, and even managed to avoid rolling her eyes. But maybe a guilty conscience was behind all her good behavior. Allison couldn't stop herself from suspecting as much.

"Well, you've been right about one thing," Flo said when Allison had finished. "There *is* more going on here than just—how did you put it this morning?—'a teacher going postal in the classroom.'"

"I know, right?"

"It sounds to me like they're all crazy. Carrillo, the boy's father, this old man Weisman. And in all likelihood, the boy's mother, too."

"Yes, babe, but crazy how? Everybody seems to be suffering from their own personal delusion. Carrillo thinks the Edwardses faked a death nobody can remember. Weisman thinks he, the Edwardses, and Carrillo *do* remember it, but that it wasn't a fake death at all. And Michael Edwards. . .I don't know what the hell he thinks, other than that I'm writing a hatchet job solely intended to destroy Carrillo's career."

"Well, aren't you?"

"No! I admit that there's almost nothing I could write at this point that wouldn't be damaging to her, but is that my fault? The story is what it is. I can't change it just to lessen its impact on Laura Carrillo."

"Good for you. That's precisely the right attitude to have."

"So I've got the right attitude. What I need now is the right perspective on this mess. Exactly what am I dealing with here? I think I get that it all starts with Michael and Diane Edwards somehow, but in what way? Carrillo's charge that they faked their son's death just doesn't make sense.

There's no evidence that they ever did such a thing and I can't imagine what their motives would have been if they had. Can you?"

"Well, the most obvious answer would be for the insurance money. But nobody bilks an insurance company out of a life insurance benefit just to declare half a year later that the insured never actually passed away."

"No, they don't."

"And yet, you say both the teacher and the old man appear to have been convinced by the boy's parents that he *was* deceased."

"Correct. But again, why? Why would they want to make two people, and *only* two people, believe that their son was killed in a car accident? And why single Carrillo and Weisman out for such a deception?"

Flo shook her head. "I have no idea. But I will say this. If Carrillo's right about them being born-again, fundamentalist Jesus freaks, any discussion of rational motive would be a waste of breath. People like that don't need a motive to do the things they do."

"People like 'that'?"

"You know what I mean. Believers. Acolytes. Subscribers to the idea that there's something out there bigger than us that hears prayers and answers them, just because it cares to."

"You're talking about people like me, Flo."

"Am I? Maybe. But not really. Because let's be honest, Ally. All you do is say the words. You believe, but you never let your belief get in the way of what you want to do. Correct me if I'm mistaken."

Allison couldn't. And much to her surprise, this shamed her.

"Don't look so disappointed," Flo went on. "Absent your lack of demonstrable faith, you and I could never be together. Peaceably, anyway."

"And if that were to change?"

"That would be very unfortunate for us. It hasn't, has it?"

"No, but. . . ." Allison had no idea how to complete the sentence. "No," she said again, forcefully this time. "Of course not."

"Miracles aren't real, Ally. God isn't real. Whatever's behind this circus you're writing about, it's not a God-given miracle. Trust me on that."

"Why?"

"*Why?*"

The question had surprised Allison herself.

"Yes, why. Why should I trust you on it?" She paused to cushion the blow of what she was about to say, painfully aware of how Flo might react. "I know you feel like an authority on the subject, after everything you went through with your father's passing and all." The accounts all ended the same way, with an angry, disillusioned little girl weeping hysterically in the back seat of a limo as the man she had loved more than all others was being lowered into his grave. "But—"

"But nothing," Flo said, whatever patience she had for this conversation on the wane. "And leave my father out of this."

"I'm sorry, babe. I didn't mean—"

"You have no idea what it was like and, if you're lucky, you never will. Watching someone you love wither away and die like a starved dog."

"You're right. I can only imagine what that must have been like."

Allison's admission seemed to take some of the fire out of Flo's indignation. "I could talk to you about it until the sun comes up, and you'd still never understand. Diagnosed in November, dead in December. Near the end, he was in so much pain, he didn't have the strength to turn his head on his pillow."

Allison started to make another attempt to apologize or commiserate, and decided to remain silent instead.

"And all the while, he prayed," Flo went on. "And I prayed. Everyone around us prayed, the church congregation and my classmates at school, day and night, twenty-four seven. All of us begging for God to show himself, to display his great mercy and power and love for my father. And of course, nothing happened. Nothing."

Her bitterness sounded brand new, as raw as the day it had been born. Flo wasn't above shedding tears—Allison had seen her cry many times, over countless other things—but her father's death was an injury she was all done being humbled by to such an extent.

"Nine years old and I thought my life was over. What a fool I was."

"You weren't a fool."

"I was a *fool!* Believing right up to the very end—to the very *end*, Ally!—that my prayers would make a difference. That this God of Moses my father had taught me to love and trust would do the impossible just because I asked." She laughed at the utter idiocy of the idea.

"You weren't a fool," Allison said again. "You just. . . ." She searched for the words, the thought occurring to her she was as much defending herself as her partner. "You just expected too much."

"Excuse me?"

"What I mean is, you probably thought it was a given. Of course God would save him. Your father was a good man, a man of the cloth, and you were his little girl. You deserved to have your prayers answered."

"You're goddamn right we did."

"But faith isn't a meritocracy, Flo. What we deserve often has nothing to do with what we get."

"Exactly. You're the same hapless victim of circumstance whether you believe or you don't."

"That's not exactly what I said."

"No, but that's what it boils down to. A god who cares for you but only lifts a finger to save you when it suits him? What the fuck is that? Who but a fool would prefer to believe that shit to believing in nothing at all?"

Allison couldn't see her way around denying it: "A fool like me, I guess."

Flo shrugged, as if to say, *Well, there you go.*

Allison fell silent.

"I don't want to talk about 'God' anymore," Flo said. "I have to get back to work."

"Flo. . . ."

"Look, I don't know what else I can tell you that shouldn't already be obvious to you. I think your instincts are right about the boy's parents. Whatever's going on, it almost certainly begins with them. But what exactly *it* is, I haven't the slightest. If I had to guess, I'd say it'll turn out to be exactly what the teacher says it is: some kind of phony miracle designed to draw attention to whatever twisted variety of Christianity they happen to subscribe to. As for the old man. . . ."

"Weisman."

"He might be the target of the whole scam. The elderly are often taken advantage of in all kinds of sick and duplicitous ways, especially if they have money."

"Yes, but—"

"I'm sorry, Ally, but that's really all the time I've got for this. If you absolutely insist, I suppose we can talk about it some more when I get home tonight, but I'd really rather we didn't."

Allison's mind turned once again to Patricia Averson. "And what time do you think you'll be home?"

"I'm not sure. But it'll probably be late. I had to cancel my afternoon class today for technical reasons, so I have to rewrite next week's lesson plan. I'd just as soon do that now as later."

Allison nodded, not able to counter such sound reasoning for being left to an empty bed again. She waited to see if Flo would send her off with a good-bye kiss, but her partner didn't move from her seat. Allison went around Flo's desk to do the honors herself.

"I love you," she said.

Flo smiled. "Me, too."

Saying the right words, but with very little feeling behind them.

TWENTY-SIX

LAURA MADE ONE MISTAKE.

Elliott had come home from work in a conciliatory mood and she was happy to forgive him. She told him her visit with the district psychiatrist had gone well, and she was ready and able to admit now that Adrian Edwards's death and burial were just tricks her mind had been playing on her, false memories produced under work-related stress she'd been in denial about. It sounded too good to be true, or course, and Elliott had to grill her thoroughly before he would believe it, but eventually, his skepticism gave way to relief. Laura had come back to reality.

She was thrilled to see her lie go over with such great success, and telling it had been easy enough, now that Allison Hope knew the truth. It was no longer left to Laura alone to speak it, to convince people Michael and Diane Edwards, and not she, were the ones who needed to be psychologically evaluated. Hope was her ally now, a professional bird dog who would ask all the questions Laura wanted asked until she discovered what the hell was going on.

Laura would be content to play the fool in the interim. While Hope did the dirty work of refuting all the evidence that Laura was delusional, Laura would pretend she had been precisely that, but was no longer. Elliott would stop worrying and believe in her again. The school district, reassured by her revitalized hold on reality and willingness to continue seeing Noreen Ives, would authorize her return to the classroom. All would be as it had been, with the exception of Laura's growing impatience for Hope to serve her purpose and make sense of the nightmare Laura had been made to live for the last three days.

It was a good plan, and it was working. As she had demonstrated in Ives's office, Laura was actress enough to convincingly fake contrition.

The quiet dinner with Elliott was the return to normalcy Laura had been hoping for.

And then Elliott found Hope's business card on Laura's bedside table.

"What's this?"

The question took her off guard. She had intended to put the card in her purse, or in a drawer Elliott rarely opened, but she'd forgotten to do either.

"What?"

"This card. From Allison Hope. She's a writer, it says."

Laura's alacrity at lying on her feet had abandoned her. She couldn't think of a thing to say.

"Who is Allison Hope, Laura?"

"Nobody. She's just—"

"Not the reporter Howard warned you about? The one who's doing a story on what happened to you at school?"

Elliott waited, and it was obvious he was prepared to go on waiting for as long as it took Laura to find her tongue.

"Yes. She was here. But I didn't tell her anything, Elliott, I swear."

"And yet you kept her card. Why?"

Laura didn't know what to tell him.

"You took her card because you talked to her. You weren't able to stop yourself."

"No!"

"What did you tell her, Laura? I want the truth."

And something about his tone, about the self-righteous inflection with which he had infused the words, turned Laura one hundred and eighty degrees.

"The truth is all I have been telling you. But you refuse to believe it."

"And Hope?"

"She does believe me. Or at least she's willing to give me the benefit of the doubt. Which is all I've ever wanted from you."

Elliott shook his head. "You're out of your mind. You told her that insane story about Adrian Edwards and this car accident that never happened? Is that what you did?"

"Yes."

"Knowing what it would mean to your career? For what, Laura? What good did you think it was going to do you to expose yourself like that?"

"It's not me she's going to expose. It's them. They're the ones who've been lying all along, not me."

"Even if that were true, how the hell is Hope supposed to prove it? How could *anyone* prove it? There's no evidence to support your story! Nobody else remembers the boy dying because he never did. There was no accident in the park, there was no funeral, and there was no conspiracy to make people believe otherwise. It's all in your fucking head! When are you going to understand that?"

This was a different Elliott than she had seen of late. For the last three days, they had been arguing constantly, Laura on the offensive, her fiancé on his heels, trying to defend himself. But now Elliott was the aggressor, his patience with Laura having finally worn thin enough to break.

"I can't understand something that isn't true," Laura said. "I wish I could, but I can't. Adrian's parents led us all to believe he was killed in a car accident eight months ago. They held a funeral for him and we all went. You, me, and a half dozen people I work with at school."

"Laura—"

"I remember the flower arrangements at the gravesite. I remember you wore that awful brown tie of yours with your blue suit, and the argument we had over it before we left home. I remember that it began to rain near the end of the service, and I turned an ankle, slipping on the pavement getting into the car. These aren't things I imagine happened, Elliott. I *remember* them. Just as clearly as you remember what you did at work today."

"That's not possible."

"Possible or not, it's what's real. And nobody's going to convince me that it isn't. Not you, not Howard Alberts, not anyone."

"And Dr. Ives? If you're so goddamned convinced this ridiculous 'truth' of yours is what's 'real,' why didn't you share it with her today instead of Hope?"

"Because I want my job back and she wouldn't have believed me if I'd been honest with her any more than you do."

"So you chose to confide in a reporter instead?"

"That's right! Who else was I going to confide in?" Laura knew the line she was about to cross, but she was beyond caring now. "I need answers, Elliott. I need someone to help me find out why this is happening to me and what it all means. And it's for damn sure I can't count on *you* to help me anymore, isn't it?"

Elliott couldn't hide his hurt. "She's going to destroy you," he said.

"Maybe. I don't know. But before she can destroy me, she has to prove me wrong. And I don't think that's going to happen."

Elliott stared at her, his anger finally spent. "I love you, Laura. I swear I do. But if you're determined to do this, to throw your whole life away, you and me included, just to keep from admitting you're sick and need help...." He shook his head again. "Then I don't want to be around to watch. I can't. I'm sorry."

He was out of the room and gone before she could utter a word to stop him.

The thought that he might never come back struck her almost immediately. She was torn between rejoicing and falling apart. Elliott was everything to her, and yet, over the last three days, he'd been almost nothing at all, just one more voice in the crowd declaring her a madwoman. She knew the hurt of his leaving would come, that she could hold the pain off for only so long, but right now she was glad to be rid of him.

Like all the others, he was wrong about her and, with or without the help of Allison Hope, Laura would find a way to prove it.

* * *

Something was different about their father, and Milton's daughters weren't sure that it was more for the better than the worse.

All his terrifying talk about killing a little boy with his car in March was done. He hadn't said a word about it since Lisa had brought him dinner three hours ago. This was the change in him she and Janet had been praying for, and Lisa was happy to let sleeping dogs lie. But not Janet. Janet had to know why their father had stopped talking about the accident. Within minutes of joining them for dinner, Janet poked and prodded him on the subject, never satisfied with hearing an answer only once. Lisa could have strangled her.

Throughout all Janet's harassment, Milton told her what he'd told Lisa that morning, that the whole thing had just been a big mistake. He'd overreacted to a nightmare he'd had two nights earlier that had confused him with its utter realism.

"Did you call that woman?" Janet asked. "The boy's mother?"

"Yes. I already told you I did."

"And what did she say to you?"

"Nothing. She didn't say anything to me."

"Daddy, please tell us the truth. What did the woman say to you when you spoke to her?"

"She didn't say anything! She told me Adrian—" Milton stopped, started over again. "She said the boy is okay, that I had to be mistaken about the accident. And I was. I was just mistaken. Talking to her helped me see that."

Milton refused to discuss the matter further.

He sat down in front of his television and lapsed into silence, acting like Janet and Lisa had gone and left him in peace. They watched him from the kitchen and debated what to do. Janet was sure their father's denial of the accident was a lie, a smokescreen he was only putting up to satisfy a need, and Lisa was inclined to agree. But what need? Certainly it had nothing to do with any sensitivity to what his children might think of him. As recently as that morning, he hadn't appeared to give a damn how insane Janet and Lisa thought he was. He'd seemed prepared to take to the grave his false memory of killing a stranger's child, regardless of the consequences.

What had happened to him since—what had this woman Diane Edwards said to him—to so dramatically change his mind?

Janet renewed her pestering and drew only more vacuous responses from him. Nothing had happened. He'd been confused and now he wasn't. They could stop worrying and go home.

They never did stop worrying, but they did eventually go home.

* * *

Milton waited for several minutes to pass after Lisa, trailing her sister, closed the door behind her, before he allowed the breath it felt like he'd been holding for three hours to escape from his lungs. He sank into the chair like a stone, lacking the strength to sit up straight for a moment longer.

He didn't know if he could do this. It was too hard, and he was too old. Adrian Edwards's father had been very clear about what he, his wife, and Milton all needed to do—proceed from this day forward as if the accident last March had never occurred—but Milton couldn't see himself perpetuating such a colossal ruse indefinitely. Lies no longer came as easily to him as they once did, and this would be the biggest lie he had ever thought to tell.

And yet he would have to tell it, over and over again. He would have to find a way. Because Adrian Edwards was alive again. Milton had seen the boy and held his hand and felt the new life in him, and as much as it terrified him to do so, Milton could make peace with only one explanation for such a phenomenon: it was God's work. Inexplicable and without any discernible point, other than to erase the enduring pain of three people.

Ever since leaving the restaurant that afternoon, Milton had done little but weigh the relative merits of alternative theories, specifically that of Adrian's teacher, Laura Carrillo, who apparently believed the accident and Adrian's death were mere illusions the Edwardses had somehow cast on, and then erased from, the minds of dozens of people. On one level, this was no more ridiculous an idea than the other, and yet, try as he might, Milton could not bring himself to buy into it. It was one thing to grant a god unlimited powers, and another to concede such powers to two mere mortals. Milton didn't know what the events of the last two days were about—he feared he may never know—but he was certain they were part of something much larger, and of greater consequence, than a man-made scam.

So here he was, left with nothing to do but believe in this miracle and accept the responsibility of helping keep it intact. If it were to some-how come undone, as the boy's mother feared it might, he did not want to be the reason. He had to live with the knowledge this incredible thing had happened while pretending to be ignorant of it. Play the senile old man who had let a bad dream shake his hold on reality, and bear all the humiliation that would earn him, resisting the lure of alcohol throughout. For one night, at least, he had managed to meet these demands.

Tomorrow, he would try to do so again.

* * *

Allison put off going home for as long as she could. In recent weeks, the house had increasingly become a place her instincts urged her to avoid. There was a funereal quality to it now that had never been there before, a chill that filled every room and permeated every corner. Day or night, lights on or off—even when Flo was there, she wasn't—and the house that had once felt so warm to Allison felt cold and empty tonight, like a warehouse stripped bare by thieves.

Much to Allison's surprise, Flo was waiting for her when she walked in, just after nine p.m. The late night at the office had apparently been put off, and Flo was sitting in the living room reading a book, or rather, sitting there with the prop of an open book in her lap, an actor setting the stage for the scene to come. Allison didn't need to enter the kitchen to know that no dinner awaited her. It was clear from the look on Flo's face that such amenities were not on the evening's agenda.

Before a word could be spoken, Allison knew everything Flo was about to say. She told herself, *Breathe. Just breathe.*

"Hi."

Flo closed the book, remained in the chair. "Hi."

"I was right. You *are* sleeping with her."

Allison could see the pretty little brunette perched there behind her desk, peering up at Flo as she laughed her sexy, deep-throated laugh. Professor Patricia Averson.

Flo shook her head. "No. I'm not." She took a deep breath, held it, then let it out. "But I want to. And it's probably just a matter of time before I do."

"Baby—"

"It's no good, Ally. I'm sorry. I can't go on like this anymore. I'm not happy and you aren't, either, and neither of us has been for a very long time."

I'm not in love with you. That would come next. It was the only thing left for Flo to say. On one hand, Allison needed to hear her say it, to make Flo utter the words just to watch her squirm. But that would be the end, a line that could not be erased once it was drawn, and even now, with their breakup a foregone conclusion, Allison wasn't ready. *No, please, no.*

"I'm not in love with you anymore," Flo said. "I've tried and I've tried, and I'm just not."

Flo never cried, but she was crying now, quietly and soberly, like everything else she did. No wasted effort.

Allison went to the couch and sat down while she still had the strength to move.

Flo forged ahead, emboldened to speak the truth now that the spell of denial had been broken. "It's not all your fault. Some of this falls on me. Maybe I expect too much. Maybe I'll look back some day and hate myself for doing this. But I don't think so. I think we're just two different people who went in two different directions, and you aren't what I need anymore."

"Because I'm not the success you are," Allison said. Her own tears were coming, oh, yes, but not until she had said her piece. She had that much pride left, at least.

"No. I mean. . . ." Flo shook her head. "I don't know."

"You think I'm a loser."

"No. I think you've tried, Ally. I think you've tried as hard as you know how. You just haven't found a way to make it work." Flo paused. "You aren't a loser, but you aren't a winner, either."

"And you need to be with someone who is."

Flo's nod carried all the weight of a wrecking ball.

They fell silent together, Flo with nothing else to say, Allison too numb to speak. She was dizzy from the pain, yet perversely euphoric. All her dread, her agonizing wait for the worst, was over. The worst was finally here.

Preparing for this day, she had built a case for herself many times. She was a good person with a big heart, solidly attractive. She was smart and eager to learn, and nobody could make Flo laugh with greater ease. Allison was loyal to a fault and open to compromise, and she'd cut her left hand off at the wrist before she'd cheat on a partner. She had given Flo everything she had.

It was a compelling argument, but she knew it couldn't counter the one Flo had used against her: Allison was a failure. Flo had a career; Allison had a dream. One was hard currency, the stuff home loans and six-figure retirement accounts were made of. The other was play money, a gambler's IOU. Flo had held that IOU for the last five years, her love for Allison strong enough to compensate for its ever-diminishing value, and now she was done pretending to believe it would ever pay off.

Flo was worth fighting for, she always had been, but much to Allison's amazement, she realized there was no more fight left in her. One could hold the inevitable back for only so long.

"All right," she said.

"I do care for you. You know that. I just—"

"It's okay. I understand. But if you don't mind, I'm not up to hearing any more about it right now." Allison pulled herself to her feet. "I'm going to go pack a bag, find someplace to be alone for a while."

"Ally—"

Allison headed off to the bedroom, determined not to let Flo see her crash and burn.

TWENTY-SEVEN

SLEEPLESS NIGHTS WERE nothing new to Michael.

For months after Adrian's death, he had endured a countless number of such nights. Eyes closed or open, it made no difference. The thought of his dead son would give him no rest.

Eventually, however, time and a fistful of sedatives would grant him some relief. A few minutes of sleep became an hour, one hour became a smattering of several. It was restless sleep, a roiling sea of dreams and memories both true and false, but it was sleep. These days, he spent only the outer fringes of every evening thinking about Adrian and the accident that had taken his life. There were still occasions when he would wake before dawn and pursue sleep again with only middling results, but these were few and far between.

Tonight was a sleepless night unlike any other.

The grief that usually drove his insomnia had been replaced by fear. Instead of his past, it was his future that held him awake now, flopping in bed alongside his wife and son like a fish on a trawler floor. Diane seemed not to notice, spooning Adrian with her back turned to Michael, the two of them the very picture of blissful slumber. But Michael was not fooled. Despite all appearances, he could not imagine Diane's sleep was any less tortured than his own.

They had talked past midnight, going over the day's events in the breathless tones of two people in the path of some onrushing doom. Things were spinning out of their control. The secret of Adrian's resurrection was now in the possession of three other people, and none could be counted on to remain silent about it. Laura Carrillo had made it clear she would do the exact opposite. Her fiancé, drawn by obligation alone to take her side, was as likely to speak openly of Adrian's return as she, and Milton Weisman—poor, old, confused Milton Weisman—was a wild card: well-intentioned and sympathetic to their cause, but only halfway convinced they weren't all insane. There was no predicting what Milton would do, or whom he might invite, inadvertently or otherwise, into the circle of those aware of God's recent handiwork.

That this handiwork was intended to be known only by the four people presently cognizant of it was becoming increasingly apparent. Others could join their ranks over time, but Michael had the sense no one would. God would have given sight to the entire world had He wanted His miracle widely known from the outset, and the more people were aware of it, the greater was the risk that word of it would spread. And then what?

Questions and accusations. Adoration and ridicule. Demands for answers no one had; not Michael, not Diane, and most certainly, not Adrian himself. Was God expecting the three of them, along with Carrillo and Weisman, to make believers out of millions all by themselves?

Michael didn't think so, and neither did Diane. Their hearts and silent prayer, offered together and alone, told them God had other plans for them. They were not being called to speak the truth but to hold it close. Defend it as long and hard as they could, and encourage Laura Carrillo and Milton Weisman to do the same. God's endgame, and His reasons for choosing the four of them to help Him achieve it, would be revealed in time. They just had to be patient, and ready to do God's bidding when their moment came. Because failure was not an option. Diane knew it, and now Michael did, too.

It was this last thought that ultimately drove him from his wife's bed, the alarm clock on her nightstand making a crimson note of the time: 2:47 a.m. He stood and watched them for a moment, the wife and son he'd thought only days ago were lost to him forever, then slipped quietly out of the room.

He went to the kitchen and made some coffee, sat at the breakfast table giving no thought to drinking the cup he'd poured for himself.

A silent sentinel on watch for something outside his powers to stop.

* * *

Diane opened her eyes.

She lay in the dark, curled into a crescent, her arms wrapped around her son. Or. . . .

She felt around, fingers encountering thin air. She was holding on to nothing. Adrian wasn't there. She started to scream—

—and woke up.

Adrian stirred in her arms but held fast to sleep. She drew him closer, put her face to the back of his head, and breathed him in. Without turning, she could sense Michael was gone. She didn't know where, but she thought she knew why. He was afraid. *She* was afraid. Fear was a dangerous affront to the power that had brought Adrian back, but it could no longer be held at arm's length. Now that her son was here in her arms, his death unraveled by the mercy of God like a spool of black thread, the thought of losing him again was more terrifying than anything Diane could imagine, worse even than the horror she had felt that morning at Lakeridge Park, racing to the spot where Milton Weisman's car had deposited the crumpled remains of her only child.

She had known doubt before. Two, three months ago, when all her praying had garnered her only silence, she would fill entire days with the business of despising herself and the faith to which she was so stubbornly, stupidly clinging. She had come close to giving up many times, to leaving Adrian in his grave and welcoming her descent into her own, but thankfully she could never finish the job. So she lived with fear as it came and went, too weak not to feel it yet too strong to let it win out.

She would have to be that strong now. This new, darker form of terror could take her but it would not hold her. Maybe she and Michael had little say in what was to come, maybe their time with Adrian was already being measured in days and not years, but whatever happened from this point forward, it would not be Diane's punishment for having lost faith. Her belief that all things were possible in God had once been strictly out of habit, guided only by instinct and desperation. But not now. Now she had a solid rock upon which to pin her faith, more evidence that God was real and merciful than any skeptic could ever ask for, and as long as she had that evidence, as long as she could touch it, and feel it, and clutch it to her breast, she had no reason, no *right*, to be afraid.

And yet she was.

She hugged Adrian tighter and hung on for dear life.

FRIDAY

TWENTY-EIGHT

IT WAS TIME TO TALK to Adrian.

The thought had occurred to Laura before. Who else could be counted on more to tell her the truth, however little of it he knew? But the opportunity to speak to him away from his parents had yet to present itself, and it had taken her this long to reach the point where envisioning herself and the boy alone in a room did not completely unnerve her. She no longer believed him to be a ghost, but neither was she convinced he was human.

Because her memories of the last eight months refused to fade, despite all her efforts to dismiss them, and they simply did not, *would* not jibe with the idea that Adrian's death had been a mere hoax. Mere mortals couldn't make one woman remember eight months that never happened, while making dozens of others forget them. Something larger than two scam artists faking the death of a child was going on here, and act of God or no, Adrian was unlikely to be the same seven-year-old boy Laura had known and deeply loved.

This was why the thought of talking to him now, as she sat at her kitchen table nursing a cup of tea in the predawn hours, frightened her so. She didn't know what he might tell her, or how much worse it would be to hear it. But Laura had no choice. They had all forced her into this corner—Howard Alberts, Noreen Ives, even Elliott—and the only hope she had of fighting her way out of it was the truth. She had risked everything taking the reporter into her confidence, and lost Elliott in the bargain. He was convinced Hope was only out for herself, in Laura's corner not for the facts but for the salacious, and if he was right, it was up to Laura, and Laura alone, to save herself.

If she could remember the old man's name, the one who'd killed Adrian in the park, she might be able to track him down and force him to talk to her. Tell her everything he knew about what was happening and why. But all she had for him still was a last name—*Weinman*—and she wasn't even sure about that. She'd tried looking him up online to no avail; adding to her growing frustration and confusion, she'd been unable to find a single word on the internet relating to Adrian's death or its aftermath. Yet another impossibility she was being asked to accept without complaint.

Laura was tired of it.

She was being used, set up to play some kind of godless patsy in whatever twisted game Michael and Diane Edwards were trying to run, and she didn't like it. Laura Carrillo was nobody's patsy. Not even God's. She had tried reasoning with Elliott and everyone else and gotten nowhere. She wasn't going to plead for their faith and understanding anymore.

It was time to talk to Adrian.

* * *

"I don't want him to go."

"He has to go."

"No. He doesn't," Diane said.

But she knew Michael was right. Keeping Adrian home from school today would be only the beginning, a concession to fear that would likely be repeated again and again. Her son hadn't been returned to her to be hidden underwing. He had come back to reoccupy the life he'd once known. Diane had the sense he was somehow at risk, that if she let him an inch too far off his leash he would evaporate like smoke, but Michael pointed out that both he and Diane were probably going to feel that way about their son for the rest of their lives. If they never learned to deal with the worry better than this, they'd go mad.

Still, it was hard to let Adrian go.

"He's going to be okay," Michael said as they kissed good-bye at the door. Adrian was already in the car, lunchbox in his lap.

Diane nodded and smiled, resigned to the inevitable.

She watched her husband get in the car, waved at their son as the Acura retreated from the driveway and vanished down the street.

Last night, Michael had seemed as frightened as she was. Morning, however, had brought him to a different place. If he wasn't exactly invigorated, he certainly appeared less inclined to expect the worst.

Diane wondered where such renewed confidence had come from.

* * *

Michael had decided the reporter was the key. Allison Hope.

Adrian's teacher would do what she was going to do; he and Diane were powerless to stop her. But that was all right because no one considered her a credible witness, and at the rate she was going—showing up at people's doors unannounced with her boyfriend in tow, ranting and raving—no one ever would.

And Milton Weisman—Michael had concluded the man could probably be trusted. They'd had only the few minutes in the burger restaurant to talk, but that had been enough. Weisman's heart hadn't been that hard to read. Michael had seen the look on the old man's face when Adrian shook his hand; Weisman had been filled with relief. This was a second chance for him, too, and to hold on to it, Weisman would surely heed Michael's warning and keep silent. And what would happen if he failed? What words would he find to tell others about Adrian that would cohere into a comprehensible whole? Even if he could articulate it all, who would hear it and not say it sounded like the first signs of an old man slipping into dementia?

Between the two of them, deliberately or otherwise, Weisman and Carrillo could make a fair amount of trouble for Michael and Diane. They might turn unwanted attention toward Adrian and force them to answer questions they didn't want to be asked. Carrillo, in particular, could hound and pester, maybe even stalk. But beyond possibly making life difficult for Michael's family for a while, she and Weisman had no potential to do them any long-term harm.

The writer, on the other hand, was not so easily dismissed.

Hope seemed harmless enough, but by virtue of her profession alone, she was dangerous. Once upon a time, a story from a freelancer went only as far as the reach of a local newspaper or the monthly circulation of a magazine. Now, however, online articles and blog posts traveled the world in seconds, regardless of their merit, and all it took for an item to become an international phenomenon was the interest of a single reader with the right social networking connections. Playing dumb for a small audience of skeptics and believers, coming at them only a few at a time, seemed to Michael a manageable task, but a rush of such people coming at he and Diane in waves?

They would have no chance.

So it was Hope's silence that mattered most. If she could be persuaded to kill the story she was writing about Laura Carrillo, the feeling Michael and Diane had that the return of their son was unraveling might remain only that: a feeling. Michael had no doubt that appealing to the reporter's conscience would hardly do the trick. Journalists with ambition didn't sit on a story simply to spare people its consequences.

To win Hope's silence, Michael would have to buy it.

He had just over sixty thousand dollars in his IRA account. It was nobody's idea of a fortune, but neither was it a pittance. Hope would at least have to think about taking it. He hadn't told Diane what he was going to do, because he was sure he could never go through with it with both his doubts and hers weighing on his mind.

He dropped Adrian off at school, drawing out the ritual of saying good-bye longer than necessary, then pulled into the lot of a nearby grocery store to use his cell. He'd kept the business card Hope had given to Weisman at the restaurant the night before. His intention had been to toss it the minute he took it from the old man's hands, but somehow he'd never made the effort.

The phone rang in his ear three times before Hope picked up.

* * *

"Hello?"

Her voice had cracked and she didn't care. Allison just wanted it to be Flo. The number wasn't Flo's but Allison didn't give a damn.

Please, God, let it be Flo.

"Ms. Hope?"

Allison didn't recognize the voice. It was familiar, but at the end of the longest night in her life, she was in no condition to hear, see, or think straight, and she had little desire to try. It didn't matter who the man was, in any case. He wasn't Flo.

She hung up.

Allison flung herself back onto the motel room bed and closed her eyes, cell phone still in hand. An empty wine bottle lay pinned under her left thigh, green glass cool to the skin, and another bottle on its way to empty sat atop the cheap bedside table next to her head. To her amazement, she hadn't once tried to call her partner—she was far from ready to stop calling Flo her "partner"—since leaving Flo's home almost ten hours ago, preferring the agony of waiting for Flo to take the initiative over the humiliation of the reverse. But Allison's pride was no more intact. Flo's silence had proven to be as degrading as any simpering plea Allison could have made over the phone, or on bended knee at Flo's feet.

Just as she began to cry again, her cell phone rang once more.

Allison remained still and let it ring, refusing to succumb to the temptation of answering the call and having her heart broken anew. The caller wasn't going to be Flo this time, either.

But the possibility suddenly occurred to Allison that he might somehow be a conduit to Flo—a go-between she trusted to say things to Allison she wasn't yet ready to say herself—and that made him someone Allison could ill afford to ignore.

She sat back up, wiped her eyes dry, and answered the call.

"Yes?"

"Ms. Hope? I'm trying to reach Allison Hope."

"This is Allison Hope. Who is this?"

"It's Michael Edwards. I need to talk to you right away. In person."

Michael Edwards. Allison couldn't believe her luck. Twelve hours ago, she would have given anything to receive this man's call. Now, she couldn't imagine what good it could do her to talk to him.

"I'm sorry, Mr. Edwards, but I don't think—"

"It'll only take a minute and I'll make it worth your while. That, I promise you. Just name a time and a place."

Allison didn't answer, her head pounding, her mind racing.

"Please," Edwards said.

And that one word tipped the scales. *Please*. Even in her pathetic state, Allison's professional inquisitiveness kicked in. Edwards really did *need* to talk to her.

"All right. One hour. Give me a few minutes to think of a place and I'll call you back."

* * *

"Hey, Milton. It's Al. I was just calling—"

"To check up on me. Yes, I know."

Milton's son-in-law took a moment to go on, no doubt weighing the merits of denying the obvious. "So, how are you feeling this morning?"

"I feel fine. I'm okay. I keep telling your wife that, but she doesn't want to believe me."

"Well, you know, you had us a little worried there for a while. Some of the things you were saying. . . ."

"Sounded crazy, I know. I know, already! But I told Janet and Lisa, and now I'm telling you: I had a bad dream. I got confused and thought it was real. Haven't you ever had a dream you thought was real?"

"Well, yes, I suppose—"

"Of course you have. It happens to everybody. It doesn't mean a man's crazy. It doesn't mean he's getting senile or has gone back to drinking again. It just means he got confused. I got confused for a while and now I'm not. What more do I have to say to get that through to you people?"

"I'm sorry, Milton. None of us means to be disrespectful. But we all love you and care about you and want to make sure you're all right."

"Well, I *am* all right." Milton sensed his temper rising, realized he was sending all the wrong messages. And neither Alan nor his daughters were guilty of anything except worrying about Milton too much.

"I appreciate your concern. Sure I do. And I know what I must have sounded like, talking about car accidents that never happened and dead children who aren't dead. If I were in your shoes, I would have thought I was drunk or crazy, too. Who wouldn't? But I'm okay now, I promise you. It was all just a mistake, a big mistake. You have to help me make Janet believe that, Alan. Please. If all of you don't stop smothering me like this, I *will* start drinking again, I swear it."

Reacting to either the sincerity or the sheer desperation in Milton's voice, Alan said, "Okay, Milton. I hear you. I'll talk to Janet tonight and convince her to lay off. Or at least I'll try. You know how stubborn she can be."

"Yes. I do."

"As for Lisa, I'm afraid you're on your own there. One Weisman daughter is about all any one man can handle."

He laughed, and Milton forced himself to do likewise, taking care to offer his son-in-law all the proper responses to avoid any further suspicion.

"You'll call us if you need us, right? For any reason, day or night."

"I will. Thanks for calling, Al."

Alan had more to say but Milton hung up on him before he could say it.

This was obviously how it was going to be for a while. Life under Alan and Janet's microscope, and Lisa's as well, until Milton could convince them all he was fine. They would watch him and test him, waiting for another word about Adrian Edwards to slip from his lips, something to give them cause to question his sanity all over again. But they would be wasting their time.

Only yesterday, Milton might have been prone to mistake. But not today. Not ever again, God willing. Last night he had slept like a rock, something he hadn't done in months, and he woke this morning with a new resolve. Whatever or whoever was behind the change his life had undertaken, Milton wasn't going to see it undone without a fight. He was happy for the boy and his parents, of course, but he had his own interests to protect as well. He wasn't a child killer anymore. That yoke of shame had been lifted from his shoulders and being free of it felt like being reborn.

Yesterday, he was afraid *of* himself, *for* himself. He was certain he would not be able to go on living a lie of omission for the rest of his days, as he had promised Michael Edwards he would. But today he knew he could, and would, keep that promise.

For Adrian Edwards *and* the new Milton Weisman.

TWENTY-NINE

LAURA COULDN'T THINK of a way to get close to Adrian that had any hope of success until she remembered Giselle Ott had yard duty Friday mornings.

Giselle was one of two kindergarten teachers at Yesler, a gentle soul and veteran of the profession, at thirty-eight, whom Laura considered a good friend. This despite the fact the older woman was an overly-affable Pollyanna. With dark brown hair that had never known a curl and a body that shared the silhouette of an unmade bed, Giselle was as unexceptional as a plastic spoon. She had always been drawn to Laura, however, and her joy in being an educator had similarly drawn Laura to her, so the two women shared a bond that made far more sense in practice than it did on paper.

Campus security was one of Yesler's greatest weaknesses, and this would mark the first time Laura had reason to be cheered by the fact. While the administration office was positioned off the front parking lot to stand as the school's first wall of defense against intrusion, its only window was the small, narrow panel of glass in the entry door. Edie Brown, the office clerk, did the best she could to keep an eye out for people slipping past, and woe be to those she caught trying, but she couldn't be both an office clerk and a security guard, eight hours a day. Trespassers were bound to get by her every now and then, and they did so with more regularity than Laura had ever been comfortable with.

Today, Laura planned to be one of those trespassers.

She dared not remain on campus long. Every minute would be a flirtation with disaster. Howard Alberts patrolled the grounds at whim and could be counted on to order her off the premises on sight. And if Alberts didn't spot her himself, Laura was confident that any teacher other than Giselle who did would feel duty-bound to make the principal aware of her presence. To reduce her risk of exposure, Laura would have to time her visit to Yesler precisely—right before morning recess—and stay no more than a few minutes.

Ten minutes would be just enough.

* * *

It was Allison's idea to meet at Lakeridge Park. She couldn't imagine where the inspiration had come from. Flo was crowding out every conscious thought in her head, and a merciless hangover was doing the rest to render Allison incoherent. But in the midst of rejecting the first two places Michael Edwards suggested—a coffee shop in Kubota Gardens and the Westfield Southcenter mall—she had blurted out the name of the site where Edwards's son had allegedly died last March.

"No," Edwards had said initially. The thought of it clearly unnerved him.

Allison hung firm, however, realizing that Edwards's reaction had to mean something. People always found it more difficult to lie where and when they were most uncomfortable, and if Lakeridge Park made Edwards ill at ease, that was where she wanted to talk to him.

A few minutes shy of nine a.m., she paused at the park entrance to locate the playground area on a map before proceeding to it. She was the first to arrive. Michael Edwards didn't join her until she'd found a seat on a bench atop a grassy knoll overlooking the multicolored, tubular play structure, which at this hour lay challenge to only a handful of children. Allison watched Edwards park and approach on foot, and wondered if she looked as horrid as she felt. She was sick to her stomach and on the constant edge of tears, and Edwards would have to be a blind man not to see the pain she was in.

He climbed the small hill and sat down beside her. "Sorry I'm late."

"No worries." She waited for him to say something. "So?"

Edwards's eyes drifted down to the playground for a second, then came back to Allison. "I want you to kill your story, Ms. Hope."

"I'm sorry?"

"I'm willing to pay you. Sixty thousand dollars. All you have to do is forget about Laura Carrillo and leave her and all the rest of us alone."

Allison was taken aback. She had thought this might be Edwards's purpose in calling this meeting, but this wasn't the tack she'd expected him to take.

"I don't understand."

"I'm offering you sixty thousand dollars to do nothing. Easy money. And, if you'll forgive me for saying so"—he gave her a lingering look—"I have a feeling you could use it."

"Is that right?"

"Forgive me if that was unkind."

"You're goddamned right it was unkind." He had come here to bribe her. Not to reason or plead with her, but to bribe her. Throw her a few dollars and make her disappear, because he thought she'd take them. That's how pathetic a creature she was in his eyes.

"I'm sorry," Edwards said again, taking pains to express his sincerity. "I don't know you. This isn't personal. But you have to believe me when I tell you, nothing good will come from this story you're writing if you go through with it. Nothing."

"Well, I don't know, Mr. Edwards. If the truth comes out of it, that'll be good enough for me."

"And you think the truth is what, exactly? Please tell me, I'd love to know."

If he had given her a day to think about it, Allison might still not have had an answer. But she had to say something. "I can tell you what it isn't. It's not whatever lie you and your wife have managed to feed poor Milton Weisman. Your little boy did not die in a car accident last spring and then rise from the dead three days ago. Of that much, I'm fairly certain."

"And Laura Carrillo? What about her? Have my wife and I fed her a lie, too?"

This time, having no ready answer struck Allison mute. Her head throbbed and her stomach was starting to churn again.

"Face it," Edwards said before she could find her voice. "Anything you try to write right now would serve no purpose other than to make a public spectacle of a good, young teacher. And all you'd get out of it is a byline and a reputation for shoddy reporting."

"You have no idea what I'd get out of it. And that's not the question begging to be asked here anyway. That question is, what are *you* looking to get out of my going away?"

"Me?"

"Come on, Mr. Edwards. Whatever's going on here, you and your wife are behind it. You proved that much just by calling me here today."

And that quickly, their roles had been reversed. Allison was the one pressing, Edwards the one pulling back.

"I'm not taking your money," she said. "Even though you're right—I *could* use it. So if that's all you've got to offer me. . . ."

* * *

"Wait," Michael said.

Hope had stood up and started off toward the parking lot.

This wasn't the fragile woman he had thought he'd be dealing with. Hope certainly looked the part—her hair was a mess and her eyes were trimmed in red, and if she hadn't slept in the clothes she was wearing, she must have pulled them from a pile of unwashed laundry—but that was where her resemblance to the hack Michael had taken her for came to an end. This woman had backbone, and if she didn't also possess principles, she had the next best thing: too much self-respect to be bought without a fight.

Hope stopped and turned around but kept her distance.

"What do you want?" Michael asked.

"What do *I* want?"

"To let this go. To walk away forever and never look back. Before—" Michael pulled up short.

"Before what?" She came back to retake her seat beside him. "What will happen if I don't walk away?"

"I've already told you. Laura Carrillo—"

"No. This isn't about Laura Carrillo. You didn't come out here to bribe me with sixty thousand dollars just to save Laura Carrillo. And you sure as hell didn't do it to save *me*. This is about you. You and your wife and your son. Adrian."

Her use of his son's name threw Michael further off balance. He wanted to leave Adrian out of this. Adrian was the very thing he was here to protect. But if he had a choice in the matter, a way to leave the park with Hope's silence assured that wouldn't cost him something far more precious than money, it evaded him.

"What do you believe in, Ms. Hope?"

"Excuse me?"

"I need to know what you believe in. If I tell you what you want to know, if I tell you what's real, you're either going to consider the possibility or reject it outright, and I'd just as soon not waste my time if it's going to be the latter."

Hope shook her head. "I don't—"

"Do you believe in God? Do you believe in miracles? Do you believe in things you can neither see nor touch, things science can neither prove nor disprove? How about prayer? Do you believe in the power of prayer?"

Hope grinned nervously. "Wait a minute...."

"I don't have a minute. I need your answer now. What do you believe in?"

He was trying to tell her in no uncertain terms: This conversation was over if she didn't tell him what he wanted to know.

"I believe that something created all this, yes," Hope said. "God, Allah, the Great Spirit—call it what you like. And that, for the most part, assuming it's a conscious being at all, it's benevolent." She shook her head. "But beyond that, I'm just not sure. To be honest with you, I don't spend a lot of time thinking about it."

"Until you need something."

This gave Hope pause. "Yes."

She was telling him exactly what he had expected to hear, but he still had his doubts about her. Her milquetoast excuse for faith would only make what he was about to do that much more terrifying. Before he could lose what little courage he had left, he said, "Where is your phone?"

"My phone? It's in the car. Why—" She answered her own question. "Oh. This conversation isn't being recorded, if that's what you're worried about."

Michael had to trust she wasn't lying. It was either that, or pat her down. He set himself, said, "It's all true. What Laura says happened here. Every word of it."

Hope let out a little chuckle. "Say again?"

"You heard me. Adrian died here last March. The accelerator stuck on Mr. Weisman's car down there in the parking lot and he lost control, drove straight into the slide while Adrian was climbing the ladder."

The same stupid smile remained on Hope's face. She shook her head. "No...."

"Come. I'll show you." Michael stood up, past any point of turning back. The lady had asked for the truth, and now she was going to hear it, in as much agonizing detail as he could stomach to relate.

Hope got to her feet and Michael led her down to the play structure, where only a single child now cavorted. It was a girl no more than four, kicking around in the sand as her mother sat cross-legged nearby, watching her with amusement. Michael pointed. "The car came across the grass this way. Hit the slide broadside and kept on going, dragging my son underneath the wheels until it slammed into that tree there and stopped."

He was fighting with all he had to remain composed, but the memory of that day was not easily ignored and his vision began to blur. "It was all over by the time I arrived, of course, but I only had to hear Diane describe it once to have it feel like something I had witnessed myself."

He paused to see if Hope had any questions, but she only stared back at him, no doubt unsure of what to make of what he was telling her. He forged ahead, turning to point at a spot in the parking lot. "Diane was sitting in the back of a patrol car there when I got here. She was in shock. White as a sheet and cold to the touch, even though they'd given her a blanket to wrap herself in. I had to get the details of the accident from the cop assigned to watch her. Adrian was already loaded into the ambulance, a sheet thrown over his face, just like in the movies. I didn't want to see him, but I had to. I had to see for myself that it was really my son."

He gave in and let the tears come, unable to do anything else. Hope still didn't speak.

"A pair of plainclothes detectives were interviewing Mr. Weisman, who was sitting on that bench there." He pointed again. "On the drive over, I had this picture in my mind of a drunken, shriveled up old fool, someone I could hate instantly without half trying. But he was nothing like that. He was just a frightened, pathetic old man. They wouldn't let me near him, for obvious reasons, but they needn't have worried. After viewing Adrian's body, I didn't have the strength to make a fist with one hand, let alone throw a punch at somebody."

A small smile crossed his face. He walked over to a familiar spot on the grass and Hope followed. "They tore the whole play structure down rather than replace the slide. Parents wouldn't let their kids on it anymore." He turned and gestured. "They put up a new one there, where those trees are now." He looked down at his feet. "And right here, they laid a plaque down in Adrian's memory. They had a ceremony and everything, with dignitaries from the city and news crews from all over, but I didn't come. Diane did, but I refused. There wasn't any point in my coming."

And that was as far as Michael could go. He was spent. If Hope wasn't ready to believe him by now, she could go fuck herself.

* * *

Edwards fell silent, his exhaustion evident, and held Allison's gaze with his own. Waiting for her reaction to determine what he would do next.

Allison sensed the weight of something much larger than the moment pressing down on her. She didn't know how it had happened, but suddenly she wasn't on the periphery of this maddening drama anymore. She was at the center of it, the player with the power to grind it all to a halt or keep it spinning, perhaps in perpetuity. Edwards didn't say as much, but he didn't have to. It was all right there in his eyes.

"I don't know what you expect me to say," she said.

"I expect you to say what you believe."

"I already did that."

"And that's still your answer?"

No. It wasn't. What Allison believed now was something far more absurd than what she had claimed to believe before. She believed *him*. Michael Edwards's words hadn't been that far removed from those of Laura Carrillo yesterday; in fact, they had aligned with the teacher's account with uncanny precision. But whereas Carrillo's telling of the tale had merely moved Allison to wonder, Edwards's had left her with no more doubt. There was a difference between reality and a reality perceived, and Allison had always been able to recognize it. What she had just heard from Edwards was the truth. A truth that coincided with no provable law of the universe, but the truth, nonetheless, and her inability to refute that fact scared the living shit out of her.

"It's not possible," she said.

"Four days ago, I would have said the same thing. I thought Diane was crazy. On her knees every night, week in and week out, praying for something that could never happen." He paused. "But it did happen."

"How? Why? *Why* would such a thing happen?"

"You know my answer to the how. But the why? I don't think we'll ever know. And you know what? I'm fine with that."

"Bullshit! There has to be a reason. Why would God do something as bizarre as all this without a fucking reason?"

She had forgotten where she was, in the middle of a playground with a small child and her mother within earshot, so infuriating did she find the man's unshakable calm.

Chastened by the looks her outburst had earned her, she lowered her voice. "You know how many children die in the world every day? You know how many mothers have spent years on their knees, begging for their return? What makes your son and your wife any different from those people? Why would God or whoever pick them out from all the millions of others he could have chosen to bestow this miracle upon?"

"I don't know."

"That's not an answer, Mr. Edwards."

"Yes, it is. I don't know. That's my answer."

"Bullshit."

"Fine," he said. "It's bullshit. So write that. If that's what you believe, write it."

He walked away.

She ran after him, right hand extended to grab his arm, but he turned on her before she could. "I've got nothing else to offer you, Ms. Hope. I've tried all the magic I know to make you understand. Nothing I've told you is a lie, or a trick, or a game, or—to use your word for it—bullshit. It's just the simple truth. If it's not simple enough for you, that's your problem, not mine."

"Please! Think about what you're asking me to do. What you're asking me to believe."

She was suddenly desperate to keep him from leaving, overcome by the vague notion that, if he made it to his car and drove away, he'd be taking something of far greater consequence with him than an interview for a story she wasn't even sure anymore she could write.

Edwards must've seen the fear in her eyes. For a moment, she thought he was going to laugh, amused to have regained the upper hand. But he softened, instead.

"Maybe you need to talk to Diane," he said.

THIRTY

GISELLE OTT HADN'T SEEN Laura coming until Laura was practically standing beside her. She was startled at first, then pleasantly surprised, because Laura hadn't answered any of her phone calls since the breakdown and it was a relief to see she was fine and back at Yesler, where Giselle believed Laura belonged.

Giselle thought it was odd that no one had mentioned Laura's return before now. It seemed like something Howard Alberts would have wanted everyone to know. But Giselle's love for the younger teacher overruled her need to ask questions, and before any could take root, she had Laura in a big bear hug.

Friday morning recess had just started and, as was usually the case, Giselle was the sole sentry manning this quadrant of the yard. The children under Giselle's charge spotted Laura immediately, particularly those from Laura's class, and before Giselle could say more than three words to her, they greeted her with disparate levels of enthusiasm. A few approached her without hesitation, some eagerly, but the rest held back, likely recalling the terrified, hysterical woman she'd allegedly been the last time they'd seen her.

To Giselle's mild surprise, Adrian was not among this latter group. The boy should have had more reason than most to avoid Laura, but there was nothing like fear in his demeanor. With time to think about it, Giselle might have stepped in to keep the two apart, but she just stood by and watched them, trusting Laura more than she probably should have.

Even when Laura leaned forward to whisper in Adrian's ear and the boy nodded in return, each smiling at the other like a more wonderful secret had never been shared by two people, Giselle saw no need to intervene. Laura Carrillo was a friend, a lovely young woman and a wonderful teacher, and Giselle remained unconvinced that she was someone to be wary of. She hadn't heard Laura's side of all the crazy stories their coworkers were spreading about her, and until she did, Giselle was going to show Laura all the benefit of doubt.

It would be forty-seven minutes before she saw the gravity of her mistake. By then, Laura would be gone and the campus of Henry Yesler Elementary School would be in the throes of its second emergency in a week, this one far more terrifying than the first.

* * *

"I won't talk to her," Diane said.

"You have to talk to her. We have no choice now."

"We do have a choice. *I* have a choice. And I'm not going to talk to her, Michael. I won't."

Diane still couldn't believe what her husband had done. When she'd heard his car pull up out front a few moments ago, less than three hours after he'd left for work, she'd known instantly something was wrong, that all the reservations she'd had about sending Adrian to school today should have been heeded. But she could have never guessed what was coming. Not only had Michael talked to Allison Hope behind her back, telling her everything they had hoped the reporter would never come to learn on her own, he had brought her here to Diane, expecting her to treat Hope similarly.

"We can't let her write her story, Diane. There's no way to know how far it'll spread if she does."

They were in the bedroom, where Diane had insisted they confer in private as soon as Michael had brought Hope into their home. The writer was out in the living room, assuming she was still where they'd left her, waiting for Diane to decide her fate.

"But you've already told her the truth and she doesn't believe you. Why should I tell her anything more if she's not going to believe it anyway?"

"Because I'm not the one who brought Adrian back. You are. If she hears the truth from you, she'll believe it. I'm sure of it."

But he wasn't sure. He couldn't be. There was no way either of them could predict what Hope would do, once she'd heard Diane's side of things, so Michael was only guessing. That, and asking Diane to trust him.

In the eight years they had been together, with only one very obvious exception, Michael had proven himself deserving of all Diane's trust, and more.

"All right," she said.

She led the way back to the living room. Hope rose from the couch, a convict watching the parole board file into the hearing room. Taking her first real look, Diane was struck by the writer's resemblance to a drunk: mismanaged hair, red-rimmed eyes, unkempt clothing. What Michael had seen in this woman to make him think they'd be better off with her as an ally than an enemy, Diane could not yet fathom.

She stopped well out of Hope's reach and said, "Before I tell you anything, I need to ask you one question."

The reporter looked at Michael—*What is this?*—but of course Michael didn't know what Diane was thinking any more than Hope did.

"All right."

Diane paused, wanting to leave no room for doubt that Hope's answer would decide whether Diane remained in the room or walked right back out.

"What's the greatest pain you've ever known?" she asked.

* * *

Allison almost laughed. *That's an easy one*, she thought.

Death came readily to mind. Her mother's in 1990, when Allison was only sixteen; her brother Jack's five years ago; and her father's only a year later. They had all hit her hard, in different ways and varying degrees. But death was an inevitability one learned to accept; the sense of loss was its only lasting mark. Heartbreak, on the other hand, inflicted pain in multiple dimensions. In the twelve hours since Flo had told her they were done, Allison had passed through a head-spinning tumult of emotion: anger and guilt, shame and self-loathing. And fear. Fear as cold and black as the farthest corners of night. And all of it, every moment, had hurt like nothing Allison had ever known.

"I've never lost a child, if that's what you're asking," she said, avoiding the question posed.

"But you've suffered the death of a loved one. Someone you cared for very much."

"Yes." Allison swallowed hard, getting angry now. "Of course."

"Do you remember what it felt like?"

"I really don't see what this has to do with anything."

Diane Edwards waited for her to try again.

"Yes." Allison had cried for weeks after her mother, only thirty-six years old, suffered a stroke and fell into a coma from which she would never emerge. Allison couldn't keep an ounce of food down, and her eyes, swollen and bloodshot, had felt like stones in their sockets.

"Good. It's good that you remember. Because that was nothing compared to what losing Adrian felt like to me," Diane Edwards said.

"I'm sure you're right."

"Humor me all you want. But I'm telling you—you have no idea what real pain is. I saw that car run my little boy over and drag him through the grass. I saw the blood and the bones poking out of his skin, his left arm nearly torn from his body."

"Diane—" Michael Edwards said. Allison saw that he'd turned pale.

His wife paid him no heed. "I held him in my arms until the paramedics pried me away. I chose the suit he wore and the casket he was buried in. Four hours after his funeral, I was still calling his name at the gravesite. Do you know why I'm telling you this?"

"No."

"Because you need to know how much pain I was in to understand how I could do it. Get down on my knees for eight months, every day and every night without fail, and pray to God for a miracle. For my baby to be brought back to me. If I can't make you see how much it hurt, how painful it was just to breathe while he was gone, I'll never be able to convince you that I never lost faith, that I never gave up believing because I couldn't. I couldn't let him go. It was either get down on my knees and pray or kill myself and risk never seeing him again, on earth or in heaven."

She studied Allison's face, as if reading it for clues as to whether or not there'd be any point in continuing. Allison had to imagine that what she saw was a woman on the brink of screaming: confused and tired, tied up in knots with her own pain, and a growing fear that soon, nothing in the world was ever going to look the same again.

"Now it's your turn," Diane Edwards said.

Allison started. "Pardon?"

"My husband's told you the truth and you don't believe him. So he's brought you here to me. Ask me a question. Any question. Whatever you need to hear in order to drop this story of yours and leave us alone, I'll tell you." She sat down on the couch, waited for Allison to take a seat on the other end and her husband to lower himself into the chair facing them.

"And after that, if you still don't believe us, you can just go straight to hell."

* * *

Michael had heard it all before, of course, but there was something different in Diane's telling this time that made the wounds feel as fresh as on the day they were inflicted. He never said a word or moved. He sat there and let the two women talk, Diane making good on her promise to answer any question Hope cared to offer.

His wife described their once tragic past in details so fine and clear, they brought hot tears to his eyes. He saw Hope make the turn. The tone of her questions changed and the space between them lengthened. She didn't take a single note. Michael had brought her here in the belief she was halfway convinced of the truth, that all she needed was a little push from Diane to surrender her last vestiges of doubt. And now he knew he'd been right. Whatever reasons she may have had to enter their home fifty minutes ago, Hope was no longer listening to Diane's story for the purpose of writing about it. She was listening to it because she needed to hear it, whether or not anyone else in the world ever did after this day.

That Hope was struggling with more than a crisis of faith was clear. She'd seemed shaken and fragile, preoccupied by an unnamed suffering, from the moment he'd first met her at the park. Michael could have ventured a dozen guesses as to why—drugs, money, love, all the usual suspects—but he had little reason to speculate. Whatever was behind Hope's state of emotional disarray, in the scheme of God's great design, maybe it was the reason she was here, poised not to reject the truth but to fully accept it.

A cell phone rang, snapping Michael from the trance his wife's voice had lulled him into. Another phone had rung twice only moments ago, in a different room of the house where it had been easy to ignore, but this phone was Michael's own, chiming at his waist. The two women watched him fumble it out of its holster, hit the button to silence it. . .

. . .and freeze.

* * *

"What is it?" Diane asked. The way Michael was staring at his phone had turned her blood ice cold.

He shook her off and took the call in the kitchen, not wanting to be overheard, but it was a wasted effort. The scarcity of his words and the panic in them told Diane all she needed to know.

She ran to his side and asked him again: "What is it?"

Hope trailed Diane into the room.

"They can't find Adrian at school," Michael said.

THIRTY-ONE

"WHERE ARE WE GOING?" Adrian asked.

They'd been riding in the car for several minutes, yet the question had not come up until now.

"Just someplace quiet where we can talk. Is that okay?"

Laura watched Adrian nod from the passenger seat beside her, as cool and unruffled as ever. He suspected nothing. A whisper in his ear back at Yesler was all it had taken to get him alone—

I need to talk to you, Adrian. When you go back to class, ask to go to the bathroom and I'll meet you outside.

—and from there, it had been a simple matter of whisking him out to her car and driving away. Adrian trusted her and was not afraid.

But Laura *was* afraid. The magnitude of what she was doing was not lost on her. She knew the words people would use to describe it: kidnapping, child abduction. Crimes that normal people did not commit. But the time for second thoughts had long passed. She and the boy were here, and there was nothing for her to do but finish what she'd started. She had to draw from him whatever details he might know about the great lie his parents were telling at her expense. She was not so far gone as to consider hurting him to extract the truth, but neither could she predict how she would react if, after all she had risked to arrange this meeting, he claimed to know nothing at all.

So yes, she was afraid.

"What are we going to talk about?" Adrian asked.

Laura turned to him and smiled. "Resurrection. Do you know what a resurrection is, Adrian?"

He seemed to give the question some thought before reaching a conclusion. "No."

If she had believed him, Laura would have driven him right back to Yesler. But she didn't. Not yet.

That she was operating on borrowed time was a given. By now, Adrian's absence would have been noticed, and if the school hadn't already connected his disappearance to her visit, it soon would.

An idea came to her, and she acted upon it before she could question its merit.

"How about some ice cream?" she asked.

* * *

It hadn't taken Howard Alberts long to imagine where Adrian Edwards might have gone. Alberts had thought of Laura Carrillo the instant he heard the boy was missing, just short of an hour after morning recess. But the principal kept his suspicions to himself, not wanting to alarm the staff, until poor Giselle Ott, reduced by guilt and embarrassment to a sobbing mess, reported her brief encounter with Laura out in the yard. Once that cat was out of the bag, Alberts was not alone in his belief that Laura had stolen onto school grounds and snatched away the child who had sent her screaming into a corner three days earlier.

It had taken several calls to reach the boy's parents, and have his father confirm what Alberts feared he would, that neither Michael Edwards nor his wife had any knowledge of Adrian's whereabouts. Both Edwardses were on their way to the school now, in a race with the police to see who would arrive first. Laura was ignoring every phone message left for her, and for the second time in one week, Yesler Elementary was on lockdown.

The only reason Alberts didn't call this the worst day of his life was that he didn't know what horrors tomorrow might bring.

* * *

In the backseat of Michael Edwards's car as they drove to Yesler, with Edwards weaving through traffic like a stuntman on a cocaine high, Allison kept thinking, *This isn't happening. None of this can really be happening.*

But it was happening, whatever *it* was, and she was right in the middle of it. Not as the objective observer she had planned to be, but as an invested participant, too enmeshed in a trap set by her own curiosity to walk away. Adrian's parents had tried to leave her behind, but Allison had jumped in their car and refused to get out, such was her need now to follow this drama to the very end.

Her certainty of anything at this point was negligible, if not nonexistent. The one thing she knew—without question—was that none of the usual explanations for people who claimed to have been touched by God could be applied to Michael and Diane Edwards. Their telling of their son's resurrection had been unique to each, yet uniform in general substance. They weren't lying or delusional. There'd been no contradictions, no hesitations before replies. Their every statement was limned with detail, the small, elementary trappings of experience that only memory found worthy of note.

Laura Carrillo had opened the door yesterday, Michael Edwards had drawn Allison through it this morning, and Diane Edwards had slammed it closed behind Allison shortly thereafter, sealing the deal.

She believed them all. She believed Adrian Edwards had been resurrected from the dead.

Everything she had thought about Carrillo she was now thinking about herself. She was deranged. It was either that or she had become privy to a seismic shift in the universe that made all the rules of the old obsolete. Even if she left God and the notion of miracles out of the equation, what was left meant, at the very least, that death didn't have to be death at all, and time could be turned back for some while left untouched for others, and that these things could happen for no other reason than one person needing it to be so.

Would any of it be easier to accept as the work of an all-loving God, rather than the arbitrary turn of a world gone mad? If Allison was honest about it, her answer would be yes. She had been clinging to her own paltry excuse for faith in the hope this very day would come, that she would be given proof the supreme being she addressed all her prayers to was more than just a myth.

And yet, there was a frightening downside to accepting not only God's existence, but His willingness to intervene in people's lives. What happened when the prayers He answered were never yours? How could you go on believing in a god of unlimited power who reserved his miracles for others? Allison had an immediate need for a miracle of her own—she was certain nothing short of that would bring Flo back to her—and asking for it in vain, knowing what God had done for Diane and Michael

Edwards, would put an end to her faith for good. Could she go on living without that faith and Flo, too?

Allison didn't think so.

Less than twenty-four hours earlier, she had been a freelance journalist with but a single preoccupation: writing a story. A story with more potential to salvage her career—and more importantly, her relationship to the only woman she had ever loved—than any she had been fortunate enough to stumble upon. There was nothing she wouldn't give now to get back to that place.

But it was gone.

So, sitting in the back of Michael Edwards's car as it careened toward Yesler Elementary, Allison teetered from this side to the other of a grave dilemma: Go all in and accept she was here by the will of God, or follow Laura Carrillo's lead and reject the idea with everything she had.

There was a pad of paper on the seat beside her, open to a crude, crayon drawing of a little girl. She picked it up and tears filled her eyes in an instant, because the little girl was black and reminded Allison of Flo. Flo, who didn't love her anymore. Flo, upon whom Allison had bet everything, and without whom she was soon to lose everything.

Flo.

Were she here now she would laugh, finding Allison's indecisiveness too ridiculous for words. For Flo, the choice between belief in a miracle and acceptance of her own insanity would have been an obvious one, and Allison's inability to see it that way now would astonish her.

Allison gently tore the portrait from the pad and slipped it into her purse, her hosts in the car's front seat oblivious. It was an odd act of petty theft, but she wanted some connection to Adrian she could claim for her own and this might be all she would ever get.

She realized such sentimentality was something else with which Flo would find fault, and for a moment, the thought stung. But then Allison decided she didn't care. She wasn't Flo and she never would be. What she chose to believe from this point forward wasn't going to be defined by anyone else's approval. This call would be Allison's to make, right or wrong, and she would live or die by it.

She'd been living in Flo's shadow too long. It was time to come back into the light.

* * *

In the beginning, they talked about nothing important.

Knock-knock jokes and cartoons on television, food that was too gross to eat and second-grade girls who screamed at the slightest provocation. What made a substitute teacher great and what made one unbearable. The twin mysteries of multiplication and ice cream-induced brain freeze.

Sharing a corner booth at a Baskin-Robbins in Bellevue, she making slow work of a vanilla cone while he sculpted shapes into two scoops of chocolate in a cup, Laura and Adrian fell into the easy small talk they had exchanged every day at Yesler before his "death." When she had thought he was a specter or, worse, an impostor, the thought of being close to him filled her with revulsion, but once she decided this was really Adrian—seeing him in the schoolyard yesterday had left no doubt—her old feelings for him gradually came to the fore. He was the jewel of her class, bright and decent, and no child had ever made her feel more alive as a teacher. So she had brought him here planning to bribe him with ice cream and jump right in, pepper him with questions she needed answers to, only to end up chatting and giggling with him instead.

And the clock was ticking. She knew that. She had kidnapped a child and it was just a matter of time before this opportunity to question him came to a sudden end. If she wasted it, she might never learn how, and for what reasons, the darkest days of her life had come to pass.

"Adrian," she said, "I need to ask you some questions. Some important questions."

The boy set his spoon down in his cup and faced her. "Okay."

"Can you be honest with me? Even if it's hard, can I count on you to tell me the truth?"

"Yes."

"Good. Do you know why I was so afraid to see you at school Tuesday? Do you know why I acted the way I did?"

"No." He shook his head to emphasize the point.

"It's because they told me you were dead. I thought you were dead, Adrian."

"Dead?" He smiled at the absurdity of the thought.

"Yes. Your parents told everyone you'd been killed. In a car accident in March. Did you know that?"

"My Mom and Dad said I was dead?"

"Yes."

He frowned, confused now.

"Well, they did. And I'd like to know why. Why would they tell a lie like that, Adrian?"

He shook his head. "They didn't."

She knew *lie* had been an unwise choice of words, one certain to put the boy on the defensive, but she couldn't resist. It *had* been a lie, a despicable one, and Adrian needed to understand that. "Yes, they did. They told everyone you were dead and kept you out of school for almost a year. That's why I was afraid of you. I thought you were dead."

"But I wasn't."

Laura's breath caught in her throat. The truth, at last. "No, you weren't. So where were you? Where have you been since March?"

"I was at school. I always go to school, except when I'm sick."

Goddamnit! "Is that what they told you? That you were sick?"

"Who?"

"Your parents, Adrian. Your mother and father. Did they tell you you were sick, that that was why you couldn't go to school?"

"When?"

He was either completely lost or faking it better than anyone his age had a right to.

Laura took a step back, seeing she was getting nowhere. "All right. Let's talk about something else."

"Okay." He took up his spoon and resumed work on his ice cream.

"Let's talk about God," Laura said.

* * *

His cell phone showed three voicemail messages when Milton came home from his daily lunch-hour walk. He always left his phone behind when he walked, contemptuous of people who couldn't demonstrate a similar degree of self-control, but now he feared he'd made a mistake by not taking the phone with him today. Two of the messages were from Janet and one was from Lisa, and listening to them, it was hard for Milton to say which of his daughters sounded more frantic. Both demanded a call back and neither gave a reason for wanting one, but it was obvious something had set them off worrying about him all over again.

He was debating which daughter to call first, or whether he was up to calling either one for a while, when the phone rang in his hand to make the decision for him. *Four* calls in forty minutes. Now he was afraid for himself.

It was Lisa.

"Oh, thank God you're home. Where have you been?"

"I was walking. I walk every day at eleven o'clock. Why are you acting like you don't know that?"

"That's all? You've just been out walking?"

"Yes. What—"

"Alone?"

"Of course alone. Your sister's been calling me, too. What's going on?"

Lisa fell silent. Janet never hesitated before blurting out the truth, but Lisa was more discreet.

"Are you watching television?" she asked.

"The television? No. I've been out walking, I just came in. I told you." It had been a difficult walk, his mind on everything and anything but the fine weather. He'd gotten out of bed this morning feeling much the same as he had when he lay down the night before, like the world was made of crystal he was destined to shatter.

"That little boy you said you killed. He's missing."

Milton put his free hand out to brace himself against the wall, his legs threatening to buckle. "What?"

"Adrian Edwards. Isn't that his name? He disappeared from school this morning. They're looking for him everywhere. Janet thought. . . ."

She didn't have to tell him what her sister thought.

"Daddy, are you still there?"

"I'm here."

"Are you okay? I can come stay with you for a while, if you want."

"No. I'm fine. I'm fine." He had to get to the television.

"Daddy, can't you please tell us what's going on? What's *really* going on?"

"Nothing's going on. I have to go."

"No, wait! The police—"

—might come looking for him. That thought had already occurred to Milton. If the boy had been taken from school by someone, who more than Milton would his parents suspect?

He hung up the phone in the face of Lisa's blathering and turned the television on. The first station he came to was broadcasting the news he was looking for.

It was a live remote from Adrian's school. Henry Yesler Elementary looked like the site of a bomb threat. Parking lot overrun with police vehicles, bystanders swarming along the perimeter, uniformed officers manning the entrance. A female reporter stood before the camera, describing the situation, her grave expression in stark contrast to her Hollywood starlet appearance. Adrian Edwards, seven years old, had vanished from the Yesler campus sometime after 10:30 that morning, and police were looking for his teacher, Laura Carrillo, in connection with his disappearance.

There was no mention of Milton.

The boy's teacher. Of course. She was the other one who knew what had happened, the atheist Michael Edwards had said was convinced Adrian's return was just a hoax. Could she have abducted the child?

Milton could not imagine a more terrifying scenario. He feared for the boy's safety, first and foremost. From everything Michael Edwards had told him about Carrillo, and everything the reporter on television was saying about her now, the teacher seemed to be a very disturbed young woman. Perhaps even a dangerous one. But whether or not she ever came to harm Adrian, the damage she'd already done was irreparable. There'd be nothing Milton or the boy's parents could do now to keep what had happened last Monday out of the public eye. Questions would be asked of all of them, by reporters like Allison Hope, the police, believers and nonbelievers, and simply repeating that Laura Carrillo was a madwoman wouldn't make them stop.

It could begin at any moment. The next knock on Milton's door could be the police, checking to see if he had taken Adrian instead. In their desperation to find their son, the Edwardses might have implicated Milton. And why not? He was old and confused and had professed to be no less skeptical of God's existence than the teacher. Why shouldn't they wonder if he was capable of kidnapping their son out of sheer bewilderment alone?

The absence of any phone messages from either the police or one of Adrian's parents meant nothing. He had never given Michael or Diane Edwards his number and it was supposed to be the kind that was blocked, so it wouldn't have shown up on her phone when he'd called Diane Wednesday night. In all likelihood, the Edwardses had been awaiting *his* call for hours.

With hands that wouldn't stop shaking, Milton picked up his phone once more and redialed Diane Edwards's number. Hoping she'd answer right away so that he wouldn't have to make this call more than once.

THIRTY-TWO

BY THE TIME DIANE and Michael arrived at Yesler, with Allison Hope in tow, a consensus had been reached that Laura Carrillo was likely involved in their son's disappearance. She had been there earlier that morning, a subdued Howard Alberts said, and had spoken to Adrian shortly before he vanished. Since then, attempts to reach Carrillo had been futile. She wasn't at her apartment in West Seattle and wasn't answering her phone. The police were being careful not to state outright that Adrian had been kidnapped and Carrillo was their prime suspect, but they seemed to be operating as if no other possibility was viable.

This was in part because Diane had yet to mention Milton Weisman, and neither had Michael. If Carrillo was the most obvious suspect in Adrian's abduction, Weisman had to be a close second. But they had no immediate way to reach him. The one time he had called Diane's phone, he had done so from a blocked number, as had his son-in-law prior to that.

In the car on the way to Yesler, Diane and Michael had hotly contested the pros and cons of putting the authorities onto Weisman, only to decide against it. He was old and unsteady, to be sure, and no one had been shaken worse by the events of the last three days than he, but Milton Weisman had promised he would keep his distance from them all forever, and neither Diane nor Michael could see where he had any reason to renege, much less steal their son away from school.

"You're crazy," Hope had said from the backseat, having remained a silent observer until then. "You have to tell the police about Weisman. For all you know—"

"We don't have to do anything," Michael said. "And I'd advise you to stay out of this."

"Michael—" Diane said, her confidence wavering.

"No. She's got no say. She's only here because I didn't have time to throw her out of the car when she invited herself in." Michael used the rearview mirror to stare the writer down. "We're gonna do this my way, lady. Adrian's my son, not yours. The minute I can't trust you to be okay with that, you're going to be gone. You copy that?"

Hope said she did.

And so far, she had done nothing to prove herself a liar. They had been at Yesler for well over an hour now, Diane and Michael being shuffled from one police interview to another—no, they didn't know where their son was; no, they couldn't imagine where Carrillo had gotten the insane idea he had passed away last spring—and as long as she was in their sight, Hope had held true to her word, speaking only when spoken to, watching and listening to everything around her without attempting to intrude.

Not that Howard Alberts gave a damn.

"Who's this?"

The principal had given Hope the side-eye the minute she, Diane, and Michael arrived.

"Allison Hope." The writer gamely stuck her hand out for Howards to shake. They were all huddled outside the bustling administration office, which the police were using as a command center. "I'm—"

"I know who you are." Alberts let her hand hang in the air and turned to Michael. "She's with you?"

"Yes," Michael said.

Alberts looked now at Diane. "I thought we had an understanding."

"We did," Diane said. "But she's not here as a reporter. She's here as a friend."

"A friend?"

"Maybe not a friend. But not an enemy, either," Hope said. "I was there when they got the call to come and I forced them to bring me along. I'm only here to see if I can help somehow."

"You? Help?"

"I interviewed Laura Carrillo yesterday. She might have told me something the police will find useful. Have they found her yet?"

To Michael, Alberts said, "Are you sure about this?"

"Have they found her?" Michael asked.

"No. Not yet. But they will."

After that, making a point of leaving Hope behind, Alberts had brought Diane and Michael into the office to meet the gaggle of police officers and detectives ensconced there, waiting to interrogate them in earnest.

The same questions were asked by different people, whose suspicion was sometimes disguised, sometimes not. Had Carrillo tried to contact either of them? When had they last spoken to her? Did Adrian and the teacher have a falling out recently? What were the reasons for Diane and Michael's marital separation? This last just a poorly veiled admission Diane and Michael were suspects, too.

And all the while, there'd been no news of Adrian.

Eventually, the police let them go, drawn to the inescapable conclusion they were torturing Diane and Michael to no constructive effect. Released on their own recognizance, they fled the office together to find Hope, who stood outside the nearest bungalow, waiting for them. That no one had asked them a single question about Milton Weisman seemed proof enough the writer had made no mention of him in any conversations she herself may have had with the police, as agreed, but Michael needed to be reassured.

"Has anybody talked to you?"

"Of course. An Officer Petrie, I think it was."

"And?"

"If you're asking whether I—"

"Yes. That's the question."

"No. Did you?"

Diane shook her head.

"Jesus! I'm sorry, but I have to ask both of you again: Are you sure you know what you're doing?"

"No," Michael said.

"If you're wrong and Weisman has him—"

"Weisman wasn't here today. Laura Carrillo was. And if we turn the police on to him and he doesn't have Adrian. . ."

"He'll tell them everything," Diane said. "He won't be able to help himself. And that will be the end. After that. . . ."

Hope eyed her expectantly. "What?"

Diane and Michael looked at her as if she were a child they would never be able to talk to on their own level.

"You still don't understand," Michael said.

"Understand what?"

"That it's all happened this way for a reason. Nobody else is supposed to know. If Mr. Weisman talks and essentially corroborates everything Laura's been saying has happened—"

"It won't just be one woman's word against yours anymore. I *do* understand. But what if he *does* have Adrian, or knows something that could help the police find Carrillo before she harms your son, or worse?"

"She won't," Diane said.

"Pardon me?"

"Laura won't hurt Adrian. She cares for him. She loves him."

Diane had always known it, but had given it little thought until Adrian's funeral, when the teacher had practically matched Diane's own show of devastating grief, tear for tear.

"It doesn't matter," Hope said. "In her present state of mind, she can't be trusted to be rational. Every minute you're silent about Weisman is a minute lost in the search for your son."

"We get it," Michael said angrily. "But there's a bigger picture here that you still don't see. You say you understand what's going on here, but you don't understand at all."

"We don't just want Adrian back safe," Diane said. "We want him back for good. He can't tell Laura or anyone else what God has done because he doesn't know himself."

"But Weisman does," Michael said. "And if he starts talking to the police, we won't be able to stop what happens next. We'll all become a carnival sideshow on a global scale, and that's not what God wants. If it were—"

"He would have brought Adrian back and left everything else as it was," Diane said. "He wouldn't have fixed things like this, given sight to only four people in the world with which to see the difference between what was, and what is."

"Five people, including you," Michael said.

"Me?" The thought clearly made Hope uncomfortable. She smiled to make light of it. "You aren't suggesting *I* play some part in this?"

"I'm not suggesting anything. But I'm not ruling anything out, either. And maybe neither should you."

Diane's cell phone rang.

She snatched it from her purse and checked the incoming number: UNKNOWN.

"Hello?"

Milton Weisman identified himself.

A uniformed police officer hovering a short distance away, no doubt assigned to keep a close eye on them, began to close in. Diane waved him off and dropped her voice to a whisper.

"Mr. Weisman, do you have Adrian?"

"No," he said. "I thought his teacher had him. On the news—"

Crestfallen, Diane shook her head to deliver the news to Michael and Hope. "Yes, I know what the news is reporting. But no one's been able to reach Laura yet and she was here at school earlier, so we're all just assuming Adrian is with her."

"Or me. Have you told the police about me?"

"No. And we won't unless we have reason to. Are you sure you don't know where Adrian is?"

"Yes, I swear it. You've got to believe me!"

"I do believe you, Mr. Weisman. But I had to be certain. I'm sorry."

The old man was silent for a moment. "So what do you want me to do? What can I do to help?"

"I don't know." Diane looked to Michael, said, "He wants to know what he can do to help."

Michael reached for the phone. Diane and Hope listened in as he told Weisman to just sit tight and wait. They would let him know the minute there was news of Adrian, good or bad. He asked for the old man's number, repeated it for Diane to record in his own phone, and said good-bye.

But not before Weisman said, "I'll pray for you."

* * *

Much to Laura's chagrin, Adrian knew very little about God.

Few children his age did, but she had thought this child would be an exception. His mother was a religious fanatic of some stripe and his father was likely another, so it stood to reason their son would bear some mark of their perverted faith. But Adrian exhibited no such mark. All he had to offer about God and Jesus Christ, the rationale for prayer and going to church on Sundays, were the same vague generalities any seven-year-old exposed to religious services and a handful of Bible classes might have posited. He couldn't cite Scripture or quote the prophets. Asked to relate his favorite story from the Bible, he just shook his head.

And as for miracles?

"*I* am a miracle," he said.

"You are?" Laura brightened, sensing a breakthrough. "How do you know?"

"Because Mommy calls me that sometimes. 'My little miracle.'"

"Do you know why she calls you that?"

Adrian shrugged. "Because she loves me, I guess?"

"Well, she does love you, of course. But maybe there's another reason. Can you think of any other reason she might have to call you a miracle?"

The boy answered with another shrug.

Laura slapped a palm on the table, creating a thunderclap that silenced the entire shop. Adrian stared at her, shaken. She was out of patience. This had all been a waste of time. She had learned nothing from Adrian of any import, and could feel the dire consequences of her actions closing in on her.

What more could she do to make Adrian tell her what he knew, what he had to know, about the game his parents were playing on her? What other method of persuasion could she use to pierce the armor of his loyalty to them? She could never hurt him; that wasn't a level of debasement to which she could ever descend, but. . . .

She remembered the gun.

The one in the car, in the glove box. The black, horrible little thing Elliott had bought for her and forced her to keep in the Chevy after she was nearly assaulted in a bank parking lot by a pair of thugs late one night last Christmas. The gun had always scared the living hell out of Laura. Surely it would scare Adrian, too.

Just the sight of it might be all the shock he needed to offer up the truth. . . .

"Are you okay, Miss Carrillo?"

She snapped to, the boy's voice calling her off the edge of the black hole she'd been about to plunge into. She'd been that close to threatening a seven-year-old with a loaded gun.

She had to save herself somehow.

Maybe it wasn't too late. She would take him back, and quickly. If they were found together, there would be no mercy; the authorities would charge her with kidnapping and brand her a felon for life. But if she brought Adrian back of her own volition, safe and sound and untouched, they might yet treat her with leniency. She was not a monster and she wasn't crazy, and maybe she could make them all see it by undoing what she had done before the chance was gone.

She glanced around the ice cream shop, certain someone was watching her. There were only three other people in the place: a uniformed girl behind the counter, a boy in the same uniform, sweeping, and an old man in a booth on the other side of the room, talking on his cell phone. Being discreet about it, the way he might were he talking to the police.

It seemed a silly thought until a car pulling into the parking lot drew Laura's eye. . . .

"Do *you* believe in God?" Adrian asked.

Oh, Jesus, Laura thought. The car was a black-and-white sedan, bearing the markings of the Bellevue Police Department, and it was moving toward the far end of the lot where she'd parked her Chevy, beyond her range of view.

She started edging out of the booth to follow the car's progress. Adrian repeated his question. "Miss Carrillo, do *you* believe in God?"

Without thinking and desperate to silence him, she spat out the truth: "No."

She left the booth and inched toward the back of the shop, where she peered out the window to see the patrol car pull into a space right next to her Cruze, the uniformed driver and her male partner exiting with some urgency.

Laura turned to grab Adrian. . .

. . .but he was gone.

The booth was empty and only the remains of Laura's order was visible on the table.

"Where did he go?"

None of the three people now watching her with interest answered. The old man put his cell phone away. The Bellevue police officers entered and went straight to the counter, looking like two more customers in the market for some ice cream and nothing else.

They aren't here looking for me, Laura thought. She had to find Adrian and leave. Fast.

"My little boy. Where did he go?"

The boy in the uniform wielding a broom stopped sweeping the floor. "Little boy?"

"Yes. He was right there just a minute ago." She pointed to the booth. Her heart had begun to race and she could feel nausea rearing its ugly head.

Again, nobody answered her, choosing instead to look at each other as if to say, *What the hell is she talking about?*

And that was when Laura knew, even before the two cops started moving toward her, that her real nightmare was only about to begin.

THIRTY-THREE

"WE WERE JUST TALKING. I swear, that's all we did, was talk. That's the only reason I took him, was to talk to him. I never—"

"About what?" the detective asked. He kept doing that to her, interrupting, and it was trying her patience, which she understood was the whole point.

"You know what about. About his parents. About this sick game they're trying to run on everyone."

"Which game is that?"

"They faked his death. They kept him out of school for nearly a year, and now they want people to believe—"

"That he's come back from the dead."

"Yes!" He'd cut her off yet again, but Laura was too tired to call him on it. They'd been here in this tiny, depressing icebox of a room, talking in circles, for almost two hours now, her refusal of a lawyer having clearly proven nothing to these people about her good intentions, and if they didn't give her a moment to rest soon, she was going to scream until her lungs bled. "Haven't you been listening to me? Haven't you heard a single word I've been saying?"

His name was Neely. With a face nearly square enough to have corners and a toupee that made a poor replacement for a hat, he seemed as prone to showing emotion as a toad. "Let's go back to the ice cream place," he said.

Laura buried her face in her hands.

"You said you and the boy were talking about his parents before he disappeared. Is that right?"

"Yes," Laura said without looking up.

"Is that all you talked about? His parents?"

"No. We talked about a lot of things. We always do. We have a—" She was about to say something she'd once considered only hers to know. "We connect in a way that's unique. Adrian's a special little boy." She raised her head, met Neely's gaze. "I would never do anything to hurt him!"

"So...?"

"We talked about religion, mostly. What they believe in, what he believes in. About God and miracles, or so-called miracles. I was trying to figure out why they...."

A thought snapped into place.

"What?"

Laura didn't answer, staring past Neely's right shoulder into space. She was playing it all back in her mind: *the flash of black and white in the parking lot, the boy posing a question she almost doesn't hear. She turns to see the patrol car, starts to ease out of the booth, Adrian asks his question again, and this time she responds. Angry and distracted, with a brutal honesty she doesn't have time to second guess.*

The cop eyed her, waiting patiently.

"Oh, no," Laura said.

* * *

Michael had seen Diane this despondent only once before, in the first few weeks after Adrian's death. She had been just a wisp of a woman sleeping through the day and night back then, her eyes sunken and dark, her voice never more than a whisper when she found the strength to speak at all. This wasn't as bad, not yet, but it was getting worse as every minute passed without word of their son having been found.

They had already been at the Bellevue police station for well over an hour, having arrived with the detectives who'd been at Yesler working Adrian's disappearance. Laura Carrillo had been arrested at a neighborhood ice cream shop, alone, and this was where she'd been brought in for questioning. Everyone was treating Michael and Diane well enough, but nobody was telling them anything, aside from Laura's initial statement: she'd brought Adrian to the shop to talk to him and he'd disappeared. One minute he was there and the next he was gone, she had no idea where.

Michael's heart had sunk at the news, but for Diane, it was the equivalent of being told their son had died all over again. The lead detective on the case—a veteran named Daniel Neely, with a sour-mash face and demeanor to match—had let slip that nobody at the ice cream shop could recall seeing a child in Laura's company, and from that moment forward, Diane was convinced Adrian hadn't simply gone missing, he'd been taken away. For good this time.

"He wouldn't have just walked off. You know that, Michael," she'd said.

And Michael did know it, but he also knew that to admit as much was to concede the point God had taken a hand in their lives yet again, for reasons known only to Him, and that Michael and Diane were right back where they started: mourning a child they would never see again in this lifetime. It wasn't a thought Michael was ready to accept. Up until last Tuesday, his wife had been the one strong enough to believe Adrian was not lost to them forever, that there was a measure of faith in God's mercy sufficient to earn the gift of the impossible, and now it was Michael's turn to carry that torch. This wasn't over.

His son would be found.

Neely and his partner, a chunky blond woman with bright blue eyes and a voice like a tugboat horn, had left them in the lunchroom to wait. Michael was standing in the hall, trying to give his wife's encroaching terror space to breathe, when the blonde finally came back for them.

"She wants to talk to her fiancé," she said, "and we think we're going to let her."

"Is he here?"

"He arrived about forty minutes ago. He says he hasn't heard from Carrillo since early this morning and didn't know she'd grabbed your son until he heard about it on the radio. Funny thing, though."

"What's that?"

"He backs up a lot of what his girlfriend says about you and your wife. About how you're somehow behind this whole thing."

She watched Michael for a reaction. Michael didn't give her one.

"You and your friend Weinman. The one she says was driving the car."

They'd already asked Michael and Diane about "Weinman," first name unknown, earlier, and been told neither knew anyone by that name. Neely's partner seemed to need more convincing. Michael recalled now her name was Rutherford.

"There was no car. And we still don't know anybody named Weinman."

"That's not what Jeffries says."

"He's her fiancé," Michael said. "She's been telling him the same story she's been telling you and her life is on the line. What would you expect him to say?"

Rutherford shrugged. They went inside to repeat the news to Diane.

"What about Laura? What did she say about Adrian?" she asked.

"Nothing new, I'm afraid. She still insists she doesn't know what happened to him. He was there at the ice cream shop with her and then, all of a sudden, he wasn't." Rutherford raised her shoulders once to convey the height of her skepticism. Diane shook her head with despair.

"You don't believe her," Michael said, addressing the detective.

"Frankly, no, and neither does Danny. If your son had been there, somebody would have seen him, surely. And the cashier receipts prove she only placed an order for one, not two. But. . . ." She waited a moment to go on. "That's not to say we're entirely convinced she's lying."

"Then. . .?"

"She stashed him somewhere. We don't think she hurt him. That's the one thing we can say with an ounce of confidence, maybe Danny more so than me. He's been in the room with her, I've just been observing. But it's for sure Ms. Carrillo knows more than she's told us so far. She has to. And maybe, whatever it is, the fiancé can get it out of her for us."

* * *

Flo called her. It was the last thing Allison was expecting.

She was sitting in the reception area near the front desk of the Bellevue police station, having no right to be here and no intention of being anywhere else. The detectives who had whisked Michael and Diane Edwards away from Yesler had stranded her there and she'd had to do some real scrambling to catch up. A fellow Uber driver had taken her back to the Edwardses' home to retrieve her car and from there, she'd driven herself to the police station. The Uber fee had tapped her out but that couldn't be helped; nothing was going to stop Allison now from finding out how this terrifying night would end for Diane and Michael Edwards.

Not that she was in any position to know what was happening. She was in the same building as the Edwardses and nothing more, killing time in the station house lobby like a dog told to sit and stay. Only the media had a worse view of things than she. They had followed the Edwardses' trail from Yesler and were gathered outside in hordes, and the only reason Allison wasn't among them was the lie she'd told the cop at the front desk: she was related to Adrian's parents. The cop had taken one look at her—an even more disheveled rag doll of misery than she had been at the park that morning—and decided it was easier to believe her than envision her a card-carrying member of the press. So he'd let her stay, to watch the steady trickle of people walking into the station to file complaints, some angry, some miserable, but all of them desperate for help.

It was worse than being in the backseat of Michael Edwards's car. In the car, Edwards and his wife had at least provided a distraction from her thoughts of Flo. Here she had no such diversion, beyond the continuing struggle between the part of her that wanted to believe this was all a dream and the part that was terrified it wasn't. The tug of war was draining her of what little strength Flo's leaving her had not already claimed.

And then her cell phone rang, and it was Flo.

"Hello?"

"Ally, where are you? Those people you've been talking about all week are all over the news. You aren't—"

"Yes, I know. I'm with them now."

It was all Allison could do to raise her voice above a whisper and put a sliver of iron in it. Flo would still know she was dying inside, but hell if Allison wasn't going to pretend otherwise.

"You're with who? Where?"

"I'm with the parents. At the police station in Bellevue." The cop at the desk gave her a look. She left her seat and moved to a corner of the room where she could huddle with the phone in peace.

"What are you doing with them? Do they know you're there?"

The question put Allison on edge. Flo couldn't imagine her being there legitimately, operating as a professional in her field. Surely Allison was only on the scene as a trespasser, soon to be discovered and sent on her way.

"Of course they know. They asked me to come, Flo."

Her partner's silence said she still couldn't fathom it. Finally: "Are you okay?"

"Define 'okay.'"

"You know what I mean. How are you doing? I haven't heard from you all day and I've been worried about you."

"Have you?"

"Yes. What do you think? You think I don't care what happens to you anymore? This is hard for me, too, you know."

"I'm sure it is."

"You think this is funny?"

"No, no. It's not funny at all, actually."

But Allison had to chuckle.

"You're laughing."

"No. I'm really not. I'm just trying to wrap my head around it, is all. How *I'm* supposed to feel sorry for *you*."

Tears filled her eyes without warning and she had to throw a hand over her mouth to hold the rest of her anguish in.

"I can see you're in no condition to talk right now," Flo said. "So I'll call back later."

"No! Wait!"

She thought she was too late, but Flo was still there. Allison had to unburden herself, let out everything she'd been thinking and feeling for the last ten hours for the benefit of someone whose wisdom she trusted, if not their promises, and she didn't know when she might get another chance.

"Something's happening here. Something I don't. . .that I can't explain."

"Something like what?"

Where to begin? With Michael Edwards's tale at the park, or the one his wife had regaled Allison with at their home? What words could she use to convey the power each had held over her, or to confess she believed them both? How could she talk about Milton Weisman without sounding like a fool?

She realized she couldn't. There would be no point. Because Flo would hear only what she *could* hear, the half of Allison's story that could withstand the tests of proof and reason. All else would get chucked to the side as sentimental rubbish, spiritual mumbo-jumbo to which only the weak-minded gave more than a passing thought.

This was the great divide between them, not love. Allison could dream and Flo could not. Flo could only plan and *do*.

"I'm sorry," Allison said, "but I have to go."

And she hung up as if it were true.

THIRTY-FOUR

"I GUESS YOUR WIFE couldn't get off work, huh?"

Milton had answered the doorbell expecting to see Janet, but he found Alan standing there instead. Milton walked back to the couch and the television without even waiting for his son-in-law to enter.

"And Lisa is at school so. . .you know how she is," Alan said.

"Yes. I know."

"And this thing with the Edwards boy has her. . .well, she's a little freaked out." Alan was standing behind Milton now, eyes on the latest television report of Adrian Edwards's kidnapping.

It appeared the boy's teacher, Laura Carrillo, had indeed stolen him away from school that morning, but now she was in police custody and Adrian was still missing. There was no evidence yet to suggest Carrillo had harmed the child, but neither the police nor the press was ruling out the possibility. Unconfirmed sources reported the teacher had suffered a nervous breakdown in Adrian's classroom earlier in the week and had been placed on suspension, pending the results of a psychiatric evaluation. In her present state of mind, the newspeople were saying, what she was capable of doing to Adrian was anybody's guess.

"Milton. Did you hear what I said?"

Alan wasn't one to raise his voice often. Milton turned around to face him. "So she's freaked out. What can I do about it?"

Milton didn't need his daughter's mothering right now, nor his son-in-law's badgering. He didn't know Laura Carrillo but he knew what she was feeling, because he'd felt the same way himself not that long ago. She would be angry and confused, terrified and overcome with doubt, and she would have no one to blame it all on but Michael and Diane Edwards.

Milton feared the worst. What little peace he'd been able to make with God and the jigsaw puzzle the world had become was quickly coming unglued, and it was taking every shred of strength he had to do what Michael Edwards had demanded of him: nothing.

Alan found the remote to the television and turned it off. Milton's jaw dropped.

"Is he here?" Alan demanded.

"Who?"

"The boy. Adrian Edwards. You know who I'm talking about, Milton."

"Is he here? Of course not! Why would he be here?"

"Because I don't think it's just a coincidence that you've been talking about having killed him in a car accident for the last two days and now he's the victim of a kidnapping. There has to be some connection. What is it? Is it the teacher? Do you know her from somewhere or something?"

"You're crazy," Milton said angrily, looking to end this line of questioning before it could begin. He put his hand out for the remote.

"Answer my question. What's your connection to the boy?"

"There isn't one! Why are you talking to me like this? You think I would help someone steal a child?"

"No. No," Alan said, retreating. "But I do think you haven't been honest with us. Something's going on with you and this boy that you haven't told us about. And I need to know what it is, Milton. Right now."

Milton faltered. "I can't."

"What do you mean, you can't?"

"I mean that it wouldn't do any good telling you. It won't change anything."

"Then you *do* know him."

There was no going back now. "Yes. But that's all I can say. I've told you enough already."

"Milton—"

"Do you believe in God, Alan?"

Alan stopped short. "What?"

"Do you believe in God? Yes or no? It's a simple question."

"Yes. Of course I do."

Alan was a good Jew, he went to temple regularly, he kept the mitzvahs. Milton would have been surprised to hear him say anything else.

"No. I don't mean the god of Abraham and Moses. I mean *this* god, the god of the right here and right now, today. Do you believe in that god?"

"I don't understand the question. What has God got to do with what we're talking about?"

"Nothing that you would ever accept as the truth. Which is why I'm not going to bother trying to explain it to you." He put his hand out again. "Now give me my goddamn remote and get away from the television."

Alan returned the remote but remained where he stood. Milton turned the flat screen back on again.

"I think I may have to go to the police, Milton."

"Yes? And tell them what? That your father-in-law had a dream about killing a little boy named Adrian Edwards with his car? You think that's going to help them find him now?"

Alan was silent.

"You want to help the boy? Sit down and be quiet and do what I'm doing."

"And what's that?" Alan took a seat beside him on the couch.

"Calling on the god you say you believe in to bring the child home safe to his family," Milton said.

*　*　*

As Helen Rutherford had suspected, the boyfriend's confab with Laura Carrillo was a bust.

Elliott Jeffries was no dummy. You could take one look at him and see that. He wasn't going to join his lady friend in the interrogation room, knowing Rutherford and her partner were outside hanging on to their every recorded word, and draw her into saying something incriminating. "He'll tell her to lawyer up," Rutherford had warned Neely. "Before he asks her question one about the kid, he'll tell her to lawyer up."

Rutherford wasn't wrong by much.

The first thing Jeffries said to Carrillo *was* about the kid: "Laura, do you know where the boy is?" But once she'd given him an answer—"Elliott, I swear I don't. I don't!"—his concerns for Adrian Edwards's welfare evaporated and his only interest was to shut his fiancé up until they could both talk to a good attorney.

Luckily for Rutherford and Neely, Carrillo remained as disinclined to seek legal counsel as ever. She wasn't worried about her own skin. She was solely focused on telling Jeffries the exact same story she'd been telling the detectives since they'd brought her in. Sobbing hysterically one minute, plainly stating her case the next, she didn't seem to know or give a damn that she and her boyfriend weren't technically alone.

When Jeffries finally withdrew from the room, shaken and exhausted, all the detectives were left with was what they'd had at the start: a suspect who either didn't know where her kidnap victim was or was not prepared to say.

"She's telling the truth," Jeffries said. "She really doesn't know where the boy is. She would have told me if she did."

"Through her lawyer, you mean," Rutherford said.

"So I advised her to get a lawyer. That proves she's guilty?"

"She's already confessed to being guilty," Neely said. "She took the boy by her own admission. What she needs to do now is prove he's still alive."

"She doesn't know where he is," Jeffries repeated. "You heard what she said. He ran away. Something she said upset him and he took off."

"Just like that," Rutherford said. "He took off and hasn't been seen since. A seven-year-old boy. Every cop in the city and half the populace out looking for him and he just went *poof!* Gone."

Jeffries glared at her. His girlfriend's story didn't add up and he knew it.

"I need to talk to Adrian's parents," he said.

* * *

"I can't do this anymore."

Milton's son-in-law turned to face him. "What?"

"I have to go. I can't just sit here like this, doing nothing." Milton killed the TV with the remote and got up.

"Wait, what are you talking about? Where are you going?"

It was the very same question Milton was asking himself. He had no inkling, but it didn't matter. The boy was out there somewhere, and if no one else could find him, maybe Milton could.

He went to get his keys.

"No," Alan said, placing himself between Milton and the door. "I can't let you leave."

"You can't?" Keys in one fist, Milton marched right past him.

Alan leapt to the door and braced his back against it. "Please. You can't do this. You don't know what you're doing." The poor bastard was practically in tears. Janet had given her husband the thankless task of sitting on Milton for a few hours until she could get free to do it herself, and here Alan was, on the brink of having Milton slip through his fingers on his way to God knew where.

"I know exactly what I'm doing," Milton said. "I'm going out through that door. And you can either put me in the hospital trying to stop me, or you can come with me. Those are your choices."

He gave Janet's husband a good, long look at the determination on his face, so Alan couldn't say later he hadn't known how serious Milton was.

"I'll drive," Alan said.

In the car, he started the engine, turned to Milton, and asked, "*Now* will you tell me where we're going?"

Without pausing to think, Milton said, "The park. We're going to Lakeridge Park."

THIRTY-FIVE

ONE LOOK AT ELLIOTT Jeffries's face and Diane knew: something had gone terribly wrong.

From the moment she'd heard Laura Carrillo's account of how Adrian had vanished into thin air at the ice cream shop, Diane had known. Her son hadn't just walked away.

Adrian had been taken back, this time for good.

"I have a message from Laura," Jeffries said.

The police had found an empty office where the three of them—Jeffries, Michael, and Diane—could talk in private, and Carrillo's boyfriend wasted no time speaking his piece, his anger as evident as the floor beneath their feet.

"But first, here's one from *me*: I don't know why you're doing this, but I'm going to find out. I promise you. Laura will never be the same. If they let her walk right now, gave her her job back tomorrow, she'd still bear the mark of what you've put her through this week, and she'll probably have to bear it forever."

"What *we've* put *her* through?" Michael said.

"That's right. If you didn't plant all these insane ideas about your son in her head, who did? You've finally got her convinced he's a dead child walking among the living. If that's what you wanted, you win. She's a believer."

"All we want is our son back," Diane said. "Where is he?"

"I don't know, and neither does she. Are you sure that *you* don't know?"

"What?"

"For all we know, the old man has him. Your partner. Weinman, is it? You and your husband have been using the boy as a straw man so far, why quit now?"

Michael took a step toward him but Diane was quicker. Her open right hand snapped Jeffries's head to one side like the sprung armature of a trap.

"Where is our son?" she asked again.

Stunned by the blow, Jeffries seemed about to strike back, only to remember Michael standing there. "I told you! She doesn't know. He just disappeared, like she's been saying all along."

Diane closed her eyes and kept them closed.

"It's the truth! She would never have hurt him. Never. I know her like I know myself and I swear to you, she didn't lay a hand on Adrian."

"Then where did he go?" Michael demanded. "If he'd been at the shop with her like she says, somebody would have seen him. And he would have shown up somewhere on the security videos."

"You're saying he didn't?"

"Detective Neely says the videos show your fiancé walk in alone and sit down alone. Adrian's nowhere to be seen."

Jeffries fell silent. Diane watched his anger seep away, giving in to something else: fear.

"You said you had a message for us from Laura. What is it?"

"She wants you to know she's sorry. That she shouldn't have taken him from school today and, obviously, she wishes she never had. She asks for your forgiveness."

The words had been a bitter pill for him, but not because they weren't true.

"No. That's not all of it. There's more," Diane said.

"That *is* all of it."

"No. She's right," Michael said. "Tell us the rest."

"It won't help you."

"We don't give a damn. Say it."

Jeffries continued to squirm, and now Diane thought she understood. He was only doing this because he'd promised Carrillo he would.

"She blames herself. Not just for the boy's kidnapping, but for his disappearance. She thinks. . . ." He had to reset himself before finishing. "She thinks it happened because of something she said."

He left it at that.

"What did she say?" Diane asked. The room was already starting to blur.

Jeffries gave Michael a look, seeking a reprieve to no purpose.

"They were talking about faith. She was trying to find out what he knew about it. He asked if she believed in God and. . .and she told him the truth." He paused to see their reaction. "It was right after that that the cops showed up. She says she only turned her head for a minute to watch them pull into the lot, and when she turned back—"

"He was gone," Diane said. At least it sounded like her voice. It seemed nothing she did now was of her own volition.

Jeffries nodded.

She reached out for a chair and would have missed falling into it had Michael not caught her. He held her tight to his chest as Jeffries looked on.

Diane began to cry.

* * *

"What are we doing here?" Alan asked. "What are you looking for?"

"Nothing. Go home. Leave me alone."

Milton was sitting on the same bench he and Diane Edwards had shared at Lakeridge Park the day before. It was after five and a gray sky was turning black, a light rain falling to complete the gloom. What few children remained on the playground were being ushered away by adults, promising Milton and Alan they'd soon have the grounds to themselves.

"You know I can't leave you here. Janet would have my head. And it's starting to rain, for chrissakes."

Milton didn't answer, eyes still scanning their surroundings, looking for something he couldn't name.

"The Edwards boy isn't here because we've looked. So what are we doing? What are you hoping to find?"

"A sign. An answer. I don't know!"

There was nothing he could tell Alan that wouldn't make Milton sound more insane than he already appeared to be. He hadn't been called to the park by reason; he'd come at the behest of impulse. He was *supposed* to be here. Hidden somewhere in plain sight, like a single pine needle among the millions littering the park, was a message only he was meant to receive. But where? And what?

He rose to walk the grounds again, as he had when they arrived. Alan let him go, weary of following Milton around like a puppy. Janet's husband had placed a call to her minutes ago and she was no doubt on her way, so Alan's sense of responsibility to Milton was waning.

The rain was holding steady but was barely noticeable against Milton's focus on the task at hand. The two men were alone now, and the only sound was an occasional jay chirping in the distance. Milton circled the play structure, spying half-formed castles in the sand. A pair of squirrels skittered across his line of sight, chased each other up the trunk of a maple tree, and disappeared among the leaves. Milton turned his head. . .

. . .and saw it.

"What? What is it?" Alan asked, seeing him stop.

Milton couldn't move, but he had to. Willing himself forward, he closed in for a better look.

* * *

In the aftermath of hearing the last words their son had spoken before his disappearance, coupled with Laura Carrillo's response to them, Diane had taken to praying without concern for discretion. Even before the detective named Neely had ushered Elliott Jeffries from the room, leaving them alone again, Diane had started saying the Lord's Prayer out loud, as if there were no one else but she around to hear. She and Michael had just learned their son had vanished on the heels of Carrillo virtually spitting in God's eye, and neither could believe one event had had nothing to do with the other.

So Michael, too, was praying, just not so anyone might notice, least of all Diane. He didn't want his wife to know her fear was his as well. All hope would be lost if she did. The logical conclusion to be drawn from what Jeffries had told them was terrifying, and Michael wasn't ready to accept it. Diane's faith had brought them this far, and now it was his turn to be the strong one. Adrian was still out there somewhere and they were going to find him. They had to.

The police were continuing the search but had decided there was nothing more Michael and Diane could do to assist them. They were operating on the assumption, and all the available evidence, that Laura was the key to Adrian's disappearance, and felt it was just a matter of time before she broke down and revealed Adrian's whereabouts. Neely offered to drive Michael and Diane home to get some rest, with Michael's car still sitting in the Yesler parking lot where they'd left it, but Michael declined. He'd seen all the police he could take for one day. Rutherford raised an eyebrow, her suspicions not yet laid to rest that Michael and Diane knew more about their missing son than they were telling, but Michael was insistent. He and Diane would find their own way home.

Neely walked them out to the front desk, where they were all surprised to find Hope waiting.

"What are you doing here?" the detective asked angrily. "I thought we left you back at the school."

"You did."

Neely waited for an explanation.

"I called her," Michael lied. Neely and Diane both turned, taken aback, but his wife kept silent.

Michael had no follow-up. He started to stammer something. . . .

"I'm an Uber driver," Hope said. She tapped her phone and turned the screen around so Neely could see the tell-tale company logo.

The detective looked back at Michael. "You called her for a ride?"

"Is that a problem?"

"If all she is is an Uber driver and a friend? No. But she told us she's a news writer, and if you tell her anything about what's happened here tonight, you can bet it's going to be all over the web and television tomorrow. You want to help us find your son?"

"'Keep your mouths shut.' We will, detective. I promise you."

"And you've got my word I won't ask them anything about your investigation," Hope said. "If I do—"

"We'll get out and walk," Diane said, for Hope's benefit as much as Neely's.

The cop wasn't fooled—only a rookie would have been, really—but he didn't have any grounds to argue.

"We've got a unit watching your home, in case the boy shows up. If you need anything or hear anything, just let the uniforms know."

He stormed off.

* * *

Outside, a gentle rain was falling in the last throes of daylight. Only a handful of reporters and newspeople were waiting to pounce on them, rather than the mob Michael was expecting. He and Diane and Hope pushed their way through with little trouble. It was as if Adrian's disappearance had already become old news.

Once they were out of the parking lot and well on their way, Michael and Diane clinging fast to each other in the backseat, Hope broke the silence.

"What happened?" she asked.

"You weren't going to ask any questions, you said. My wife told you what we'd do if you did," Michael said.

"Please. I need to know."

"Need?"

"Yes, *need*. I'm involved in this now, almost as much as you are, and maybe not by accident. You told me that yourself, only hours ago."

Michael didn't say anything, and neither did Diane.

"For God's sake, look at me! You think I give a shit anymore what kind of *story* this will make?"

They made her say the word again: "Please!"

Michael finally turned to Diane, seeking his wife's permission. Off her silent nod, he told Hope everything, in the broadest strokes he could devise.

"But you guys aren't thinking—"

"No. We're not."

Hope didn't ask any more questions, but Michael could practically hear the wheels turning inside her head, doing the same math he and Diane had when Jefferies offered them Laura Carrillo's account of how, and precisely when, Adrian had gone missing. Coincidence was always an inadequate explanation for the improbable, but this. . . .

There was next to no conversation after that, save for a pointless apology Hope made for the unkempt state of her car. Michael paid her words no mind and Diane was unlikely to have heard them at all. Then, only blocks away from home, Diane's phone rang.

She sat up, gave Michael a look that was a mixture of dread and cautious optimism.

She hit the phone's answer button. "Hello?"

The call was painfully brief, Diane's part consisting of only two questions: "Who?" and "Where?" With Hope stealing glances at them in her rearview mirror, Michael could draw no conclusions from the strained look on his wife's face but one: this wasn't good news.

"That was Milton Weisman's daughter," Diane said after hanging up, all color drained from her face. "She said Milton's at Lakeridge Park and there's something there he needs us to see."

THIRTY-SIX

IT HADN'T HAPPENED all at once.

The change had come over the park in pieces, like segments of a painting being filled in over time. Milton would blink, and something would be different. Small details that slowly and inexorably kept adding up to larger ones.

It had started with the lamppost, the one his car had clipped on its way onto the playground, and then the tree that had brought the Honda to a halt. After the accident, the post had been replaced, but not in its original position. To better light the new, larger play structure, the city had moved the lamppost several feet. Not much more than twenty-four hours ago, when Milton had been here with Diane Edwards, the post had been in its old familiar place, in perfect harmony with everything else in the park that had traveled back in time to the days before Adrian Edwards's death. But now, to Milton's horror, the lamppost stood in its new position, shedding light where the old metal play structure had no use for it.

Of course, Alan and Janet, who'd raced to the park at her husband's call with the urgency of a paramedic, were oblivious to the metamorphosis going on all around them. Nothing Milton did could make them see what was happening, and he'd finally given up trying. All they cared about was getting Milton home and, he imagined, in bed asleep, so they could plot out the steps necessary to have him psychiatrically evaluated or placed in a rest home as quickly as possible.

He'd had to beg Janet to call Diane Edwards. His daughter and Alan were loath to facilitate Milton having any further contact with Adrian's parents, convinced the two were somehow at the root of Milton's delusions, if not their son's disappearance. But Milton needed the Edwardses there, to witness what he was seeing and to tell him—*convince* him—it did not imply what he feared it did.

In his rush to leave the house earlier, he'd left his cell phone behind, but in his pocket was the note with Diane Edwards's phone number that Janet had given him two days ago. Milton had forced it into Janet's hands tonight until she'd had no choice but to make the call.

By the time Diane Edwards arrived, accompanied by her husband and, much to Milton's bewilderment, the reporter Michael Edwards had warned him never to speak to again, the transformation of the park was nearly complete. Only one large piece of the puzzle remained to be fitted into place.

Milton hurried over to greet the trio as they piled out of the car, and already he could see the astonishment on all their faces.

* * *

No, Diane thought. *No.*

"This isn't possible," Hope said.

The rain had stopped, but night had come to Lakeridge Park in full. The six of them—Diane, Michael, Hope, Milton Weisman, and a man and woman Diane assumed were Milton's daughter and her husband—had the playground all to themselves.

"I thought I might find the boy here," Weisman said. "That's why I came. But instead. . . ."

Diane pushed past him, leaving the others to follow as she closed in on the play structure, walking as if in the quicksand of a dream.

"No," Diane said.

The playground was caught between two worlds: one that included an all-wooden structure and another that held only half of a brightly colored metal one.

As she looked around, Michael and Hope doing the same, Diane made note of all the other ways the park had changed since yesterday, reverting to what it had been only five days before. The tree Weisman's car had plowed into after running over her son was once again missing, the new water fountain that had been added in its place was back, and the plaque forged in Adrian's memory was once more set into the grass in its usual spot, its surface slick with rain.

Someone began to gag, and Diane turned just in time to see Michael retch into a trash receptacle, body convulsing.

"My God," Milton's daughter said. "Will someone please tell us what the hell is going on?"

Diane felt no need to answer, but Hope said, "You wouldn't understand."

"No? Try me."

Hope shook her head, warning her: *This is not the time.*

It had all been for nothing, Diane thought. All the tears, all the prayers, all the days and nights on her knees. The miracle was no more. Her son was gone and this time, he would not be coming back.

"Why?" Michael bellowed. "What the fuck did we do?"

Diane turned to face him. She wanted to cry but couldn't, wondered if she would ever be able to cry again. "We didn't do anything," she said.

"Then why? What was the point? If we didn't do something to cause this—"

"This isn't about us, Michael. It never was."

Diane knew it to be true, though she didn't know how. They all looked at her as if she'd spoken in tongues.

"What do you mean?" Hope asked.

"I mean that this was a test of faith, but not ours. We didn't fail Him. She did."

"Laura Carrillo?"

"The rest of us believed and kept on believing. Even you. We wouldn't be here otherwise. But not Laura. She may believe now, like her fiancé said, but—"

"Now it's too late," Michael said.

"No," Weisman said angrily, stepping to the center of the group. "That's bullshit! That can't be what happened. God wouldn't do such a thing!"

His daughter came to his side to take his arm. Diane had the feeling she'd never heard him talk about God this way before. "Come on, Daddy. It's time to go home." She glared at the others. "I don't know who these people are or what they've done to you, but we're going home right now."

The old man jerked his arm away. "No. Leave me alone!"

The man Diane took for Milton's son-in-law moved in to help his wife, but Weisman threw up his arms to ward him off. "Get away from me! Both of you."

"It's over, Milton," Michael said. "There's no reason for you to stay. There's no reason for any of to us stay now." Diane recognized this voice. It was the one he had used in the months before their separation, when he'd resigned himself to his misery and become contemptuous of Diane for refusing to do the same.

Weisman said, "I'll leave when *she* leaves." Staring at Diane, he said, "If you tell me to go, I'll go."

Diane didn't want to be responsible for him, but she understood his need to stay. Addressing his daughter, she said, "I know what this must look like to you. We all must be insane. And maybe we are. But we share something with your father that we could never fully explain to you. He'd like to stay with us here for a little while longer, and we'd like to have him stay."

"No. I don't—"

"Please. If you could give us just a few more minutes alone, I promise you he'll be all right. And that we'll never see or talk to him again."

"Why should I believe that?"

"Because I believe it," Weisman said.

His daughter studied him, then glanced at her husband.

"What about your boy?" the man asked Diane. "Did the teacher really take him like they say, or. . .?"

"If you're asking us if we killed our own son," Michael said, "the answer is no."

There were other questions the man could have asked, but Weisman's son-in-law, either intimidated by Michael's tone or sympathetic to his possible loss, chose to let the matter drop. He turned to give his wife a small shrug. It was her call.

"Ten minutes. That's all," she said.

"Fifteen," Weisman insisted.

She gave him a hard look before allowing her husband to guide her to his car.

* * *

Laura had never been so afraid in her life.

They had placed her in a holding cell and told her she would spend the night in city jail. The thought chilled her to the bone. Here in the bowels of the police station, she could hear sounds that belonged only in nightmares.

But this *was* a nightmare, after all. The living, breathing, interminable kind from which there was no escape. She knew now Diane Edwards was neither crazy nor a con artist; her miracle had been exactly that. But no more. Adrian would never be found and the blame for his disappearance, or worse, would fall squarely on Laura's shoulders. She had no defense that was credible. She had admitted stealing the child away from Yesler and could not account for his whereabouts since. She would face kidnapping charges to start and, when Adrian never turned up, possible murder charges later. And all she'd be able to say was, this was how God apparently wanted it. She had only done what the master scheme of Diane Edwards's Heavenly Father had preordained she must.

There would be little point in attempting to make anyone believe it, aside from receiving whatever sympathy from the court an insanity plea might buy her. Whether she relied on silence or the truth, she would be doomed. And why? What crime in all her twenty-six years on Earth had she committed to deserve the starring role in this sick, extravagant exercise of divine power? Who was she to have been chosen for such humiliation and ignominy?

She had answered a simple question honestly: she did not believe in God.

How that made her any different from all the millions of other atheists in the world, Laura could not fathom. She wracked her brain trying to find it, the quality of disbelief that separated her from the rest, the thing that made her uniquely worthy of all she was being made to suffer, and failed. Her only insult to God had been apathy. A quiet comfort in never needing Him to exist in order to survive and prosper.

So she had denied Him. Why in the hell would He have cared? What difference did one grain of sand make to the caretaker of an endless beach? In the days when she had entertained the possibility of God, the hurdle of faith she could never get past was the randomness with which He seemed to operate. It was inconceivable that a so-called loving god's ministrations could be so haphazardly applied, to the guilty and innocent alike. But now she could see this must be precisely how God worked: not to reward those He favored or punish those He condemned, but to toy with both.

He had given Diane and Michael Edwards their little boy back, only to snatch him away again in a fit of pique because Laura had failed to pay Him proper due. Laura did not deserve to carry that kind of guilt. She loved Adrian, and she loved children, and she loved Elliott most of all. But who could love her now in return? Would she ever be loved again?

Lying on the hard and fetid cot in her cell, giving no thought to sleep, she closed her eyes and considered the great irony.

She believed in God now. Oh, yes.

God was most definitely real.

* * *

There was no God, Michael thought.

He felt like a fool for having ever thought differently. What had happened to all of them—Michael, Diane and Adrian, Milton Weisman and, perhaps most of all, Laura Carrillo—may have been the work of the devil, but not God. God was a dream. God was a false hope. God was what you believed in rather than face the fact life had no meaning beyond what the vagaries of fate provided.

The transformation of the playground was complete. The fragment of the old play structure that had been there when Michael arrived was gone, replaced in full by the new wooden one, and the only conclusion to be drawn from the exchange was clear: the clock had been turned back five days, taking Lakeridge Park—and Adrian—along with it. Michael knew that if he cared to look for them, there would be other signposts: his son's grave, returned to its place at Forest Glade Cemetery; Michael's apartment, no longer cluttered with Adrian's toys and clothes; Adrian's room in Diane's home, once more resembling the pristine memorial to a dead child it had been one week earlier.

And why? Because one woman had failed to believe in something Michael only barely had himself? Was he supposed to blame poor Laura Carrillo for the way this day—the second longest in his life—had ended, as Diane seemed more than willing to? If so, he didn't have it in him. Laura Carrillo was not the villain here, and neither was God.

Because God did not exist.

Michael could not imagine what life would look like after this night, but he suspected the three people on the playground with him might offer some clue. Diane sat on a motionless swing, feet dragging in the sand, staring into space. Milton Weisman sat on a rain-soaked bench, waiting with the dread of a condemned man for his daughter and son-in-law to take him home.

And Allison Hope stood alone, off to one side, her head down and eyes fixed on the spot of grass where a bronze plaque bearing Adrian's name and face had once more taken root.

"I can't believe it," Allison said as Michael Edwards, moving like a wraith through a fog, came up beside her. "I can't believe any of it."

"It doesn't matter what you believe," Edwards said. "It is what it is."

She turned to face him. He was an empty shell.

"What will you do? How are you and your wife—how the hell are any of us supposed to go on after this?"

Edwards shook his head. "Maybe we won't. Maybe we won't want to. Either way, we'll have no say in what happens. We've got no say now, and we never really did. Or haven't you figured that out yet?"

His words stung, but she couldn't argue with them. In the last twenty-four hours, Allison had seen all the proof she would ever need that reality was an illusion, time was elastic, and the fates of men and women were as much in their control as the stars in the heavens. Whatever power had brought Edwards's son back to life, only to return him to his grave—the word *god* seemed too kind for it now—would do to them what it would.

Edwards and Allison lapsed into silence and her attention turned to his wife, propped on a swing like a mannequin that had been posed there and forgotten. No one's devastation could be as great as Diane Edwards's. Her investment in the dream that was Adrian's resurrection had been all encompassing. For eight months, she had given herself over to the unwavering faith of a disciple. And then, suddenly, God had been moved to respond. He placed her son back in her arms again, as alive as Diane was herself, and brought her husband home to both of them. To have the boy torn from her grasp again only four days later, for no offense of her own commission, had to feel like having her heart cleaved right down the middle. What else could she be thinking now, Allison mused, but that she'd been betrayed, and that no prayer she had ever offered to God had been worth the time it took to utter it?

It was a thought so disheartening, it brought Allison to the brink of tears, the latest round of many since they'd arrived at the park. She was reminded of the crayon drawing in her purse, the portrait of a little girl Adrian had left in the backseat of his father's car. Allison had stolen it like a common thief, as if it were something to which she was entitled, and she wondered now how she could have been so arrogant. Consumed by guilt, she reached into her bag, dug down deep to retrieve it.

"I don't know why I did it," she said, handing the rumpled sheet of paper to Michael Edwards, "but I took this from your car this morning. I'm sorry."

Edwards took the page with some hesitation, realizing what it was almost at once. Admiring his son's handiwork, he smiled, eyes alight, and actually laughed. "He always made the noses so small," he said.

Allison laughed, too. He was right. The nose on the child's face was barely a scratch of brown above her oversized mouth.

"I've seen that girl before."

They turned, startled. Milton Weisman was standing behind them, peering past Edwards's right shoulder at Adrian's drawing. His daughter and son-in-law had returned for him, and on his way to their car, the old man had stopped to see what Allison and Edwards were examining.

"In a dream," Weisman added.

It was the first time Allison had heard him sound this way: ancient and tired. And maybe a little bit deranged.

"A dream?" she asked.

But Weisman's daughter, as aware of the change in her father as Allison was, steered him away with her husband's help, lest any more damage be done to him by this band of what she could only believe were certifiable lunatics.

Weisman craned his neck to throw one last glance behind him before he was dragged out of range. "She was at his funeral. She ran away."

That was all he said. He was in his daughter's car, strapped into the passenger seat, before he could add another word. Weisman's son-in-law raced to his own car and the two vehicles sped out of the lot, approximating a movie chase scene complete with squealing, rain-soaked tires.

"What did he mean? Were there children at Adrian's funeral?"

"A few," Edwards said. "I really don't recall. I was barely there myself."

"Then why—?"

"It was a dream. He wasn't there. After all the poor bastard's been through, he's entitled to be a little confused, don't you think?" Before Allison could answer, Edwards held his son's drawing out to her and said, "Here. You wanted this, you should have it."

"Me?"

"It would just be one more thing making it impossible to let him go." He pushed the portrait toward her. "Please."

Allison felt unworthy of such a gift, but the last thing Edwards needed was an argument over something trivial. She took the drawing back and willed herself to smile.

"Thank you."

* * *

Diane stood up from the swing. There was nothing more here for her to see.

She went to her husband and said, "Let's go home, Michael."

Michael and Hope looked at her with some surprise, and Diane thought she knew why: she wasn't acting like the walking dead anymore. She had been, she knew it, but now she was done. She was still mired in the depths of depression, and maybe would be for the rest of her life, but she had decided to fight it, one minute at a time, to see if she could get to a place she hadn't been in over seven years. A place where life without Adrian seemed worth living. She owed it to Michael to try.

As for God, she would never call on Him for anything ever again. She had said her last prayer. What she had learned tonight, more than anything else, was not that He did not exist, nor that He didn't care who lived or died, but that His will was too impenetrable to place designs upon. Why ask for miracles that were only yours to borrow, not to keep? God's mercy was too flighty, His compassion too sporadic.

So Diane was done with prayer. Whatever role God chose to play in her life from this day forward, He would have to do it without any entreaties from her.

Michael took her hand, his grasp firm. This much, at least, had been salvaged from the wreckage of the last few days, and Diane was determined to hold onto it. Together, they had some chance for survival. Alone, they had none at all.

"Your husband gave me this to keep," Hope said, showing Diane the sheet of paper in her hand. It was a drawing that was clearly Adrian's work, a portrait of a little black girl with pigtails that was not unlike all the other still lifes of children Adrian had loved to draw. "I hope you don't mind."

For a brief moment, Diane thought she might. The impulse to cling to every last reminder of her son was compelling. But then she reconsidered. Hope had come too far on this journey with them for Diane to send her off empty-handed. Adrian had touched her life, too. Diane tendered the gift with a shake of her head.

Minutes later, the three of them were in the writer's car again, headed for Yesler. Diane and Michael had decided to have Hope drop them where they'd left Michael's car that afternoon, rather than go home and leave the trip to Adrian's school for the next day. They had no fear the police would be waiting for them there. As the absence of media outside the Bellevue police station upon their leaving had foretold, the world's interest in their son's disappearance was a thing of the past, just as Adrian was himself. In fact, Diane thought, it was doubtful Laura Carrillo was still being held at the police station, rather than in her bed at home, locked in fitful sleep.

After a ride that was silent and swift, they rolled into Yesler's parking lot, where Michael's Acura sat in the dark lot alone. Hope mumbled a faint condolence by way of farewell, and Diane and her husband piled out of the car, too spent to do anything more than nod in return.

Hope was still sitting there in the lot, watching, as they drove off for home.

THIRTY-SEVEN

THEY WOULDN'T TAKE HIM HOME, so Milton ended up at Janet's. Her eyes and Alan's were never off him for a minute. Lisa had joined them for dinner, as if no suicide watch was complete without at least three people on duty at all times.

The good news was, they weren't hounding him with questions. They were just studying him closely and attending to his every need, having squirreled away every ounce of wine and liquor in the house.

He knew what they had planned for him. All the questions they were hesitant to ask now would be posed by doctors later, one after another, until it was decided where he should live the rest of his life and under whose care. Because he certainly couldn't live in his own place alone anymore.

He had destroyed his computer because it wouldn't google results for an event that had never happened. He had become convinced he'd killed a little boy who, until this morning, had been very much alive and, hopefully, remained so. He had talked about God when he'd never before had the slightest interest in His existence, and he'd become involved with people whose own sanity and motives seemed questionable at best. Tonight, he had wandered around Lakeridge Park with the wide-eyed horror of a man who could see things no one else could, and he'd left mumbling about a dream he'd had of a little black girl he had no reason to know, running through a cemetery he almost certainly had never visited.

And now, he was saying almost nothing at all, offering them no resistance, moving like a sleepwalker who might never wake.

Of course they were afraid for him. But not nearly as afraid as he was for himself. Because Milton couldn't help thinking they had to be right, that the only explanation for all he had done and said was the most logical one: he was crazy. Something had happened to him on Tuesday, something he couldn't recall or lacked the insight to pinpoint, and it had broken his hold on reality.

And yet. . . .

He didn't want to believe it. He preferred to believe in the impossible, the alternate reality that, for a brief moment in time, had given him reason to hope life was not entirely without meaning, that every man, woman, and child ever born was not at the mercy of chance and chance alone. Something was in control, its name didn't matter, and sometimes it could be moved to make incredible things happen. Beautiful, merciful, inexplicable things.

Miracles.

But Milton was tired.

He had tried so hard to do his part in keeping Diane Edwards's miracle whole, and it hadn't been enough. Little by little, in the space of one day, things had come apart at the seams, for reasons Milton still didn't fully understand, and now there was nothing left but his fading memories of them. Adrian Edwards was back in his grave, and Milton was once more the old fool who had put him there.

Tomorrow, his daughters and Alan would remember things exactly that way. Milton was sure of it. History would have completed the counterclockwise run it had started tonight, until all was as it had been last week, when neither Janet nor Lisa had looked at him strangely for talking about the little boy he had killed. They would recall the boy, too, and share their father's shame for having taken his life.

So Milton let them plot his future, bandying the names of doctors and psychiatric hospitals about. None of it would come to pass, because in hours, they would no longer think him insane. Life for all of them would be back to "normal": ordinary, predictable, godless.

All Milton had to do was make it through the night.

* * *

They never did take Laura off to jail.

Someone brought dinner down to her holding cell, and then they all just seemed to disappear, not unlike Adrian had hours earlier. The lights dimmed in the cell and darkness closed in all around it, attended by an eerie quiet that would have been well-suited to a crypt. Laura called out through the bars once or twice, but no one answered her. It was as if the entire police station had been shut down like a shopping mall after hours, its lone prisoner forgotten down in the building's catacombs.

The thought occurred to her that someone could be playing a joke, poking her as if with a stick to see if they could get her to scream. She was, after all, a monster to them: a deranged young woman who'd stolen a seven-year-old boy and then killed him. Who wouldn't derive some pleasure from torturing such an animal? Or maybe this was the detectives' way of turning the screws, of forcing a confession from her. *Even crazy people,* she could picture Neely telling Rutherford, laughing, *could be made to fear the dark.*

But time kept moving at a crawl, and no one came to see her, and the idea that she might be here all alone began to solidify.

She needed Elliott desperately. She wanted to know he still loved her, and that Diane and Michael Edwards had received the message she had entrusted to his care. He had said all the right things in the interrogation room, given her every reason to hope he would be there when she got out of this accursed place, but after what she'd told him—that she believed her rebuke of God in Adrian's presence was the reason he'd disappeared—she wasn't at all sure her fiancé hadn't already left her, in spirit if not in the flesh.

Adrian.

His mother had brought him back once. Were there any words Laura could say now, humbled and down on her knees, that could bring him back again? If she begged and pleaded, screamed until her throat was raw, would that undo all the damage she had done?

No, Laura thought. It wouldn't be enough.

She went to the bars of the cell and called out one last time. No one answered and no one came.

She wondered if anyone ever would.

* * *

Michael had seen this movie before, and now he was living it himself.

For weeks after Adrian died, Diane had known no peace. She lay in bed for days at a time, curled up in the tightest ball she could form, opening her eyes only long enough to make her way to the bathroom and back. She ate little and had no use for words; crying was the only activity she had the strength to pursue. Weight fled from her body like water squeezed from a sponge.

Michael had sought similar solace in sleep, but he couldn't go on that way forever. His bitterness would not allow it. To stop living and wither away would have been all-out surrender, and he wasn't ready to bow down that far to whomever or whatever was responsible for the death of his only child.

It was God he hated, of course, but he couldn't admit it. It shamed him to do so, and he was loath to counter whatever magic Diane's fervent prayers might bring to pass. In any case, it was rage that had taken him from the bed and set him on his feet again, and it was rage that had driven him from the marriage when Diane could not find it in herself to feel the same.

And now the cycle was destined to start anew.

They had come home, unlocked the front door, and stumbled straight back to the bedroom, neither of them pausing to turn on a single light. Diane crawled onto the bed first and Michael was right behind, both fully clothed, their shoes still on their feet. He was half expecting his wife to object to his company, so little comfort would it purchase for her, but she let him join her on the bed without a word. He put his arms around her and held on tight, trying not to think about the night before, when they had lain here just this way with their son sound asleep beside them.

Michael didn't understand what had happened and was certain he never would. Diane believed Laura Carrillo was the reason for it all, that Adrian had been brought back to life strictly to test the teacher's belief in God's power to heal, but that was bullshit. None of them was the "reason." Not Carrillo, not Diane, and certainly not God. The glue holding the world together had simply come undone. They'd all been trapped in the resultant void, and now that the rift had repaired itself, the normal order of things was falling back into place. Time was once again in sync with the universe, and death was as immutable as ever.

He would never be able to convince Diane of this, but he didn't care. Having lost Adrian twice, he would need her love now as much as she needed his, and he wasn't going anywhere. Whatever he had to do to stay right here, in this bed in this house with this woman, he would do it.

But he would pay no homage to her god.

* * *

When Diane's tears finally came, it was in a torrent that shook them both.

Her pain was unbearable but her fear was almost worse. Though suicide had entered her mind many times after Adrian's death, it never held. Between her faith in God and her love for Michael, she'd always found the strength to hang on. But this time would be different. Her faith was shaken and Michael could not be counted on to stay. What else besides death offered relief from this torment?

Sleep was not the answer, but for now it would do. And so she cried and went on crying, working herself to a point of exhaustion that would force sleep upon her. Her husband soon followed, burying his face in the back of her neck to weep, mumbling things into her hair she could not decipher.

Eventually, she drifted off, a slow descent into the black. She seemed to grow lighter as she fell, and she realized with some surprise that her memory of the past few days was fading, piece by piece. Laura Carrillo's fiancé offering her apology at the Bellevue police station. The transformation of Lakeridge Park. Howard Alberts's call, alerting them to Adrian's kidnapping. It all melted away. Her pain evaporated. Diane was free.

By the time sleep took her in full, there was nothing left to remember, and nothing more to mourn.

THIRTY-EIGHT

WITHIN MINUTES OF RETURNING to her motel room, Allison had begun to write.

It was the last thing she would have thought herself capable of doing. She had left Yesler Elementary expecting to do nothing all night but cry, thoughts of Adrian Edwards and Flo taking turns tearing her apart. She had even stopped for another bottle on the way, certain she would not be able to sleep without drinking herself into a torpor. Instead, she had walked into the room and gone straight to her laptop, filling the screen with lines of text as fast as her fingers could type them.

She wasn't writing as much as disgorging, relieving herself of something she could no longer hold within. She was driven in part by the fear it would all be gone tomorrow, her memories wiped clean like the world of Adrian himself. There was no guarantee a file on her computer would survive the purge, but she didn't care. For now, just the act of transcription was keeping her sane, and once she started, she couldn't have stopped herself even if she wanted to.

She began with the events of the last several hours and worked her way backward, skipping about in time as her muse dictated. The fresh bottle of Pinot Noir was opened and poured, but barely touched. Tears came and went as the minutes turned to hours and the pages piled up. At some point, Adrian's crayon portrait had come out of her purse and taken a place on the desk beside her laptop, and every now and then she'd catch a glimpse of the little girl with braids and a whisper of a nose staring up at her.

Unanswered questions accumulated like raindrops in a barrel. Ten became twenty and twenty became a hundred, each more confounding and frightening than the last. In the end, one demanded an answer more than all the others: what did any of it mean?

What point could there have been to it? Michael Edwards, his faith in God spent, had told her there was none, that his son's resurrection and disappearance, and all the equally inexplicable things that had occurred in between and after, were just the work of a chaotic universe unbound by order. Anything could happen to anyone at any time, good or bad, beautiful or tragic, and looking for the reasons behind it was futile. It was as viable a theory as any, and yet Allison couldn't accept it, even now. She could not believe life was so devoid of purpose, that it could be tied to nothing more substantial than the whimsy of fate, which was wont to change the rules of the game, and then change them back again, at any moment.

But it was no easier for her to accept the view of Edwards's wife, Diane, which approximated the dictum that "God giveth and God taketh away." That was only Michael's stance dressed in pious clothing, and it amounted to something far worse: any cruelty was possible if God chose to make it so. Unspeakable things could happen to you not by chance, but by the conscious design of a supreme being that ruled over all. Religious texts were filled with depictions of God as ruler of heaven and earth, meting out terrible punishments to those who displeased him, but Allison had never subscribed to that characterization and she couldn't do so now. If God was the author of the heartbreaking theater she had witnessed over the last three days, He hadn't written it simply to demonstrate his capacity to inflict pain.

At Lakeridge Park, Diane Edwards had implied that Laura Carrillo had been the object of the exercise all along. It was Carrillo's faith God had been testing, and her faith that had failed Him, leaving Him no choice but to take back the gift—Adrian's return—He was offering her. But this, too, was a premise Allison couldn't accept. Not because she didn't think God could possibly care that much about a single individual, but because the individual involved had possessed no faith to test. Carrillo was an avowed atheist. What was to be gained by bribing her to acknowledge something she could not abide by of her own free will?

And yet, Diane Edwards's words kept coming back to Allison as she wrote: *This was never about us.* Allison had that sense, too, but she didn't know what to make of it. For whom, if not the Edwardses or Laura Carrillo, could God have gone to so much effort, to reshape time and space, and reverse the very polarities of life and death? Milton Weisman?

Allison couldn't build a case for him, either. The old man had done everything he had been asked to do, demonstrating great courage and self-sacrifice, stretching his own apparent agnosticism to a degree that would have made the punishment of Adrian's return to the grave unjustifiable.

That left only Allison herself, the most unlikely candidate of all. She was only an observer to the drama, an outsider who had wormed her way into it out of desperation, and her faith in the Almighty was paper thin. There was no way this was about her. God had not invited her to this dance; Flo had, three nights ago when she'd stumbled upon Betty Marx's online report of Carrillo's meltdown at Yesler and brought it to Allison's attention. Never imagining Allison would latch on to the story and run off with it like a dog with a stolen bone.

The thought of Flo, and that night in their bedroom, brought Allison's gaze once more to Adrian's portrait of the little girl. Weisman had said he recognized her from a dream, in which she'd been fleeing Adrian's funeral. She tried to picture the scene, the child in pigtails racing away from her classmate's gravesite, and decided Michael Edwards had to be right: it couldn't have happened. Weisman was confused. Because Edwards didn't remember it, and it didn't seem like the kind of detail he could have forgotten.

Unless. . . .

Allison had picked up her glass of wine at some point, but now she put it back down, taking the crayon portrait in hand instead. She studied it for the first time without sentimentality and realized Michael Edwards had been right about something else: the nose *was* too small.

But Adrian had gotten the eyes and mouth exactly right.

* * *

Allison told Flo the story much as she had written it back at the motel, in an unbroken stream that could not be held back once unleashed.

She could tell by Flo's reaction this wasn't at all what she had been expecting. It was another late night for Flo at the office, and Allison's ten p.m. call to plead for an immediate meeting had probably foreshadowed a different kind of discussion. Flo had tried to beg off but Allison wouldn't take no for an answer, so here they were in Founders Hall at Bothell, practically alone in the dark and silent building, talking about things that had nothing to do with the shattered relationship only one of them felt the need to repair.

Flo had listened with a tinge of exasperation at first, her patience for the subject of Diane and Michael Edwards's circus of the absurd exhausted, but as Allison went on, her interest became acute. When Allison was done, Flo seemed almost anxious for the opportunity to interject.

"It's incredible," she said. "Not entirely believable in places—that whole shape-shifting bit in the park, in particular—but I'm sure it'll make a fascinating piece. Still, you could have waited until morning to tell me about it, Ally. I know this is important to you, but—"

"I'm not going to write a piece," Allison said.

Flo didn't follow. "You aren't? Why not? Not because of what's happened between us, I hope."

"No."

"Then what's the problem?"

"It's not what I'm meant to do. None of it happened for my benefit. Or the boy's parents'. It happened for yours."

Flo smiled, as if she couldn't be sure she'd heard Allison correctly. "Excuse me?"

Allison had left her only evidence for last. She passed it over to Flo. "This was the drawing Adrian made. The one I took from his father's car."

The portrait's effect on her was more than Flo could disguise. She opened her mouth to speak, only to close it again. Allison imagined there was more in the portrait she found familiar than just the child's face: the clothing and hair, maybe even the colored bands around her braids.

"Of course, I thought of you immediately. There isn't much that hasn't made me think of you for the last two days. But tonight I realized it's more than just a resemblance I see. That's you when you were a little girl. Isn't it?"

Flo's answer was slow in coming. "No. That's ridiculous."

"And it wasn't a classmate of Adrian's Milton Weisman saw in his dream, running away from his funeral. It was you, running away from your father's."

Flo had only told Allison the whole story once, so painful was it for her to relate, but as Allison had reflected upon it at the motel tonight, she had seen how open to interpretation Flo's telling had actually been.

"You told me you how you stayed in the car while he was being laid to rest. I always thought it meant you refused to attend the gravesite. But you did attend it. You went and then ran away."

"Stop it, Ally."

"Didn't you?"

"It doesn't matter. This isn't me," Flo said. "It can't be." She tried to hand the portrait back, but Allison wouldn't take it.

"I knew how hard it would be to convince you. I knew you'd refuse to believe it. But you're a practical woman, babe. You don't put much stock in coincidence. Do what you always do and do the math. Put everything I've just told you together with that drawing and ask yourself what it means. What it can *only* mean."

"I don't want to hear any more of this. . . ."

"All these years you've been thinking God betrayed you, that your father died in spite of all your prayers because no one was listening. But He *was* listening. He did hear you. Adrian Edwards is the miracle *your* faith made possible, Flo, not his mother's. The faith you used to have and can have again. Nothing else matters now."

"You can't be serious. You're trying to say this is all about *me?* That *I* have the power to bring him back?"

"Yes."

"Ally. . . ."

"I can't explain it. I'm not even going to try. But what the hell difference should it make, whether we understand it or not? Adrian will be back with his parents. An old man won't have the death of a child on his conscience. Who gives a damn if it makes any sense?"

"I do. What you're talking about is impossible."

"Impossible or not, I know it to be true. I know it with all my heart, Flo. I've never been so certain of anything in my life."

"That's enough, Ally."

"You can't believe it. All right, fine." Allison got down on her knees at Flo's feet. "Then believe *me.*" Tears began to fill her eyes but she wouldn't give in to them. Not yet. "Just one more time."

"No," Flo shook her head. "No." She tried to rush off but Allison took hold of her wrist, held it firm.

"Please. You've got to try. Try to remember how my word used to mean something to you. The trust you had in my judgment. All I had to do was say it and you believed it, simply because *I* believed it."

Flo had loved her that much once, before doubt and failure had seeped in to drive them apart, and if Allison could still recall such a time, Flo could, too.

"I know that's all gone now. I do. But you have to get it back. Just long enough to do this one last thing for me. Please, baby."

"Let go of me, Ally."

Allison held on.

"I can't do what you're asking me to do!" Flo wrenched her arm free.

"Yes. You can." Allison held her hand out for Flo to take. "You must. He's gone forever if you don't."

Flo didn't move. Allison could see she couldn't, caught between two disparate worlds: the one she'd found comfort in for the last twenty-five years and the one that had torn her to pieces before that. One demanded nothing of her, and the other everything she had.

Flo stood there, peering down on Allison, one foot rooted to the floor and the other turned to run, until Allison finally lowered her hand and began to pray.

Knowing her voice alone would not be enough.

SATURDAY

THIRTY-NINE

IT RAINED ALL the next day. Hard enough to loosen the shingles on roofs and make wading pools out of intersections. It came down at a sharp angle that pounded windows and rendered the sighted blind.

In the morning, for a fleeting moment, Milton Weisman thought about going out. But he knew better than to try. His daughters were baby-sitting him again and they would have pounced at his first move toward the door. They loved him so it was difficult to complain, but the two watched over him as if terrified of what he might do. For the life of him, Milton couldn't figure out why.

He had his occasional mishap, certainly. What sixty-eight-year-old didn't? He nicked a finger with a knife while making dinner. He bruised a knee, banging it on that damn table in the hall. But he'd never seriously injured himself, nor had a single accident in the car. The only person he had ever really hurt was their mother. His children had no reason to worry about him.

Milton Weisman was good.

Laura Carrillo spent the afternoon at home. Her fiancé Elliott Jeffries had built a fire in the fireplace and they snuggled on the living room couch before it, she working on her lesson plan for the week while he read a book, their legs occasionally intertwined. At moments like this, Laura's mind always turned to her children—the ones she taught and those she planned to have someday—and she couldn't help but smile. If someone had asked her, she would have said she was happy, though she still wasn't sure what the word was supposed to mean.

Shortly after four p.m., Allison Hope was driving for her third Uber rider of the day. She needed the money. The motel room she would have to call home until she could make other arrangements was nowhere for a lovesick, unemployed writer to be sitting, drinking red wine and listening to the rain crash down to earth. Out on the road, the relentless downpour making her windshield a watercolor wash of gray, she had too much to think about to shed more than a few tears at a time over her estranged partner, Flo Davenport. Avoiding an accident, for one, and absorbing the wild stories her passengers seemed compelled to tell, for another. She still had the idea she could make a career out of her writing someday, Flo's skepticism notwithstanding, but she needed a story worth telling. If she listened to the world closely enough, eventually one would find her and she would write it. That was what she prayed for every day, and that was what would happen. She was sure of it.

While Allison was driving her third Uber passenger of the day to his desired destination, Flo Davenport lay in the bedroom of the home they used to share, leafing through a book she hadn't picked up in years. The house felt empty without Allison and Flo was restless in her absence. The book was one that had once belonged to Flo's father, a reminder of his death to cancer she was constantly tempted to throw out but, for some reason, never could. As a child, she had possessed a copy of her own, and had loved it, but she'd had no use for the book since her father's passing, which in her mind had made a lie of its every word. But today her father's dog-eared copy had called her to its place in storage, and now it was in her hands, waiting to be read. Afraid and excited at the same time, she turned the pages, seeking a random place to start, and landed on a parable she remembered as one of her favorites: Luke 15:11.

And he said, a certain man had two sons. . . .

That evening, a melancholy Diane Edwards labored in her kitchen, fashioning a simple dinner for two. She never missed her son Adrian more than when she was cooking for only herself and her husband Michael, every course something Adrian would have likely rejected. If Michael felt the same, she wouldn't know it. He had learned to put Adrian out of mind whenever necessary. He and Diane were trying to hold their marriage together, and on nights like this one, he insisted they behave and speak as they had in the beginning, like a childless couple in love who needed only each other to feel complete.

Still, dicing up asparagus stalks that would have moved Adrian to groan, Diane thought about her son and smiled. He would be home tomorrow, after his sleepover at his Aunt Vicky's was complete, and if the rain saw fit to stop, they would all go together as a family to Lakeridge Park.

It was Adrian's favorite place in the world.

ACKNOWLEDGMENTS

The author would like to express his deepest gratitude to the following people, whose generous contribution of time and expertise made this book possible:

Rabbi Zoe Klein
Temple Isaiah

Doselle Young

Honey DeRoy

This book was set in Adobe Jenson Pro, named after the fifteenth-century French engraver, printer, and type designer, Nicholas Jenson. His typefaces were strongly influenced by scripts employed by the Renaissance humanists, who were in turn inspired by what they had discovered on ancient Roman monuments.

This book was designed by Shannon Carter, Ian Creeger, and Gregory Wolfe. It was published in hardcover, paperback, and electronic formats by Wipf and Stock Publishers, Eugene, Oregon.

CPSIA information can be obtained
at www.ICGtesting.com
Printed in the USA
LVHW112105241120
672180LV00034B/508/J